Running Wild

Running Wild

LUCINDA BETTS

APHRODISIA

KENSINGTON BOOKS
http://www.kensingtonbooks.com

APHRODISIA BOOKS are published by

Kensington Publishing Corp.
850 Third Avenue
New York, NY 10022

All Kensington Titles, Imprints, and Distributed Lines are available at special quantity discounts for bulk purchases for sales promotions, premiums, fund-raising, and educational or institutional use.

Special book excerpts or customized printings can also be created to fit specific needs. For details, write or phone the office of the Kensington special sales manager: Kensington Publishing Corp., 850 Third Avenue, New York, NY 10022, attn: Special Sales Department, Phone: 1-800-221-2647.

Aphrodisia and the A logo Reg. U.S. Pat & TM Off.

ISBN-13: 978-0-7582-2216-9
ISBN-10: 0-7582-2216-5

First Kensington Trade Paperback Printing: December 2008

10 9 8 7 6 5 4 3 2 1

Printed in the United States of America

For WTT, always.
For SKK, may her red pen and wit never run dry.
For JLP, whose breathtaking images grace my e-world.

1

Silence smothered the dunes as the officiating *klerin* held up his arms, his black sleeves rippling in the hot breeze. "We will begin," he said deliberately when all eyes were upon him. "We will greet the morning sun to initiate the marriage ceremony, joining the lands of the Sultan and the Raj through the beds of Raj ir Adham and Princess Shahrazad."

Shahrazad stifled a shiver. Haniyyah should have been wedding the Raj, but instead her head stared at her from the Pike Wall, her cousin's once lustrous skin now waxy and pale. Talking to the soldier had been enough to negate the engagement, but touching him . . . What had possessed Haniyyah to touch a man? Shahrazad would never do such a thing.

"Please, begin," the Sultan commanded the *klerin* from the opposite dune. "The sun awaits your salutation."

The *klerin* nodded, closed his hands together over his heart, then turned toward the sunrise. As the *klerin*'s salutation flowed from one asana to another, he took the warrior's stance, the same one he had used to behead her foolish cousin. God hold her in his eyes, she would miss her.

The hot sand burned through the soles of her slippers, but Shahrazad didn't move. She didn't lift her eyes. She had never spoken to an unrelated man. And by God's eyes, she never would touch one. Ever.

"Princess Shahrazad?" a man's voice asked from several steps behind her. She jumped, and the tiny golden bells on her wedding veil jangled in the desert's morning heat. The *klerin* glared at her interruption.

"Hush," her mother-in-law-to-be whispered to her. "Do not embarrass my son."

"I heard a man—" she started to whisper, but her nurse, Duha, caught her eye and gently shook her head.

"There is no man in the women's tent," the old woman said, her lips barely moving. Her kohl-rimmed eyes didn't leave the *klerin* as she added, "How could there be?"

Despite the sun beating down on the silk canopy, the words chilled her—she had heard a man's voice.

"Princess, come to me," the intruder whispered again, his words sliding over her like a snake.

Who was he? Her husband-to-be stood below, his broad face impassive, his blond hair tucked neatly into his gold turban. She caught another glimpse of her cousin's head, Haniyyah's black hair floating around her lifeless face. Shahrazad felt faint, and the desert seemed to swim and ooze around her. Was she hallucinating?

"You will come to me," the stranger said, his words more insistent. Wasn't that his robe brushing the backs of her calves? She couldn't be imagining that. Why didn't her mother-in-law-to-be stop him? Why didn't her nurse?

"You'll not belong to the Raj ir Adham," the stranger said in her ear. Now she could feel the heat of his body through her silk *oraz*, smell his oddly feminine scent of gardenia blossoms. If he leaned forward . . .

If he leaned forward and touched her, her world would crash. If he touched her, she was ruined.

"You'll belong to me."

Something in her snapped. She jerked her chin hard, making her bells ring again, loudly this time.

The noise made the *klerin* stop in the middle of his sun salutation, and he glared into the women's tent. "Obey the rules," her mother-in-law-to-be said as Duha looked at her, worry etched in her ancient face.

"Look behind me," Shahrazad whispered. "Who is it?"

Ignoring the glowering *klerin*, her mother-in-law-to-be looked quickly where directed. With a tight expression, she shook her head. "There is no one," she hissed. "How could there be? What in God's eyes is wrong with you?"

"But—"

The woman hardened her features and pointedly looked away, and the *klerin* continued his chant.

She heard a shifting of robes behind her. "You'll be mine," the stranger said. "And you'll enjoy every heartbeat of it."

She froze absolutely, like a mouse hypnotized by a cobra's gaze.

And then he touched her. He actually ran his fingertips over the small of her back. He stroked her flesh. "I can grant your heart's desire," the stranger whispered in her ear, his breath heating her skin.

Before she could move, before she could draw in one more breath, shame enveloped her. She was spoilt—and she'd ruined her family's chance to survive the *shitani* invasion.

She could not bear this.

"Leave me alone!" she said, turning toward her assailant, her bells jangling even after her voice died. Below her the *klerin* stopped speaking, but more chilling, Shahrazad saw no man, only an empty spot where the man should be standing.

"I will take you from here," her mother-in-law-to-be hissed. "My son will wed a more stable woman."

Was she insane? Shahrazad's eyes fell on the Pike Wall and her cousin's dead eye seemed to wink at her. *You'll join me here*, she seemed to say. But Shahrazad couldn't let that happen. The *shitani* would lick up her land with their demonic tongues, tear it up with their demonic claws.

"I am sorry, mother-in-law-to-be," she said, keeping her eyes down. "I don't know what's come over me."

"I'll come all over you," the man breathed in her ear.

Channeling her rage, Shahrazad realized she needed to do something drastic. She was not crazy.

The heat of the man's body told her exactly where he stood, even if her eyes hadn't seen him. She knew where to strike. Lifting her foot so gracefully that not one of her bells rang, she kicked back with all her might, aiming for his groin.

Her face hit the woman standing in front of her, bruising her lip. Her mother-in-law-to-be fell into her neighbor as Shahrazad's elbow slammed into her chest. A masculine yelp started to come from the throat of her assailant, and then—silence.

She stumbled again as the body behind her unexpectedly vanished.

Duha sent her a worried glance, the wattles on her old neck shaking as she clutched Shahrazad's arm and refused to release it. Her aunts and cousins stared too, but her mother-in-law-to-be tightly shook her head, refusing to dignify the fiasco.

The invisible stranger hadn't doubled over in pain as she'd expected—he'd simply vanished.

And Shahrazad thought she might faint. The touch from this disappearing man could mean only one thing: a magician had cursed her, cursed her marriage.

And no one defeated a magician.

* * *

His sister, the co-ruler of House Kulwanti, had vanished—and Prince Tahir took full responsibility. He'd run her off.

"The other Houses are beginning to suspect," Queen Kulwanti said. "Queen Kalila must be found—now."

"Who suspects what?" he asked, hating the guilt. He'd never meant for Kalila to flee. He'd just suggested she refuse the Impregnation.

"Queen Balqis expressed overly enthusiastic admiration for my ability to rule without my co-ruler . . . and then she asked how you were faring. She hadn't seen you hawking lately, she said."

"By the Sun Goddess's eye," Tahir said, anger tightening his muscles. "How can I hawk when I'm fulfilling Kalila's duties?"

"I believe that was her point."

"Perhaps if we Impregnated her daughter instead of one from House Casmiri—"

Imperious as ever, his mother held her hand to silence him. "Political machinations won't save us now. We have a bigger problem looming on our horizon."

"And what is that?"

Queen Kulwanti relaxed her gnarled fingers on the table. All vestiges of bitchy mightiness dropped away. "The augury was here this morning."

"What did she say?"

"If Kalila isn't found in a month and a day, *shitani* will invade our land—and conquer it."

He let out his breath, wishing he'd never urged Kalila to stand up for herself. Was his land going to fall because of this? "That's a prediction directly from the nine hells," he said.

"Yes." His mother ran her fingers around the edge of the table. "Not only did the augury's knucklebones make this claim, but she also saw snaketrack sign and some bizarre celestial portent pointing to the ascension of the *shitani*."

So many signs, he thought. If he'd only kept his advice to himself. "That seems definitive."

"There's more." His mother looked older than she ever had. "A woman—someone with eyes the color of honey—she is supposed to help restore Kalila. This woman is from the Land of the Moon."

He thought about this prediction for a moment, confused. "How could any of those women help?" he asked finally. "They're nothing but chattel." As he was himself.

"Be that as it may, the augury declared it as truth. The old sorceress is seldom wrong."

"I'll go." To save his land, he'd rectify this problem or die trying. "I'll find her."

"No." Queen Kulwanti wrapped her crooked hand around his, her hard silver ring winking in the afternoon sunlight. "I couldn't bear the thought of losing both my children."

For a moment Tahir couldn't speak. His mother had treated him like property for so long he couldn't believe she thought of him as blood, as something she treasured. "Mother," he said, "Are you well?"

She brushed his hand away. "My heart is sick," she said. "The *shitani* have been quiet for so long I thought we'd have time to build an unassailable land. Instead, I hear they're coming, my co-ruler is missing and inadequate, and the rival Houses are nipping at my heels. You—" She jabbed him with the nail of her index finger then stopped speaking.

"Me, what?" he asked.

"You could have ruled by my side—if the matriarchy had been open-minded enough." She paused, her eyes focused unseeingly on the window. "I should have pushed them harder."

Tahir was too shocked to respond.

"I need to unite these Houses," she said into the awkward silence. "And I cannot do it without Kalila—who'd rather be anywhere but here."

"Kalila won't let the *shitani* invade her home," he said with more assurance than he felt. "I'll bring her back."

"The Warqueen Abbesses will bring her," she corrected. "I'll select the best ones this evening."

"You'll send the Warqueens to the Land of the Moon?" He didn't keep the doubt from his voice. "The Sultan won't thank you."

"Don't dictate policy to me, boy," she said, standing with royal haughtiness. Her brief show of vulnerability was gone. "I want you to Impregnate House Casmiri directly after you leave these chambers. They've earned the right."

"House Nouf would be better—"

Again she held up her hand. "You will Impregnate House Casmiri now."

As Tahir left her chambers for the Impregnation chamber of House Casmiri, he stifled his frustration. The queen gave with one hand and took with another—said he would rule well but then forbade him to speak about policy.

It wasn't that he'd loathe impregnating whatever woman House Casmiri deemed worthy. Fucking was enjoyable, almost regardless of his partner. But the Land of the Sun was in jeopardy, and it was his responsibility to fix it.

And he could not meet that responsibility while obeying his queen.

2

─────────

"Read your bones for me," Shahrazad said. "What does my future hold?" No magicians, she silently pleaded. No Pike Walls. Only marriage to the Raj. Only the safety of her land.

Duha shook her head, folds of skin obscuring her expression. "Seeing the future is not a good thing, my darling."

But Shahrazad needed hope. "It's important." She couldn't shake the feeling something big lurked on the horizon—something big and terrible. "If you read them and they refuse to work, we've lost nothing."

The old woman sighed again. "Very well. I'll do it." Duha wiped the last of the oil on Shahrazad's braids, then dug the knuckles from her pocket. She closed her fingers around them, and Shahrazad wondered if she'd changed her mind. Finally the old nurse poured the things into Shahrazad's palm.

"Think about your future but only in the most general terms. Don't ask a question or focus on something like your wedding—just think about tomorrow and the next day. Think about your family and the mornings and nights."

Shahrazad closed her eyes, holding the bones. Letting images of the rising sun fill her mind, she imagined sumptuous meals eaten with her mother-in-law-to-be and new moons rising above the dunes. She imagined her father's paddocks filled with new foals. She tried to imagine her husband-to-be, the Raj ir Adham, but his face wouldn't focus.

Instead a rangy man with hawklike features came to mind. His hair, black as a well's bottom, grew long, past his shoulders. He had broad shoulders, and he was smiling, his gaze locked on hers. His eyes were a delicious brown, as delicious as his skin, and his expression reminded her of—

"Give those bones back, my darling," Duha said, holding out her white hand.

But Shahrazad couldn't obey. Her hand wouldn't move, and the vision of the man wouldn't dissipate. Now, his dark hair was tied back in a neat club, and he was wielding a bow, his long fingers pulling the string and arrow. His silk shirt had melted away, and muscles rippled through his powerful arm. The planes of his chest called to her fingertips, her tongue. She longed to feel the texture of his skin and the hard play of his muscles beneath her palm.

"Shahrazad?" His voice was deep, melodic even. She could imagine him humming to a belly dancer's drums.

Through the vision, he looked at her and started, like he hadn't expected to see her standing there. Then he smiled, a luxurious expression that matched his voice. He set his bow aside and embraced her, flaunting the rules of her land.

She couldn't step away from him. She wanted to feel his strength, have those mighty arms wrapped around her. Inexorably, he drew her to him, and she didn't mind. Not a bit.

"Who are you?" Shahrazad asked him, her nose buried in his shoulder. He smelled masculine, of sandalwood and . . . his own musk.

But he had no answer. Instead, he kissed her. Only this was no chaste kiss like those she'd received from uncles and brothers and her father.

First, his lips grazed hers, and she smelled the sweetness of his breath. Then his kiss stole her ability to think, to breathe. As his tongue wrapped around hers, her knees buckled and—

"I need my bones back, darling," Duha said, shaking Shahrazad's shoulder. The touch and the harsh movement evaporated the vision. "You've had them long enough to talk to them."

"But I think they spoke to me," Shahrazad said, still enthralled by the image. The slick heat between her thighs wasn't something she could ignore. What dark beauty that man had possessed. Who was he? Could he be the magician? But there'd been no danger in his eye—only in his lips.

"What did they say?" Duha asked, her voice practically vibrating with some unnamed emotion. Her gaze was locked on hers.

"They didn't use words. I just . . . saw something. Someone."

"Something or someone?" Duha tossed the knucklebones on the long table as if they burned her hand. They landed softly, not clattering on the polished wood. "Who was it?"

"I don't know."

"A man?"

"Yes," Shahrazad said. He'd definitely been a man. "But no one I recognized. Not the Raj. Not any of my uncles. Certainly not the Sultan."

"Hmph," the old woman said, and relief filled Shahrazad as Duha tore her attention away from her face and examined the bones scattered over the table. They gleamed in the morning sun.

"What do the bones say?" she asked. "That I'll be happily married, give birth to three fat, happy children, and—"

"They didn't speak," Duha said, cutting her off. "The bones said nothing—just as I predicted."

Shahrazad looked at the knuckles scattered across the table, knobs up and down and every which way. They meant as much to her as snaketracks in the sand. But Shahrazad knew a falsehood when she heard one.

"What do they really say?"

"They say nothing." The old woman turned away so Shahrazad couldn't see her face.

"You should tell me—they read my fate."

"Your fate is your fate, regardless of what the bones say. It is immutable."

From deep within the palace's heart a throaty bell rang the hour, and Duha turned toward her. "Are you ready for the ceremony?" she asked, eying Shahrazad critically.

"You dressed me yourself. You know I'm prepared."

"Well, your mother-in-law-to-be selected that *oraz*, and I wasn't certain about it." Duha lifted the silken hem with a doubtful expression. "But I have to admit the orange color suits your complexion." She made a wistful sound. "Your skin is so lovely, the color of the darkest honey."

"Duha, stop. I want to know what the bones said." Did they refer to the evil magician who'd touched her?

"Just remember," the old maid breathed in her ear.

"Remember what?" She didn't understand why they were whispering. They were alone in the princess's chambers, as dictated by the rite of the ceremony.

"Remember this: Let no man touch you—not until your wedding night."

"Of course I wouldn't." But fear raced through her as an image of her cousin's dead eyes danced in her mind. The magician . . . he had touched her. She deserved to die. Shahrazad took a deep breath. "Do the bones foresee my death?"

"Worse," the old woman breathed. "If you let a man touch you, our land will collapse. The *shitani* will invade."

He stepped toward Casmiri's Impregnation chamber, knowing it was a man's lot to blindly obey. If he had his way, he'd be building an alliance with House Nouf.

House Casmiri couldn't help them against the *shitani*. Not only were their lands placed non-strategically, but they had no Warqueen Abbesses. They were nearly useless. Their lands sat between Kulwanti and the *shitani*, and they had a strong army. True, Casmiri's ancient lineage brought power and respect among the Houses, but the *shitani* cared little for human formalities.

Still, his mother said to service House Casmiri, and service he would.

And perhaps this chore wouldn't be particularly odious—lush as melted butter, the warm scent of passion curled through the air. "Prince Tahir," a voice called.

"Yes?"

"Please, come here." The desire in her voice was clear, and he had no doubt she was ovulating. "Come now."

"But where is your eunuch?" Three or four Casmiri women, all ovulating, should be standing before him, waiting for the Impregnator to make his choice, waiting for the Kulwanti Way of Pleasure.

"I am alone. Please, approach."

Tahir began to obey, but something stopped him—a nagging question. Why was she alone? Perhaps she outranked all other fertile women? Perhaps the Casmiri delegation had only one ovulating woman today?

Or perhaps this was some sort of trap.

"Prince Tahir?" she purred. If her body matched her voice, the speaker made delicious bait.

But when he saw her, all rational thought fled. The woman lying in the silk nest oozed lust. She wasn't young, but the flush on her cheeks and the ripe curves of her naked breasts screamed fertility. The scent of her desire filled the small room, nearly overwhelming the cloying scent of gardenias.

"I hope you're ready for me, Queen Casmiri."

"I hope *you're* ready for *me*," she said, her voice husky, almost dreamy.

The laughing challenge in her eyes made his heart beat faster. This woman would be perfectly fuckable between the sheets. "I'm not known for leaving women wanting," he said, surprised at the thickness of his voice.

"Which of your characteristics bring you the most notoriety, then?"

"You could discover that for yourself."

"Are you up to the task?"

"For you, yes." But he was more than ready; his cock throbbed. Looking at her, he knew in forty weeks, House Casmiri would have another child of Kulwanti descent, another brick in their alliance.

Assessing him, she toyed with the silk sheet covering her midriff and thighs. The friction of the sheet hardened her nipples. He'd sink his teeth into her breasts, wrap his tongue around that dark bud.

"You are far more handsome than I was led to believe," she said, running her hand over her breast. She caught a nipple between two fingers and squeezed, making herself as hard as he was. "And I had high expectations."

"Is that so?" His voice was almost a groan. He couldn't remember a woman as forward as this. "I hope your informative source found herself satisfied with my services."

"Looking for flattery?" she asked. With her eyes locked on his, she licked her finger, slowly. Then she slid it around her nipple.

"I think I found what I was looking for."

"Your hair," she said. "I love men with long hair. It gives me

something to grab when their head is buried between my thighs."
She sat and pulled the leather tie from his club with a flirtatious
tug. He stood still, letting her come to him.

"And your profile," she said, lying back to assess him. "You
look like a hawk."

"Would you like to soar? I'll give you wings."

"I'm no bird. Your muscles interest me more." She eyed his
arms, bared by his camelskin vest. "Why don't you bring them
here? I long for something . . . harder . . . under my palms."

"I aim to please." He kept his voice steady, but as he examined her face unease crept through him. Her dark eyes were
sultry and long lashed, and her lips were swollen, just begging
to be kissed. But he didn't recognize her—and he'd memorized
the names and faces of all highborn women.

There was no chance in the nine hells he'd have forgotten
this woman.

"Looking at you isn't difficult either," he said. Slowly he unbuttoned his vest. Normally he liked to tease his women before
he serviced them. But for this woman, he sought time. "Looking at you is like looking at the Sun Goddess herself—beautiful." He paused, then added, "And hot."

She smiled at the compliment—at least her lips did. And
while part of him wanted to suck that fake smile off her face
until her eyes rolled back in pleasure and she screamed his
name for the entire palace to hear, the rational part of his brain
wanted to know her identity.

"What would you like me to call you on this sizzling afternoon, Queen Casmiri?" he asked.

She rolled onto her stomach so that the silk sheet molded to
the curve of her ass. "That's an interesting question," she said.
"And I like the implication."

"That being?" He worked yet another button—slowly.

"That I might have a different name tomorrow," she said.
"And the day after."

"Would you?"

She laughed, a rich song that wrapped around his cock and pulled. "I haven't told you my name for today. How can I speak about an ephemeral tomorrow?"

Perhaps this woman came from a rival house, one that would leverage his blood against the queens'. "Would you like me to suggest a name for you?" he asked, letting a smile dance on his lips although he wasn't amused. *Like Queen of House Nouf?* he thought to himself. *Or perhaps House Tefertiri?*

"Perhaps you'd need more information before you gave me something so personal as a name," she said. She cocked her hip so that the paper-thin silk molded against her cunt. Her wetness dampened the sheet, and his cock pressed against his trousers.

He eyed her. "You're giving me quite a bit of information."

"And yet you stand there—alone. If I didn't know better, I might worry you were balking, avoiding my bed and the touch of my skin."

"Never that."

"Then I hope you're not one of those men who prefer the helplessness of younger women."

Tahir grinned. He couldn't help himself. The challenge she presented made him want to bite her ass until she screamed in delight. "Not particularly," he said. "Though I do my best to please the more tenderhearted when I find them in my bed."

Languidly, she rolled to her back and retrieved a golden rope from the side table. She held it up, and yellow tassels dangled from the ends, teasing her plum-colored nipples. Her warm gardenia scent filled the room. "You could tie me, if you like helplessness. Try to restrain my . . . enthusiasm."

"Curbing your enthusiasm would be neither in your interest nor mine." Which was true.

She laughed, her lips curving and her white teeth flashing. "I could tie you up, if you're man enough to take it."

Knowing he couldn't prolong the inevitable, he shrugged

out of his vest. Likely she was from House Nouf . . . and perhaps that wasn't a bad thing. If he impregnated her, that would force his queen into an alliance with them.

Of course, that was high treason. But if it buffered his House against the *shitani*, shouldn't he at least consider it? Perhaps giving House Nouf their alliance with House Kulwanti was exactly the right thing to do.

"What do you say?" she said, dangling the golden rope with a smile dancing around her lips. "Want to play?"

"I'll tie you."

"I can grant your heart's desire," she whispered.

Her words disturbed him, though he couldn't have said why. They made sense in the context, but something about them tempted him beyond the rational . . .

His heart truly ached with desire, and it wasn't for this woman, as beautiful as she was. He wanted his sister's power.

Slowly he took the rope from her hand, and he covered her naked body with his half-clothed one. Just as deliberately, she arched her bared breasts into his chest and sucked his neck. Her teeth scraped against his skin in a way that brought equal parts pleasure and pain to his brain, and his cock.

He growled in desire. This woman wanted to be dominated, and he wanted to dominate her. She'd seen to that.

And he wanted to rule.

But he wanted that leadership honestly. He couldn't fuck this imminently fuckable woman. Not yet.

Snaking his hand through her hair, he caught her lips in his, just barely keeping his lust in check. He wouldn't let himself be used in whatever game she was playing, but she certainly had his attention.

When she sunk her teeth into his lip as she pressed her hot cunt against his cock, his ability to think vanished. Blood—his own—tantalized his mouth, and he drew back as she laughed.

"You like it rough?" he asked. He grabbed her wrists and held them above her head as she struggled, but his strength didn't appear to daunt her. Her nipples were rock hard, begging to be tasted as she rubbed them against him.

"I like your consideration," she said, "rough or otherwise." Sinking her teeth into the flesh of his chest, she rolled her thighs against his cock. "You like mine, too, I see."

He was balanced precariously between control and abandon, and she was definitely pushing him. She was pushing hard.

Something in him snapped. He'd given up everything to camouflage his missing sister. Every time he covered for Kalila, he risked his life—and this wanton succubus would take it all from him.

He wouldn't do it.

He wrapped the cord around her wrists and began to pull her hands above her head.

"You can tie me up," she said. "But I won't be helpless." She wrapped her legs around his waist and pulled his cock tight against her cunt to make her point.

"I think you want to be helpless," he said. "You want to forego that power. Maybe it rests too heavily in your heart."

Her dark eyes met his unflinchingly. Her irises were a shocking violet, the color of the sun leaking across the desert as it set. "The kind of power I have cannot be foresworn," she said.

With her love of the sensuous, he didn't doubt it. He caught one of those plum-colored nipples between his teeth and bit, firmly enough to get her attention but not enough to make her bleed.

It didn't seem hard enough for her though. When he inhaled and sucked, she gasped, pressing her cunt against his cock. Her wet heat saturated his trousers.

"Bite harder," she said in her husky voice. "Harder."

For a moment, Tahir nearly lost control. She wanted him.

She was begging for him. Fucking her would be the easiest thing in the world. He could sink his cock so deep into her that he'd lose himself, lose his ambitions.

Instead, he sucked harder and wrapped the rope more firmly around her wrists.

"Yes," she hissed as he tied the ropes to the wrought-iron bed frame. "Now we can play."

She kicked off the thin sheet that'd been covering her waist, and appreciation raced through him. She'd completely shaved herself, and a gold stud glittered in her clit. He didn't know anyone who wore such jewelry, not even the bold women of House Nouf.

He pulled his belt from around his waist, his gaze locked on that jewel.

"Yes," she said, her eyes languid with anticipation. Even when he wrapped the supple leather around her ankle and bound her foot to the bed frame, the stranger writhed in pleasure. The undeniable scent of her desire filled the air—as did the perfume of ovulation.

Finally, when he had her arms and one leg tied, he broke character and stood, relieved to have some distance between them. "Who are you?" he demanded. "Who are you really?"

"Ah," she said, undulating so that her breasts shimmied. But she crossed her thighs so that her gold stud was hidden, and Tahir was disgusted to find himself disappointed. Maybe the matriarchy was right in their belief that intact men were good only for servicing women, all cock and no brain. "I thought you were too smart to fall for my little ploy," she said, "but a girl can hope."

"Girl?" he asked. "You haven't been a girl since the day your mother birthed you. Now tell me who you are. Who sent you?"

"Do you care?" she asked, running one foot over his cock. Never had he been happier to remain clothed in the presence of such a beautiful, naked woman. "You look like a man seeking something . . ." She licked her ruby lips and smiled. "Power, perhaps? Something to call your own? I don't think you can get that here."

"If you don't tell me your name now," he said, angered to find she'd struck so close to truth, "I'll call the guards. I'm sure Queen Kulwanti would love to see which House is posing as House Casmiri."

The coy gaze dropped away, and she stopped slithering. "But I can grant your heart's desire."

And again, Tahir knew—knew—she wasn't promising sex and lust. What she was promising he couldn't fathom. A lesser man might feel afraid. "Who are you?" he asked.

She spread her legs, her jeweled clit glittering. "Why don't you come find out?"

And it was tempting. He could plunge his cock right into her. She'd arch to meet him, scream his name in pleasure. She'd welcome him.

Which was why he couldn't do it. "Fucking you won't answer my questions."

Her red lips made a beautiful moue that begged to be kissed from her face, and she said, "But you can't leave me like this. I need satisfaction, and so do you." She slid her perfectly formed thighs together and said, "You know I'm right."

He leaned toward her and ran his fingers over her clit. She pressed toward him. Her wet heat welcomed him, and he moved his fingers slowly, making the caress last. Then, almost as an afterthought, he slid a finger inside her.

"Please," she begged as she bucked against him. The expression of unfulfilled hunger on her face seemed genuine, and his cock throbbed in response.

He slid his finger out, caressing her clit. Then he pushed two fingers into her, deeper this time. "I'm not a cruel man," he said, watching pleasure pulse across her face. Her eyes, heavy lidded, were rolled back in desire. His cock ached for her. "I don't have to leave you longing."

"Then don't. Fuck me."

He leaned forward and sucked her clit hard, keeping his fingers sliding inside her. She tasted of fertility, like the verdant sedges on an oasis.

"I can fuck you without impregnating you," he said, just as he felt her muscles quivering with an impending orgasm. He flicked his tongue over her clit, then said, "Would that be satisfying? All this effort to seduce me, and no child in forty weeks?"

"Fuck me," she said again, her voice as gravelly as a pipe-smoking *vizier*. Her hips sought his face.

"I think I'll do this instead." He leaned forward and sucked again, not gently. His thumb slid hard over her clit, and his fingers sought that spot deep inside her that promised satisfaction.

And he found it. She climaxed hard against his fingers, yowling like a cat as he sat back to watch her beautiful face.

"Your performance appeared theatrical enough for any dramatist," he goaded after her internal storm died back. He stood and adjusted his trousers, a part of him amazed he'd stood up to this woman. She exuded such power, and men were not permitted to question their queens. "Now tell me who you are."

"You're not going to fuck me, are you?"

"Not for salvation from all the nine hells."

The sexy mien dropped away like a stone down a well. "You can untie me then," she said. "We need to talk."

"I think we can have a civilized discussion just like this," he said, tugging the belt holding her ankle. "I like you tied up."

"You don't like me enough."

"Are you finished in your attempts to seduce me, or can I cover you—not that I don't appreciate the view but I am a man, after all. We're not to be trusted with much."

She sighed and closed her free leg over her tied one. "Cover me, please."

He did, admiring the slide of the silk over her creamy skin. "Did you want to discuss House Nouf's bid to ally with House Kulwanti?" he asked.

She laughed. "Is that what you think this is about? An alliance?"

He looked at her, daring her to change his mind. But she'd raised a frightening question: if she wasn't from House Nouf, which House directed her?

"It's logical." She sighed again, shrugging as best she could with her hands tied above her. "But untrue. I'm not from Nouf."

"What is true, then?"

"I'm not from any House."

This caught his attention. Tahir had never met a woman not associated with a House. "Who are you?" he asked. "And I want an answer, or I will call the guards."

"You're not asking the right question."

"Ayoob!" He called the eunuch's name out the door, almost loudly enough to be heard.

"My name is not important," she said, fighting the bonds to sit.

With his booted toe, he pushed her back into the silk sheets. "What is?"

"The location of your sister."

"My sister?" He couldn't keep the shock from his voice. What did this stranger know about Kalila's absence?

"Queen Kalila has been gone since the dawn of the Festival of Madeeha. And I can tell you how to find her."

I can grant your heart's desire. Her words echoed unbidden in his mind. But what was his desire? Did he want Kalila restored and his normal life back, or did he want recognition for the work he did in her stead? Either way, he wanted the safety of his land.

"After the Festival of Madeeha, my sister retired to her personal palace for a period of deep meditation," he said, telling her the propaganda his mother had concocted.

"And I'm carrying your child," she said, "seeded by your talented tongue and heat-seeking fingers."

"Believe what you want." Then he flashed her a grin of his own. "Although I like to think my tongue is talented."

"Do you want to know where to find her or not? Perhaps you like risking your life to cover for her?"

"I've no fear," he said as she searched his face.

Perhaps reading something there, she grinned, a feral expression that reminded him of a desert cat. "Perhaps you enjoy people underestimating your intellect while they sing praises of Queen Kalila," she said. "Especially after she ran away, and you complete her duties?"

"She did not run away." Again this woman had hit too close to the truth with her sarcasm. Still, his bitterness would never provoke him to treason. Never.

"I think," she said, goading him, "you'd be happy if Kalila never returned."

The spitfire spoke subversion, but she was tied and at his mercy. "How do I find her? Where is she?"

"She's been kidnapped by Badr the Bad."

"The magician stole her? A man stole her?" Shaking his head, Tahir could hardly believe it. "That's why the matriarchy castrate all but a handful of men—just to prevent violence like this."

The beauty at his mercy snorted. "I should have been more precise. She went willingly to Badr the Bad, who then prevented her return. He's holding her captive."

"That she went willing to the magician is impossible to believe." He tried to weigh this possibility for any grain of truth. "How would she even find him? Men such as he aren't permitted in the Land of the Sun."

" 'Men such as he'," his prisoner taunted. "You mean men with their own minds—and balls—intact."

"Under the reign of the queens, there've been no wars for seven generations. Every child is cared for, educated, and fed. Every adult has a meaningful position."

"Every *girl* child," the beauty said.

"Boys too."

"Only if castration falls under your definition of 'cared for'."

"Look at the Land of the Moon," he said. "Those men kill heedlessly. Blood soaks their sands. Women are treated as chattel. How does your society behave, judgmental one?"

"My apologies, Prince Tahir," she said with mock humility. "I didn't get myself tied up in the bed by your capable hands to discuss politics. I came to tell you how to retrieve your sister."

"So tell me."

"Badr the Bad is looking for an assistant, and you fit his needs. Assist him for a month and day, and you can save your sister."

"Assist him?" Tahir tried—and failed—imagining his mother accepting this idea. "House Kulwanti will attack to return their queen to the throne. He'll die in a puddle of blood."

"That would not be in your best interest."

"You seem to think my opinion matters."

The red-haired beauty smiled, making the corners of her violet eyes crinkle. "Don't sell yourself short, Prince Tahir. I've seen your actions cause impressive results."

"But have you seen Queen Kulwanti?"

"I know things. You're substituting for Queen Kalila, unbeknownst to anyone. Did that idea originate with you—or your mother?"

Of course he'd invented the plan. He heard her point but said nothing.

"You wield more power than you realize, and as soon as you embrace that truth, your world will change for the better."

"You speak in riddles, woman."

"You force me to speak when I'd rather fuck."

"And give you a child to leverage against House Kulwanti?" he asked. "I think not."

"And you say you wield no power. You wield it now."

"Many people have power between their thighs," he said. "As I'm sure you know."

"Your skills are wasted here, Prince Tahir."

He ran his hand through his hair, unwilling to hear such enticing treason. "Where's my sister?"

She shrugged in her yellow binds, the tassels dangling near her elegant wrists. "You can find Badr the Bad in the Cavern of the Sixty Thieves," she said.

"Tell him to expect my mother's army," he said, reaching to release her. He'd send one of the Warqueen spies to track her to the magician's nest. "The Warqueen Abbesses are a sight to behold, a match even for the soldiers in the Land of the Moon."

"I'll tell him as you wish." The red-haired woman chuckled and snapped her fingers, filling the chamber with gray smoke.

With a curse, he lunged for her ankle, but his hand met only silk sheet.

The red-haired beauty had vanished, leaving only the lingering scent of gardenias in the haze.

3

Tahir let Kateb gallop west, toward the Cavern of Sixty Thieves, toward the magician who had his sister. He'd defied his mother, but that was the price he had to pay for running off Kalila and losing the fake Lady Casmiri. His short service to Badr could restore House Kulwanti's queen and stop the *shitani*. He owed it to his land.

As they galloped, Tahir noticed a thick scent of gardenias, which made no sense—water wasn't available for leagues. Why would desert air smell like a succulent tree?

A piercing cry speared the dusk air. Kateb stopped in his tracks. Snorting through dilated nostrils, his short neck vibrated with tension. Tahir pulled a dagger from its sheath as he scanned the dunes.

Shitani, he thought. The demons must have awakened—as predicted by the auguries. Did he have even the promised month and a day?

Again a shriek filled the air, only to be cut off mid-cry. This time Tahir recognized it. It wasn't a *shitani*—it was a woman. Kalila.

Silently dismounting, he palmed a second dagger. The gardenia scent was thicker here, cloying. Tahir looked down the escarpment. Below, a *shitani* lurked over a captured woman, and the creature looked just like the ancient drawings in his mother's library.

Who was the victim? Tahir squinted in the fading light. *Not my sister,* he prayed to the Sun Goddess. *Please, not my sister.*

He couldn't see the woman at first. All angular, bony, and green, the *shitani* stood in his way as it wrapped its unnatural tongue around the woman's breast. Everywhere the creature's tongue lapped, her flesh disappeared—just as described in the ancient texts. Her entire left leg was gone, although the rope that had held her ankle to the stake remained taut. Her right breast, lush and dark, was vanishing as he watched.

The woman was not his sister. This woman had skin the color of amber. Kalila was darker, and she didn't have a purple gemstone winking from her belly button. At least, she hadn't last time he'd seen her.

The creature moved down the woman, burying its head between her legs. The woman opened her eyes, and her honey-colored gaze met his.

Tahir snapped. He'd never seen eyes of this color. This was the woman from the augury.

He leaped, daggers extended, and he landed atop the demon, which collapsed beneath him with an angry squeal. He didn't think—he acted, grabbing the thing's chin, pulling it taut, and slicing the length of its neck. Hot blood poured into the desert sand as the body quivered in death throes. The earthy scent of copper momentarily overpowered the flowery perfume.

The dark-haired woman began bucking against her ties, her gold-tipped braids flailing. Tahir threw the *shitani* corpse to the ground, rushing to cut her binds.

"No!" she cried. He realized that the gardenia scent came from her. "Wipe the saliva from me first. Please!"

Tahir looked at her, wondering if she'd lost her mind, but she pointed to her left with her chin. "Use that."

He picked up the implement. It reminded him of the tools grooms used on horses to scrape them dry after they'd bathed them.

"Wipe the saliva off me before it dries, or I'll waste the tiny bit of spit I managed to collect for all this effort."

He began by scraping her invisible toe. The demon saliva was unlike any he'd seen. It had the consistency of olive oil and a deep, rich fragrance—gardenia. Her toe, then her foot became visible as the spit came off, thick and viscous. It accumulated in the groove of the scraper, and he started to shake it clean.

"Don't throw that away," she said, her tone exasperated. "There's an amphora over there. You need to collect it."

But as he picked up the clay jar and carefully let the oily liquid into it, he realized he hadn't saved her—he'd interrupted her.

"You meant to do this, didn't you?" he asked. "You came here to collect *shitani* spit. Why do you want to be invisible?"

She didn't answer as he slid the scraper over her thigh, making it reappear in its glorious perfection. The warm muscle begged to be caressed, and she actually trembled as his fingertips accidentally touched flesh.

"Who was going to scrape you clean?" he asked, letting the saliva drip into the jar. Her flesh felt warm in his palm, alive and toned.

"Badr the Magician."

"Where is he?"

"You must have frightened him off."

Only then did he realize he recognized her voice—the redhaired beauty who'd tried to get him to fuck her, the fraudulent Lady Casmiri.

"You," he growled.

"Who else?"

"What game are you playing?" Tahir stood, letting the

scraper drop to the sand. "A heartbeat ago, you were dark skinned with tanzanite in your belly button. Your hair was black and braided with gold tips. Your eyes were gold, not purple. You were . . . beautiful."

She looked at him from behind lidded eyes and said, "You don't like red hair and white skin?"

"You didn't have red hair when the demon ran its tongue over you."

"Are you certain?" she asked, her voice sly. "Could you see in the odd light?"

"I saw your hair perfectly. It was black and braided. It's neither now."

She shrugged, an elegant gesture he recognized from the Casmiri Impregnation chamber. It didn't inspire rational thought. In fact, he wanted to fuck her. Which was exactly why the matriarchy castrated most men. Reining in his lust, he looked at her, running his hand through his hair. "I could walk away and leave you to the snakes, one of which probably spawned you."

"I'm a pawn in all of this, too." She sighed. "Please, don't let the demon saliva dry on me."

"Why shouldn't I?" he demanded. "You liked the creature's tongue rolling over you."

"Jealous?" she shot back. "Either scrape me clean or let me do it myself, although more of the spit gets wasted that way."

He would have liked to walk away, leave her to her own misguided plan, but the sight of her with her breast missing unnerved him, and he couldn't leave her tied in the desert, waiting for a magician who may or may not appear. Tahir picked up the scraper and began to clean off her thigh again.

"That was the first demon," she said. "They'll come more often now, and in greater numbers."

"Are you certain that was a *shitani*?" he asked, cleaning her neck. "They've slept for so many generations, perhaps it's just some desert monster."

"Green skinned, pointy eared, and orange eyed? It was *shitani*."

"But how do you know that?"

She paused while he scraped the spit off her cheek. "Nothing else has spit that makes you invisible, does it?"

Her logic was flawless. The scent of her desire filled his nose, as it had in her supposed chambers. "You're still ovulating."

"That's what attracts the *shitani*—ovulating women."

He knew the feeling.

He knew the feeling, but he didn't want this redhead. He didn't trust her, didn't know her agenda. And even as he scraped the spit off her small breast, revealing another miracle of perfection, he craved the lush, dark woman he'd seen while this one had been in the demon's thrall. In his mind, he saw the other woman's honeyed gaze, and he craved that, too.

Although why that should be true, he had no idea.

"The *shitani* are searching for a new human to rule them. The scent of ovulation and competence makes them seek a queen; the scent of masculine competence makes them crave a king. Either would do."

"They think you're their queen then." He kicked the cat-sized corpse. "It was certainly worshipping you."

"If I were the queen, there'd be more *shitani* in this desert than there are hairs on your horse." She shook her head and looked at him speculatively, almost as if she were testing him. "But perhaps you're their new king?"

He snorted in disbelief. "Where I come from, men do not rule."

"Tell the *shitani* that."

"As you command, oh Queen of the *Shitani*." He gave her a mocking bow, curving the scraper through the air with a flourish. But she didn't acknowledge the humor.

"I'm not their queen, and woe to the woman who is."

An image of honeyed eyes flashed before him again, but he said nothing. He'd caught only a glimpse of her lips, full and kissable, and he wished he could see them again. "I'm almost finished." He dripped the last of the saliva into the amphora, closed it with its stopper, and put it in his pocket.

"That's my jar," she said.

"I think I'll keep it. Who knows when I'll need to become invisible."

"As you wish," she said. He would've been angry if he'd been her, but instead resignation crossed her face. And then he saw that sly look again. He couldn't shake the feeling that she'd expected him to keep the amphora, that she'd arranged for him to take it. "Untie me, at least," she added.

He looked down at her and saw that she was once again completely visible. She was also beautiful and ovulating, and the Impregnator in him found her difficult to ignore. "You like being tied at my feet."

"And you keep resisting me." She managed to look coy, tied in the sand and just wiped clean of demon spit. "But I can be very, very nice, you know."

"I can imagine." He flicked his dagger over the rope tying her wrists to the stake and freed her arm. "It's your mouth that stops me. And your cunt. I won't be a traitor to my House."

"Your House doesn't appreciate you."

"Let Badr father your child."

She choked out a laugh as she stood, and Tahir saw her point. If the magician fled at his arrival, he wasn't a very brave man. "I left my clothes here," she said, striding toward a rocky outcropping. "Let me dress, then we can go to the Cavern of Sixty Thieves." She stopped midstride, apparently unbothered by her nakedness. "I take it you're here to serve as the magician's assistant? You wish to be his for a month and a day?"

"That is the price. House Kulwanti needs Queen Kalila restored."

The red-haired woman shrugged into her robe. "And what if she doesn't want to return?"

"Our augury read the bones. If Queen Kalila isn't returned, the Land of the Sun will fall to the *shitani*."

"And you think she'll care?"

Tahir was losing patience with this woman. He whistled for his horse, and when the seasoned stallion approached, he leaped on his back. "Would you like a ride?"

When she accepted his offer, he wasn't surprised she pressed her breasts against his back or ran her hands too high up his thighs. What surprised him was that the image of the dark-skinned woman with the amber eyes kept haunting him.

"Who was she?" he asked, gently pushing her hand from his cock. "The woman with the braids."

"I don't know what you're talking about," she said.

"You do."

"Go west around those rocks, and we'll find the Cavern of Sixty Thieves."

Tahir refused to be distracted. "When the *shitani* was licking you, your form shifted. Into another woman."

She laughed. "Would you be more willing to lay with me if I looked more like her?"

Tahir didn't answer. He was the Impregnator. He could service the ugliest woman alive if need be. But something about the dark-haired woman haunted him. . . . Something in her amber eyes.

"Here's the cave," she said, jumping off. "Go in. I expect Badr will be waiting for you."

"You won't accompany me?"

"I don't have to."

"Why not?"

"Are you certain you'll serve the magician for a month and a day?"

An image of his sister flashed through his mind. "I'm certain," he said.

"Then you'll replace me." She laughed. "I'm free!"

He thought he saw a lie behind her eye, something that warned against this course of action.

But as her gleeful words sizzled through his mind, he felt something shift, like something in his mind had been shackled, and for the first time since he'd agreed to this quest, fear snaked through his veins.

His mind was no longer completely his own.

A good daughter would have remained silent throughout the entire moon salutation on the second day of her wedding ceremony, but Princess Shahrazad was no longer a good daughter—she was a desperate one.

And she was a daughter who saw the magician arrive. With flashing wings, a golden *pegaz* soared over the Amr Mountains, ridden by someone in a black robe.

"Father." As her voice floated over the silent wedding party, the *klerin* froze. She felt the women next to her still, waiting for the terrible repercussion.

"I'm beginning to loathe you, Princess Shahrazad," her mother-in-law-to-be whispered. "Must you ruin every ceremony?"

But Princess Shahrazad refused to be daunted. She gestured to the approaching *pegaz*. "Look!" she commanded. If her father and her husband-to-be couldn't help her fight this evil, no one could.

"What is it?" the Sultan demanded. Then he squinted into the sky, puzzlement clear on his expression.

"It's a . . ." Her old nurse stopped, perhaps stunned at the words about to come from her lips. "It's a *pegaz*." Her hand went to the bones in her pocket. "And it's more beautiful than anything I've ever seen."

Shahrazad could only nod in sick agreement. With wings as stunningly huge and gleaming as any storybook painting, the horse swept through the sky with power and might. The hot sun shone on the beast's massive wings, making them shine like gold as they beat the air. An emerald bridle glittered in the morning light.

"It's the magician," Princess Shahrazad said to the Sultan, hoping all the evil he embodied was captured in her meager description. "Don't let him land his beast here." *Don't let him ruin this marriage.*

"You do not command your father." The Raj ir Adham said these words calmly, but his mother turned to her and slapped her mouth.

"And you do not speak during the wedding ceremony," the older woman whispered.

Shame washed through her, stinging her like the pain hadn't. She'd never spoken out of turn or lifted a demure eye in her entire life. That she had to do so now . . .

"Please, father," she called across the dune, ignoring the taste of blood. "Can you forbid him to land?"

"Willful bitch," her mother-in-law-to-be hissed. But her father ignored her altogether, gesturing to the archers who loaded arrows into their dark bows and pointed them at the *pegaz*.

Only then did Shahrazad see the rider, the face of her assailant. His black robe rippled in the wind, and his thin mustache twisted down his face, trailing in the wind over his shoulders. Silver embroidery winked, and she saw his bared chin, which was as pointy as his nose.

And then words whipped through her mind. *I can grant your heart's desire.*

The *pegaz* adjusted the sweep of her wings so that her flight slowed. She stretched her legs as does a horse about to land after a great jump, and then she touched the ground with a silent grace.

I can grant your heart's desire. The words were a torment— like a mirage seen while crawling through the desert. By jeopardizing this marriage not once but twice, this magician had taken her heart's desire from her.

The mare galloped a few steps through the deep sand and then stood, her fine legs gleaming in the sun. Her long, elegant neck arched beautifully, and her face bore a lovely dish. The light breeze toyed with her golden forelock.

"Greetings, Sultan," the magician said to her father, sliding from the *pegaz*. His voice radiated a terrible power.

Her father responded by placing his hand on the hilt of his scimitar, a scowl clear on his fine-boned face. His bodyguards put their hands on their hilts, too.

"Who are you, sir?" the Sultan said, his voice carrying majestically across the hot sand. "Who are you to intrude upon this most sacred ceremony?"

The black-robed magician unfastened his cloak and shook it. The action sent sand whirling near his feet, and a large dust devil spun near the mare's withers.

A second man appeared from the swirling sand, stepping forward toward the wedding party with lanky grace. He was taller than her father and more broad shouldered than her husband-to-be. Shahrazad couldn't see his eyes from where she stood, but his sharp cheekbones and the elegant line of his nose reminded her of a bird of prey. His long, dark hair fluttered in the breeze for all that it was tied back in a club.

But when he turned toward her, she gasped. He was the same man she'd seen in her vision. He'd given her a secret smile and pulled her toward him like she'd belonged in his arms. He'd stolen her thought and her senses with his kiss.

As he met her forward gaze, his expression was too tight to

read, but then his eyes widened when he saw her, as if he, too, were surprised.

Suddenly the small of her back burned, just like someone held a lit torch to her skin. Her defilement ached.

"I ask again, sir," her father said to the magician, apparently unimpressed by the creation of a full-formed man from nothing but a flapping cloak and swirling sand. "Who are you? And if you fail to answer, my men will fill you and your assistant with arrows."

"Forgive the intrusion, my Sultan," the magician said, bowing low to her father, his expression humble. The tips of his mustache fluttered just above the sand. "I want nothing more than to help you celebrate the Festival of Nooroze, to help welcome your lovely daughter"—he bowed toward the canopy where she stood—"and your stalwart son-in-law"—he bowed to the Raj—"into marital bliss."

Seemingly not convinced, the Sultan raised his hand in an elegant gesture, and his archers drew back their bowstrings. "You have not answered my question."

"My Sultan, I am Badr, Great Magician of the Moon's Land and the Sun's. I bring a gift to you, to celebrate this marriage between two great houses." He stepped toward the mare's head and held her reins toward the Sultan with his long fingers. The huge moonstone ring he wore flickered in the sunlight.

"Badr the Bad," the Raj said, his disgust clear. "You seek to trick us."

"I do not trick, as you say."

"I know your reputation, sir," the Sultan said, but his gaze offset his forbidding tone. Even from this distance, Shahrazad could see his eyes drink in the winged mare. Shahrazad could almost smell her father's lust for the beast. "I know your name," the Sultan said, "and you are not welcome here."

"Very well." Badr bowed. "I will leave as you ask." He turned toward his mount, the picture of compliance.

Relief sang through Shahrazad, swamping the sorrow at the beast's departure. If the magician left, her life could continue as planned. Perhaps the burning pain across the small of her back would fade like a forgotten dream. The man with the warming kiss would vanish, too.

And when Badr the Bad grabbed his mare's mane to mount, Shahrazad actually let out the breath she hadn't known she was holding.

But then the magician paused and turned toward her father, and her breath once again refused to leave her lungs.

"What is it?" the Sultan asked. "Why do you hesitate, unwelcomed guest that you are?"

"Please forgive me," Badr said, bowing low again. "It is only that I have a question for you." A breeze swept over him, sending the tips of his long mustache fluttering against his narrow chest.

"What is your question?"

"Send him away, Father!" She couldn't contain herself. She didn't want to hear the question; she didn't want her father to hear it. "Send him now!"

But the magician answered the Sultan before the Sultan could stop him. "Are you certain you wish to send me off—when I can grant your heart's desire?"

Your heart's desire. With those all too familiar words, a strange squeak filled the women's tent, bounced off the silken ceiling and the surrounding dunes. As her nurse grabbed her arm, Shahrazad realized the cry had come from her own mouth.

"I beg your pardon," the Raj said, stepping out of his wedding tent. "But *I* am giving the Sultan his heart's desire."

"And what is that, sir?" Badr asked. "If I may ask with nothing but the deepest respect in my heart for you."

"Don't answer!" Shahrazad shouted, pushing Duha's powerful hand from her arm. "Don't engage him!"

"I will denounce this wedding if one more word falls from your mouth," her mother-in-law-to-be said.

But her husband-to-be ignored her. "With our two lands joined together in marriage," the Raj growled, anger resonating in his tone, "our great armies can protect all the Moon's Land from the *shitani* insurgence, God hold us in his eye."

The magician straightened from his bow. "Perhaps, if you find it too onerous to accept this gift from me—" Badr held up the golden reins. "You'd like to take her for a ride? A quick flight over the Amr Mountains to view the Land of the Sun on the other side?"

Oh, Shahrazad wanted to ride the winged mare more than she'd ever wanted anything. If her father felt any portion of the same longing she felt, he'd be unable to refuse. He'd fall right into the magician's trap.

"Father," she called over the dune. "Don't ride! It's a trap!"

But could any trap be sweeter, more perfectly baited?

"Perhaps your willful daughter should ride instead," the magician suggested, flapping his cloak as if shaking out dust. It was the same gesture, Shahrazad realized, that he'd used to make his assistant appear.

"Perhaps my willful daughter should ride instead," the Sultan repeated.

The women surrounding Shahrazad gasped and muttered. They certainly realized her father shouldn't allow the nearly wed princess—even one who continually spoke out of turn—out of sight for even a heartbeat. "No!" one of them shouted. Shahrazad realized it'd been Duha, who'd never said a word in the presence of a man, much less the Sultan.

"Do you wish your daughter to ride my *pegaz*?" Badr asked the Sultan, his dark eyes inscrutable at this distance.

"She rides better than most men in this land."

"Ah, but that is not the question," Badr replied. "This *pegaz* is most compliant. Your daughter will be quite safe in her care." The magician shrugged his black-clad shoulders, sending silken ripples across his elegant robe. "The true question is one concerning the character of your daughter. Do you trust her to return when the arching sky does nothing but invite?"

"How dare you!" the Sultan said, his face flushed. "She will return. Princess Shahrazad is a humble and obedient daughter. She will ride. She will return."

And she would. She could no more disobey her father—even her ensorcelled father—than she could sprout wings and fly.

The dark-haired assistant from her vision stood next to the magician. His eyes met hers across the dune, and she caught her breath. What would it be like to trace the planes of his cheek with her fingertips? With her lips? But he was shaking his head. *Do not obey*, she read. *Do not ride the* pegaz. And she knew he was correct.

"Do you trust her to ride?" the magician asked.

"Bring her down," the Sultan instructed her sisters, who immediately formed a phalanx around her and led her across the dune toward the men.

As Shahrazad stepped into the flat area where the ceremony had been conducted, she kept her gaze on her feet as trained.

The Sultan took the proffered reins from Badr and held them toward her. Shahrazad made to take them, wondering how she would ride in her wedding *oraz*, but Badr interrupted.

"Oh, allow me," he said, shaking his dreadful black cape again.

As before, dust swirled into a small tornado, but this time it enveloped Shahrazad. She felt rather than saw her father step back as the wedding guests cried their concern. For a moment she could see nothing but a swirling wall of sand.

Self-reproach filled her heart. She'd known—known with every bit of her mind—that Badr meant trouble. And here he was kidnapping her. She'd walked obediently toward her fate, knowing her father himself damned her.

But before she could cry out, the sand was gone. Several grains danced over the tip of her sandal. Only she hadn't been wearing sandals. Shahrazad realized that Badr had changed her clothing. Gone was her bridal gown with its belled veil and long flowing robe. Now she wore the most perfect riding pantaloons of violet silk. A modest top billowed to her hips, and the silver sandals laced up her calves.

"What have you done?" a man from the groom's tent called. "You've violated her purity!"

The Raj looked at her darkly, and she knew the reason. Another man had unclothed her in public. No matter that she'd had no choice in the matter, no matter that no one—including Badr—had seen anything through that wall of sand, her husband-to-be might imprison her for the transgression. He might do worse.

"I'm thinking we should kill this man and take that cloak," the Raj said to the Sultan. "Forget the beast."

"Ah!" said the magician, holding up his hands. "There is no need to kill. The cloak is yours for the asking. Only be warned." He handed it to his assistant, who shook it in a manner identical to that used by Badr—and nothing happened. "The cloak is useless without proper instruction."

"We can get those instructions from you," the Raj muttered, almost under his breath, "in my dungeon."

For a moment, for less time than it takes a man's heart to beat, flames enveloped the Raj's clothing. Blues, yellows, and oranges erupted from the air around him and coalesced into crimson. For that eye blink, the Raj wore nothing but red fire.

Before he could shout, before his mother could do more than gasp in horror—before the Sultan could lower his hand to release his archer's arrows, the Raj's wedding finery reappeared, completely unruffled.

Shahrazad wondered if she'd imagined the flames, if the heat of the morning sun intoxicated her brain. But the magician left no room for doubt. "Threaten me at your own peril," he said.

The Sultan held up his elegant hand. "Enough," he said. "We won't be robbing this magician." He turned toward her and said, "Here, daughter." He held out the reins again in invitation, his gaze still distant. From the spell? "Take this beautiful mare for a ride. Tell us what the Amr Mountains look like from above."

Shahrazad walked toward her father, slowly, her eyes on her new sandals. Violet gems like the ones in her belly button adorned the straps.

The crowd was quiet as she approached the beast, and she sensed the magician's assistant's gaze upon her, smelled his masculine scent. As in her vision, he smelled of sandalwood, and his hair was the color of black onyx.

She took the reins from her father. Without a word, she put her hands on the mare's neck and launched herself onto the animal's back.

Shahrazad had executed this move hundreds of times, maybe thousands. She felt her right leg fly over the mare's back, just as expected. She felt the mare remain quiet and steady beneath her hands as she vaulted.

But something went terribly wrong.

Instead of landing squarely on the mare's back, she sank *into* the animal. She became the animal. Which made no sense, but she embraced the truth of it nonetheless. She lost her depth perception, and all the colors in the world shifted to shades of gray.

Did Shahrazad suddenly have hooves? Really have them? She looked down at her feet, fully expecting to see her gem-encrusted sandals. But before she could make sense of the shining onyx hooves prancing where her feet should be, before her mind could do anything but sort out all the crazy impressions assaulting it, something—no, someone—vaulted onto her back.

"I won't let you do this," someone—a man—shouted. "Not to her." Then powerful hands grabbed her mane, and mighty thighs latched onto her shoulders.

The magician.

No man could touch her, and live. She screamed in rage, only her voice sounded like a horse's, high pitched and frantic. Trying to reach behind her and pull the creature off her back, she found herself instead bucking like a newly captured horse. Her hooves churned the sand around her. Shahrazad threw her head down and tossed all of her weight into her hands—her forefeet. She kicked her hooves as high into the air as she could, following some instinct she didn't realize she had.

But still the creature remained on her back. His powerful thighs squeezed her hard, cutting off her breath.

"Stop," the man on her back said. "Princess, stop!"

She'd had enough. She jerked her head with all her might, throwing her nose into the air. Tasting blood, she then threw all her weight back and reared up, pawing the sky. Still, her rider stuck on her back, refusing to fall.

Her legs trembled from supporting all of her weight, but she wouldn't concede to this madman. Once again she ripped her mouth against the bit to free her head. Once again she reared up, pawing the sky. Her front hoof hit one of the Sultan's soldiers, but she didn't care. She'd kick all of them. But her quivering legs couldn't support her, and she fell over backward, hitting the hot sand hard.

"Stop that thief!" Badr the Bad cried from the Sultan's side. The archers turned in his direction, but he was pointing at her as she scrambled to her feet. She watched the magician flick his cape. The archer's arrows turned to snakes and slithered into the dunes. The magician tried to run toward Shahrazad, but her father stopped him with a hand on his shoulder.

"My *pegaz*," Badr cried.

As Shahrazad threw herself onto her forefeet again, twisting and leaping, she realized Badr wasn't on her back.

Who was it? What black evil had hold of her?

The rider gave her no time to wonder. As Badr took his cape and madly shook it, the man on her back leaned over the far side of her neck. She felt something—a spell, maybe—sizzle ineffectively through her mane. What was happening to her?

The rider jerked one rein to his knee and kicked her flanks. She had no choice but to twist around herself. Pain, fear and exhaustion closed all other doors.

With her head twisted to her side, she again saw the magician attempt to swish his cloak. Shahrazad lurched to the side as her rider pushed with his powerful thighs. Her rider reached down and grabbed the magician's cape, snatching it from his bony hands.

"No!" the magician cried, grabbing for the cape. But the Sultan wasn't letting the magician go anywhere.

"Where is my daughter?" the Sultan bellowed. Shahrazad saw his hand clasped onto the magician's shoulder, apparently unafraid. "You tell me now!"

"Stop that man!" the magician cried, pointing at her rider. "He has her."

Suddenly, her rider released her nose, letting her lurch straight. She took advantage of the opening, leaping toward freedom, nose down to buck him off her back. But then he kicked her side viciously and she leaped into the sky—and flew.

Come to me, she heard in her head. It sounded like a chorus of oily voices.

"Fly, Princess!" her rider called, his voice as solid as the voices in her head were not. He loosened the rein and released her head. "Fly!"

4

An arrow flew past Tahir's ear, past the princess's swooping wing. "Puss and pox," he cursed under his breath. The arrows were too close.

Why? he asked himself, wiping sweat out of his eyes. Why had he done this crazy thing? He could have served out his short time with the magician, saved his sister and the Land of the Sun. But no—he'd been unable to let Badr take the princess, not this princess.

Another arrow whizzed past them, this time just missing her hindquarters.

And had the magician allowed him to escape? That was the question. Near the Cavern of Sixty Thieves, he'd felt the magician lock part of his mind away from his control. Had Badr let him do this? Surely, Badr could've stopped him.

But he hadn't.

Leaning forward, he kicked the princess's sides again, squashing the guilt racing through his veins as she lurched forward. "Fly!" he urged again. "Faster!"

With a swoosh of wings the princess obeyed, but blood

dripped from her mouth, splattering across her chest and his shins. He imagined it wrapping around the bit in her mouth and trickling onto the sand far below them.

He'd done that to her. He'd jerked the bridle and ripped her mouth. Beneath his thighs, her flanks were soaked, and white foam frothed in the crease where her wing joined her side. The princess needed to rest—especially if he was going to use her to save his sister.

Now that he'd broken his contract with Badr, he'd need all the help he could get.

"Do you smell water?" he asked as her wings beat downward. Her golden ear flicked back, so he knew she heard him. "An oasis nearby?"

Her barrel expanded beneath his legs, and Tahir guessed she was sniffing, searching for that water. She nickered, a short sound muffled by the whoosh of her wings.

"Good." He loosened the reins and relaxed the grip on her sides. "Go there then," he said. "And we'll rest. You must be thirsty."

As he tucked the magician's cape firmly into his sack, she shifted her direction a little south. Taking her time, she shifted a little more. He welcomed the breeze on his face as he let her coast.

She banked a little toward the south again, and he eased with her, but then suddenly Tahir recognized a small crop of mountains shaped exactly like the silhouette of a *shitani*; he and the princess had flown over them when they'd left her home in the rain of arrows.

"You sneak," he said, resisting the urge to jerk her mouth again. "You've doubled back home."

A thought struck Tahir, right in the heart. She must really love the man she'd been about to wed. And if she loved her husband-to-be, she'd hate him—Tahir—for stealing her.

"You're only making this more difficult for yourself." He

said the words for her, but he meant them for himself. Not jerking the reins but letting her know he held them, he added, "You can't rest in the middle of the sands of this desert. We need water and shade—and we're not going back to your palace for it."

Her head hung low, humility pouring from her body language, but he'd seen the culture she'd come from—women knew how to appear yielding.

A resigned-sounding huff came from her nostrils, and with a powerful swoop of her wings, her body shifted beneath him. Her muscles slid so smoothly, so powerfully, that he needed to grab her mane to keep his seat, and wind from her wings ruffled his hair. She'd changed directions again, this time heading northeast.

By the time he could see the oasis, a puddle of green in a sea of tan, she was exhausted, but the grace with which her hooves touched the ground and the smoothness of her gallop as she slowed to a stop impressed him. She approached the edge of the oasis, wings tucked neatly against her flanks.

Looking at her still-heaving sides, he squashed that guilt again. He'd do whatever necessary to save his sister, his land. No regrets.

Knowing that hunger and thirst must be leaving her weak, Tahir led her to the lake, a gentle hand on her shoulder. He felt her flinch from his touch, but he ignored it, keeping his palm in place. She immediately drank, so thirsty that she submerged half her nostrils to better get the water.

Wanting to share the quiet of the moment, he leaned over the lake and drank himself, letting her stand over him, letting her dominate him—while he held her reins.

"I'm not going to hurt you," he said slowly, wiping the cool water from his face. But then immediately he felt like a fool. He'd already hurt her. "I'm not going to hurt you more," he amended.

She turned as far as she could, given her tether.

With deliberate slowness, he walked toward her, his palm down and toward her. She eyed him, nostrils flared, but he kept his step unhurried, his shoulders down. She didn't step back, and he shortened the rein. Now she couldn't bolt away from him without hurting herself. "Don't be afraid," he said in a low voice. "Not of me."

When she allowed him into her space, he let his palm glide down her muscled neck, and he rested his hand on her shoulder, feeling the damp heat pouring from her.

"See?" he asked in the same low voice. "This isn't so bad, is it?" Then, with the same deliberate slowness, he unbuckled the saddle and took it from her back. He quietly set it into the long shadow growing from the palm tree.

Sweat soaked her fur where the pack had been. "I've removed it now. Does that feel better?" he asked. "I can make it better yet."

She stepped away from him, pulling the reins taut.

But Tahir was undaunted. Locking his gaze on her dark eyes, he took a silk handkerchief from his pocket. He dipped it into the cool water and, not looking away from her, he squeezed. The sound of the drops hitting the lake filled the quiet night.

This time when he stepped toward her, she remained still. Only the heavy breath from her dilated nostrils belied her nervousness.

Good, he thought, let her feel a little nervous. His gentleness would have more meaning this way. Taking his time, he ran the cool cloth around her ears and under her forelock. He wiped the lather from under her jaw, and when he came to the still-bleeding wounds where the steel bit met the corners of her lips, he said, "I'm sorry I hurt you."

She pinned her ears back but didn't move, not even when he wiped the blood clean and exposed the sore to the twilight air.

"Let me clean your wings," he offered. "You'll feel better."

He held out the cloth to show his intent, but she didn't approach him.

But she didn't step away either as he purposely walked toward her. He ran the cloth over the long line of her wing, and he felt the play of muscle beneath the stiff golden feathers. With a careful hand, he wiped the crease where feather met fur, inhaling the warm scent of her.

"I have to make something clear," he said. "I didn't change you into a *pegaz*. I cannot control this."

She pinned her ears and swished her tail.

"I believe you're going to change back to human form when the sun fully sinks below the horizon," he said, wiping the sweat from the tendons of her forelegs. Did she appreciate the trust he laid before her as he prostrated himself at her feet? "And I have nothing to do with it. I can't stop it. I can't change it. When the sun comes up in the morning, you'll change back into a *pegaz*."

With swiveling ears, she looked at him. If he were her, he'd have many questions.

"When you touched the magician's *pegaz*, you were trapped by a spell. You were cursed. You'll change with the sun until the spell is broken."

She looked west, no doubt inspecting the sun's position. Half the red orb was already gone, but he kept washing the lather from her, cleaning her chest and the small spot between her forelegs. He dripped cool water over the sweat mark where her saddle had lain, and then he used his hand to wipe away the excess water and sweat.

She could have bitten him, lashed him with her hooves as he did this. She could have killed him—but she didn't.

Tahir took that as a good sign.

"You're probably hungry," he said. He let cool water drip down her flanks, then he wiped it away with the side of his hand. He had only moments before she transformed. "When you change, there'll be dinner provided by the cloak—at least there was every time Badr opened it."

The sun finally sank below the horizon, washing the sky in ambers and pinks. The beams bathed her, too, drawing long and strange shadows around her. Then he realized the strange planes weren't some trick of light.

Amid silvery sunbeams, her forelegs shortened and hooves retracted. Her sand-colored mane gave way to a wealth of black hair plaited into complicated braids. The golden tips of the braids caught the setting sun and sent glittering confetti over the soft oasis grass. Her skin darkened from palomino horse-flesh to the color of the darkest honey. And her breasts . . . high and firm, curved through the purple silk.

The woman who appeared before him was a stunning beauty, something he hadn't appreciated as he'd watched her from across the dune at her wedding. Her amber eyes nearly glowed in the fading light, and thick dark lashes fell over elegant cheekbones. Her lips were kissable, full, and her loose purple silk did little to hide the curves of her waist. His hands longed to caress those curves, memorize them and make them his own.

But that was never going to happen, he could clearly see. She was as angry as a *shitani* trapped for eternity in a bottle.

"Do not touch me," she said, her eyes flashing but not quite meeting his. "Ever."

Tahir took a step back, raising his hands. The damp cloth he'd been using fell to the sand with a quiet plop. "I'm sorry," he said, trying to meet her gaze.

"I don't know what edicts the *klerin* have against men touching pure women when the women are in animal form, and I don't care to find out."

"And if I tell you I don't understand to what you're referring?"

"You only need to understand one thing," she said, putting

her hands on her hips, making the purple silk ripple over her lush curves. "You are not to touch me. Your head and mine may very well end up separated from our bodies and decorating Pike Wall if you do. The rules of my land do not permit it—in fact, my cousin was recently beheaded for just this transgression. She permitted a soldier to touch her. I will not be that foolish."

He took another step back, giving her as much space as she needed. "I won't touch you." Here he paused, unwilling to start their relationship with a lie. "Except to ride you." Hearing those words, he almost choked. "In *pegaz* form only, of course."

Her eyes flashed in anger, but when he tried to meet her gaze, let her see his lack of evil intent, she wouldn't look at him. Then he remembered her wedding party, the separate role women played from men. No woman made eye contact with men.

"You are not to speak to me either," she said, her tone as imperious as any queen's. But . . . did she sound afraid? "No man may speak to me save my male relatives—which you are not."

"I have food," he said, still trying to gain some goodwill. "At least I believe I do. And if I'm wrong . . ." he inspected a towering date palm, ripe with fruit. "I'll climb the tree."

But she turned her back to him, ignoring his words.

"Look," he said. "We're stuck here in the middle of an oasis. We need to help each other. That generally requires communication."

But she kept her back to him, implacable.

"Princess, listen." Tahir looked at the elegant lines of her shoulder blades as the purple silk rippled over them in the fading light. "No one will know we've spoken. There're no humans around for leagues and leagues."

"Please!" she said, walking toward the sandy shore of the small lake. "No man may speak to me. You must stop. My father will have your head—and mine. My cousin—" But she broke off, saying no more.

Tahir ran his fingers through his hair, at a loss. She must be hungry, and he had to convince her to help him. How could he convince her if he couldn't talk to her? He opened his mouth to speak again, but she was writing something in the damp sand.

How is this enchantment broken? she wrote. *My marriage to the Raj must take place, and he cannot wed a horse.* She'd underlined the word *must* several times.

He erased her words and took the stick. *Eat first*, he wrote in the sand. Then he added, *Can I talk aloud to myself?*

She hesitated for a moment, then shrugged, still refusing to meet his gaze.

"As sure as my name is Prince Tahir of House Kulwanti in the Land of the Sun, I can't remember the last time I was this hungry." He directed the words to the date palm trees, away from the princess.

She didn't respond. "I wonder if I can get this cape to create dinner for us?" As he said this, he retrieved the black cloth. If he'd observed Badr correctly, it was all in the fingers. "If I cross these first two fingers together . . ." He crossed his fingers in example. "And shake . . ." He shook the cape. "A meal should appear."

And it did. The meal appeared on a blanket before them— figs and dates, honeyed loaves of bread, pomegranates, and wine. A small lantern sat on the corner, their only protection against the coming dark.

He looked at the luxurious meal, appreciating how nice it would be if he could sit next to this beautiful woman and share the food with her. But he guessed that wouldn't happen. If she couldn't look at, touch, or speak with a man, he doubted she could eat with one.

"I think I'll walk over to the other side of the oasis," Tahir said—to himself. "I'll make sure there's no one here. No lions."

Ignoring his hunger, he began to walk away from the meal.

But warm sand hit the back of his knee and trickled to his ankle. She'd thrown sand at him.

Sit! she wrote in the sand. The letters were hard and deep. Perhaps she was as exasperated as he was. *Eat.* The princess herself sat with a pointed deliberateness—and grace. Her legs were curled neatly around each other, and her braided hair fell to her shoulders.

If the fraudulent Lady Casmiri had had this much beauty, he doubted he could've resisted her. But then he realized: it wasn't beauty that Lady Casmiri had lacked. She'd had plenty of that. But this silent, stubborn princess had something else. . . . Her spirit, her very essence called to him. He could do no less than obey her.

He sat.

With her mustache fluttering in the hot breeze, the magician watched her *pegaz* fly off toward the Amr Mountains. Her teeth were clenched in something that might have resembled rage if she hadn't had four hundred years to master such a basic emotion.

The prince wasn't supposed to have gone with the princess, and he wasn't supposed to have taken her cape. Not that she needed the cape, but she wanted the Sultan to think her powers came from an external object rather than her herself—and without the cape . . .

Well, she hadn't been magician for the last half a millennium without learning anything. If the Sultan thought she lacked power without the cape, she'd take advantage of that misconception. She had her ways.

The fact that her true powers were slipping was something no one needed to know.

Especially her minions.

As if prompted, one of her minions spoke to her. *The Sul-*

tan, one of the *shitani* called in her mind. Had it known she was thinking of them? They didn't used to read her mind. They didn't used to have that ability. *He could rule us*, the *shitani* said. *Inspect him, too. He can replace you.*

She bristled at the command—she was supposed to give *them* the orders. She turned away from the receding *pegaz* in a cold fury.

Several steps to her left, the Sultan's guards gave her an apprehensive look. The hot scent of urine filled the air, and she knew one of them had wet his pants, probably when she'd turned the arrows into asps. No one liked the idea of asps slithering around their ankles, not even mighty soldiers.

Well, they'd do more than wet their pants if she convinced the Sultan to replace her as the magician.

Scanning the wary crowd, she found the commander, the man with the undeniable aura of authority. She looked him in the eye.

Arrest me, she told him silently. Without a strong link between them, without physical contact, he'd think the idea originated in his own mind. *Arrest me now*, she commanded, trying to keep all doubt at bay.

Thankfully, this power still worked.

"Come with us, mighty magician," the commander of the Sultan's guard said. He grabbed her arm firmly, giving no indication of the fear she knew he must feel. "You are under arrest."

The soldier marched her past the Sultan, and she met the ruler's placid eyes. His lack of fear wasn't feigned. No tightened shoulder muscles, no shifty expression, no scent of nervous fear existed in him.

Perhaps the *shitani* were correct, she thought reluctantly. Perhaps this Sultan would make a good replacement. In him she recognized a man who'd met adversity and survived it.

But he'd never met her before today. He'd never met the *shitani*. She'd see what he was capable of surviving.

Interrogate me, she thought at the Sultan, her gaze locked on his regal eyes. The compulsion would fall on him and stick like a spider web—at least that would be true if her powers remained in place. *In my cell*, she added. *Interrogate me.*

Her successor might have to come to her willingly, but willingness could be . . . encouraged. And the blank glare the Sultan sent her gave her no encouragement. He didn't appear to be a man interested in interrogating anyone, much less Badr the Bad—who could change arrows to asps.

The oblivious commander opened a cell door for her and locked her inside the iron bars, and for a moment, panic raced through her heart. Orchestrating these various scenarios didn't used to be so difficult. She wanted a successor. To achieve this goal, she needed control. Did she have it?

She sat on the floor, set her palms on her crossed legs, and closed her eyes. Badra rubbed her thumbs over her third finger, and she chanted the sound of creation almost under her breath. The earth's strength began to pour through her, and her extremities trembled.

Three millennium ago, the first magician, Faruq the Great, had harnessed magic to control the dark *shitani* power. Before Faruq's mighty works, the *shitani* burst from their caves and plagued the land like locusts. Badra had inherited that mantle from the fifth magician in his line—but that was so long ago she could barely remember being human.

As she repeated the sound of creation in an increasingly loud chant, she recalled ruling her desert clan and ruling well. In a watery way, she remembered craving a child; she'd slept with hundreds of men, hoping any seed would take hold. After years of failure, she'd stolen her sister's babe—she remembered that. Her family had turned against her then, and she'd been forced to chose: become the new magician or face death by stoning—by her mother, her siblings, her father.

It wasn't until she'd replaced her predecessor that she understood the magician had rendered her barren, if not exactly forcing her brash actions then certainly fanning the flames of her weakness. If she needed to step in her predecessor's proverbial footprints to accomplish her goal, so be it.

The breath-of-fire focused her strength, focused her mind. She envisioned the Sultan's spare face, pictured the depth of his gaze. *Interrogate me*, she sent again to the image in her mind. *Come to me. Question me.*

She should have kept sending the message. If she had any power left, always a question after spending as much as she had today, he'd be pounding down the hall toward her as she breathed this very breath. But did she have power left? No certainty there.

And no focus left either. Like the *shitani*, her mind kept sliding away from her control.

Her mind kept sliding back to a child. Her child. Her unborn child. After becoming a mage, she could have borne a child; she could have healed her barrenness with one small spell. She could have seduced a man or simply asked to be fucked and been obeyed.

But she hadn't.

She redoubled her effort now, refocusing on her breathing, refocusing on her bid to get the Sultan into her cell. But it wasn't working. The Sultan didn't arrive, and her mind kept going back to that unborn child. She'd punished herself for the pain she'd caused her family. No child, she'd said. Not as long as she ruled as a magician.

But her period of self-inflicted punishment was nearing its end. She no longer possessed enough strength to rule the demons. Once she found a replacement, she could rest. And forgive herself.

And the sound of footsteps filled the corridor, interrupting her. The Sultan. The wave of hope that surged through her nearly brought tears to her eyes. Maybe he was the one. Maybe he'd release her from this life. It didn't lack for rewards . . . in the right hands.

"Badr," the Sultan said, loudly enough to echo down the hall. "I know your ilk. You'll not cast your spells on me—I will not interrogate you."

Hope turned to dust in her veins.

My pretties, she called in her mind to the demons. Could she control them now? Many still slumbered deep within the Amr Mountains. But some . . . some were Awake. *Come to me,* she called. *I need you—one of you. Wake, my pretties.*

She sensed angry reluctance from them, a shocking wish for her demise. *We don't want to, Badra,* they said in their rasping mind voices. *Leave us be.*

"Badr," the Sultan said, interrupting her shock. How dare her minions speak to her in such a manner! "Tell me, man," the Sultan called from down the hallway. "Where is my daughter?"

With quiet dignity, Badra slowed her breathing to something approaching normal. The Sultan cared about his land; the *shitani* had recognized that. For him to accept her mantle, she needed to play this flawlessly.

In the door's window, the Sultan's head appeared, topped by his pristine white turban. His men opened it. "Where did you order them to go?" he asked quietly. "Where has your assistant taken my daughter?"

She stared blankly at him, amazed at his focus. Perhaps even envious of it. He'd known she'd cast a spell on him, but he'd pushed that knowledge aside, thinking only of his daughter. Why? Because he loved her? Or perhaps because she was his last route toward an alliance with the Raj?

She needed help. If love of his daughter motivated him, well, she could continue her search for a replacement. If his love of his kingdom drove him to this, however . . .

Which of you will come to me? she asked the *shitani*, hiding her fear from them. If they didn't obey even these simple commands, what would she do when they all Awoke? *It is time, my pretties. One of you must come to me now. You have work to do after years of napping.*

She said nothing to the Sultan.

Our queen, we won't obey. We're tired . . . of you. Tomorrow perhaps.

"Answer me, man," the Sultan said, calmly. "If I don't find my daughter and marry her to the Raj, this whole land could fall to *shitani*. Not even you would wish that upon us."

I command you now, she said to the demons. *You will obey. Now.*

Our dark queen! she heard in response. *We don't want to help you! We're hungry. We're tired. Leave us be.*

"Would you like more power? " she asked the Sultan, provoking him, inspecting his fault lines. Where were his weaknesses? "Would you like to rule this land and others for a thousand years? Would you like powers you cannot—as yet— imagine?"

"Every ruler craves power," the Sultan said, his expression unchanging. "But every good ruler knows such power comes with a cost."

"Is that so?"

"And every good ruler knows the costs of wielding power increases as the amount of power wielded increases."

"That is a cryptic answer," Badra said.

"An appropriate answer to a cryptic question," he answered. "What do you truly offer me, locked as you are in my dungeon?"

Badra closed her eyes, the picture of serenity.

You want to obey me, she said to her demons. Locking an image of the Princess Shahrazad in her mind, she sent the tempting picture to the *shitani*. *Find her. She might be your new dark queen. She might rule you should the Sultan prove unworthy.*

Delicious! they cried after a moment inspecting her image. *Juicy!* They loved huge human breasts, and Shahrazad had them, so their reaction didn't surprise her—but the pang of jealousy ripping through her stomach did.

Put perhaps we want a king instead, one of the demons said. *Perhaps we want your Sultan.*

That was promising, too. She might be able to hand this mantle over to this ruler on a silver platter. *Help me now,* she told the demons, *or you'll get no one.*

Don't leave us alone!

Like she'd ever leave them without a leader. Without a strong magician, the abhorrent creatures would overrun the lands. They'd rape the women—and the men, at least that's what Faruq's ancient texts claimed. They'd consume all the crops and drink every oasis dry. As their strength grew, they'd take control of the minds of every sentient being. Women would give birth to wretched hybrids, and humans would become a distant memory. Only magicians kept the demons in check.

Not that the *shitani* needed to know any of that.

Perhaps irked by her silence, the Sultan waved his hand in front of her face. "Are you enthralling anyone as we speak?" he asked, his face gleaming in the afternoon sunlight.

She stood, taking care to lengthen her legs just enough so that she stood taller than the Sultan. Thankfully, that ability still worked.

The Sultan looked her in the eye for a moment, tilting his head to do so. She supposed he was trying to take her measure, but more than five hundred years of living had made her more than difficult for most people to read. Sometimes she felt like she couldn't read herself.

"That is none of your concern."

"Can this power you offer help return my daughter—safely—to this palace?" the Sultan asked.

"She is where she is." Again she closed her eyes and smiled like some ancient religious icon.

You spoke with a pegaz, *a flying horse,* she told the demons. *You must find her before dawn. You must stop her from returning to her palace.*

But why? We don't want to work.

We don't want her here, or you'll have no queen, no king. Ever. And thanks to Faruq the Great's workings, they believed her.

"I'm losing my exceedingly short patience," the Sultan said. "You called me down here when my counselors needed me. You attempted to trick me into believing this visit to you was of my own design. What is it you offer?"

She sensed dissatisfaction among her minions. Had her threat worked?

"Your luscious daughter wouldn't have tried to ride my *pegaz* if you hadn't yearned for freedom yourself. She sensed your dissatisfaction and acted upon it." If nothing else, five-hundred years of living had given her a lot of insight into human motivations. "You offered her her heart's desire, and now . . ." Badra let her hands flutter at her side like a flock of birds.

Without warning, the Sultan slapped Badr with the back of his hand. His ruby ring slit her lip open, and she tasted blood, thick and coppery. Still, she did nothing.

"What power do you have over that, old man?" the Sultan asked.

"Your fingers reply your own query," she said, flinging her mustache behind her shoulders.

"What do you mean—" he asked, but as he glanced at his hands, he hissed in a breath, answering his own question. Her spell had worked. His fingers turned to asps, dropped off his hands, and slithered under the cell's bed. For a moment, his hands lacked any fingers at all.

"Your fingers may return now," she said, letting him believe her words held her power.

"That is an impressive talent," the Sultan said, and again, Badra admired his control. He would be well suited for her position.

"It is yours for the taking."

How? her demons demanded, either not realizing or not caring that they'd interrupted her. *How do we stop the princess from coming home?*

Go to my cave, my pretties, she replied, relieved that they'd come to heel. *Bring the white turban you find there to her. She will understand the meaning.*

The demons might disappoint her, but the Sultan . . . he showed only promise. She would make her offer now, let him see a glimmer of truth.

"I can grant your heart's desire," she said, in Badr's masculine voice. It shook with simulated fear. "Take my place as magician—take it willingly. I'll save your land, from the demons and your rivals. You'll inherit my powers."

"Fool," the Sultan said. "Do you not think I've consulted my own auguries? Why do you think I'm so desperate for my daughter?"

"Love?" Badr said, without sarcasm. If she had a daughter, she'd be unable to do anything but love and protect her.

"Love!" the Sultan said in one clipped sound. "Love! You must have boiled your brain out there in the sun. According to the augury, Shahrazad must wed the Raj—or else the *shitani* will invade. The augury said nothing about replacing a magician."

"The auguries are not infallible," Badr reminded him.

"I trust you like I trust an asp." The Sultan shook his hands.

"You seek to trick me. Why would a magician need a replacement?"

"Even magicians get old." Badra looked at him. She let the mirage of the toothless old magician fall away, and she permitted her true self to shine through. Her mustache and wrinkles gave way to smooth, supple skin; her hunched back gave way to a sprightly figure. Then she held out her hand and twitched her fingers. His turban of white linen turned to gold.

The Sultan took the thing from his head and looked at it in amazement. "What trick is this?"

"No trick," Badra said in her true voice. "Only power. Power that could be yours. Power to control the *shitani* and live forever." She nodded. "I've judged you worthy," she said, using nearly the same words her predecessor had used on her.

The Sultan looked at her a moment, her small breasts causing his gaze to hitch, but only momentarily. "I trust an asp more," he said, and he spat on the floor.

"Positions have been known to change," she said to him.

"Just as tigers have been known to change their stripes," the Sultan said, closing the cell door behind him.

But all was not lost. By dawn's rise, Princess Shahrazad would be running. The Sultan would have no choice but to turn to Badr for succor. And with Shahrazad running—from her father, from the meddling Prince Tahir, from the demons—she'd run right toward the magician's arms. Another potential replacement. Perhaps a more willing one.

The *shitani* liked her well enough.

5

As Prince Tahir sat opposite her on the blanket, Shahrazad couldn't breathe. She'd never dined with a man, not even her father. But she'd demanded this. Now she had to accommodate it. With her eyes demurely downcast, she poured wine from the bottle into the two glasses provided by the magic cloak. She set one in front of him, careful not to touch his knee.

Let no man touch you. Her Duha's words still rang in her mind. Well, she hadn't let one, not purposefully, but the magician had still managed it, and now the magician's black promise rang through her mind. He said she'd never wed the Raj.

But she would. She must. Despite this handsome prince sitting across from her, despite the wings that would sprout from her back tomorrow, she must wed the Raj. And to do that, she must find the magician and convince him to lift this curse—because she simply couldn't imagine the Raj purposefully marrying a *pegaz*.

Prince Tahir broke the honeyed loaves into two parts and spread softened goat cheese onto half. Handing a chunk to her, she saw how careful he was not to graze her skin with his fingers, which, she noted, were long and powerful, just as in her vision of him. Remembering that vision brought his kiss to mind, and she quickly shoved it aside. This was not the time. In fact, the time for that memory did not exist.

Setting the bread carefully on the blanket, she erased the command she'd written in the sand and replaced it with a question. *Do you believe the* shitani *will awaken and invade the surrounding lands?*

Soon. He underlined the word deeply. *I've seen one.*

She nodded and erased his words. Then she wrote: *If I do not wed the Raj, my land will not withstand the* shitani *invasion. Father needs this alliance if he wishes to maintain human rulers.*

Tahir read this, she noted from beneath her lashes, with seriousness. She added another sentence. *I must wed the Raj now. But I cannot until this curse is lifted.*

He ate some dates, and she wondered if he cared about her predicament. Perhaps she was just a silly girl to think this outsider cared three-grains-of-rice about her land. But then he looked directly at her, and she wished he wouldn't do that. The pressure of his gaze made her feel . . . uncontrolled.

Finally, he picked up the stick they were using to write. *I need the magician too. He has my sister. I have less than a month to restore her. Else* shitani *will invade.*

He dropped the stick, presumably so she could retrieve it without touching him. Shahrazad doubted the *klerin* would smile upon even this blameless and distant form of communication. It was their job to suspect, and they did it with exuberance.

Underneath his words, she answered, *My father will have him imprisoned, perhaps executed.*

Tahir shook his head with apparent certainty. *Not dead.*

How do you know?

He shrugged, his dark hair shining in the moonlight, and he tapped his temples. *We're linked somehow. I'd know.*

She had nothing to say to this, horrified for him. What would it be like to be harnessed to such evil?

Tahir seemed less bothered by the attachment. He pushed the bowl of figs toward her and poured the last of the pomegranate wine for both of them. *We'll find them tomorrow,* he wrote.

She nodded.

Only as she finished her meal did she realize that she was going to have to spend the night in an oasis alone with Prince Tahir.

"Princess!" The word confused her half-sleeping mind. No man could speak to her, but one did. The magician!

"No!" she shouted, jumping from her warm nest in the sand. "No!"

"Shh!" he said. "It is I, Prince Tahir." Then he ran his fingers through his hair and whispered to the palm tree next to her. "I won't hurt the princess. I won't touch her. But she needs to dress. Now."

Tension tightened his voice, and she picked up the stick. *What has happened?* she wrote, trying to ignore the fact he'd spoken directly to her.

"I think someone's coming."

Formalities be damned. She paused for a moment and listened. She heard nothing, but the thick scent of gardenias hung in the predawn morning. Odd. She'd seen no flowers yesterday. She hadn't smelled them either.

"No time to explain," he said. "Put on your shoes. We need to leave now."

Keeping her eyes down, she laced her sandals around her ankles while Prince Tahir collected the magician's cape. But before she laced her last shoe, the nine hells erupted into the oasis.

Cackling like a crazed hen, something she couldn't see jumped onto her shoulder and grabbed her ear with cold fingers. Without thinking, she screamed and jumped, shoving it away from her. Its claws dug deep furrows into her shoulder, but it landed in the grass with a thud and a whine.

She looked down, trying to see it, but she saw—nothing. Perhaps the dim light hid it. But then she saw the oasis grass wave, as if by some invisible force, and again something whipped through the air and landed on her shoulder.

"Help me!" she cried, spinning and flailing at the thing. From the corner of her eye she saw a white object floating through the air. She realized that the invisible monster was carrying something. "Get it off me!" she shrieked.

But Prince Tahir was already swinging his sword at something she couldn't see in the dim, early morning light. He slashed the air at the ground near his feet. What was this madness?

Invisible fingers twined through her braids, almost lovingly, and she screamed again, slapping blindly. Finally her hands hit the invisible creature on her shoulder, and again it fell from her with a thud.

"Where is it?" Tahir cried, looking up from his own battle.

But she didn't know how to answer. She couldn't see where it was. Instead, with a scream of rage she stomped the ground where she'd heard it land. And her foot hit something. The creature screeched like a child, and she blindly stomped again. This time she found nothing.

In the rising light, she saw several blades of grass ripple, and Tahir swung his sword near her feet.

The grass erupted in blood, and the red fluid coated the invisible creature, which lay still, apparently dead.

"What was that?" she asked, looking at its distorted features. Its ears were too big, its neck too small.

Prince Tahir nodded at a second body. "There were two of them. *Shitani.*"

Trying to control her breathing, still ragged from fear and exertion, she asked, "Are they dead?"

"They—"

But another demonic screech emanated from the palm tree, and Shahrazad felt the air whip past her face. She screamed and jumped, but the *shitani* landed on her head and grabbed her ears. She felt something hot and wet lap her neck, and revulsion made her throw herself to the ground to try to rub the demon from her body.

"Stop," Tahir shouted to her. "Still yourself."

But she couldn't obey. Dreadful fingers carressed her neck and the tops of her ears. Frantically, she grabbed for the thing, wanting it off her now. Now! She swung wildly.

Finally she knocked it askew. She felt it hanging onto her braids, swinging like some crazed monkey. "Get it off me!" she screamed, beating her braids. "Please!"

And he did, swinging his closed fist through her hair. The creature hit the ground with a thud, and a second thud followed it.

Tahir raced to where they'd heard the thing hit and began slicing the ground with his sword, using it like a peasant hoeing the dirt.

Just as its death-scream filled the morning air, Shahrazad spied the thing it'd been carrying. "That's my father's turb—" she started to say, but the rising sun cut off her words.

The change was upon her. For a moment, a haze of glittering silver light prevented her from seeing anything, and the sexual tingle coursing through her body to her very core left her helpless. She could do nothing more than register the enchantment licking the veins in her wrists, behind her ears, through her breasts.

She regained herself only to find those wrists, ears, and breasts changed. "Tahir," she tried to say, but the word came out as a nicker. When she drew in a breath to try again, she smelled something underlying that cloying gardenia scent—something both warm and reptilian.

Shitani.

We are shitani, she heard in her head. *And you will love us. We've told our queen we will love you.*

Ignoring the horror of those words, her equine eyes registered nothing. But she smelled at least three demons in the tree. Where was Prince Tahir? She blinked, trying to accustom herself to the strange black-and-white vision, and then she saw him, bending over her father's turban . . . just as the *shitani* launched itself from the palm tree toward the prince.

Panic surged through her. If they had her father's turban, he must be besieged! Her palace. Her land.

She squealed and leaped toward Prince Tahir, turf tearing beneath her feet as she did. He looked at her just as she heard a demon land on him. With a speed worthy of a snake, he swatted the thing from his back, and she jumped on it, crushing it beneath her hoofs.

Prince Tahir wasted no time. Turban in hand, he jumped in her saddle and collected the reins. "The cloak. We must retrieve it." Understanding, she galloped the ten paces to her makeshift bed. He leaned precariously over her side, snagging the cloth on the first try.

"Now, fly!" he commanded. "Far away from here!"

But he'd wasted his breath because she'd already launched herself into the sky. As she soared over the palm tree, she heard three more *shitani* gnashing their teeth.

Don't leave us, she heard. *Come back to us.*

Somehow she knew the *shitani* were speaking in her head. She'd been marked, brought to their attention. And it all came back to Badr the Bad: he'd touched her back, he'd turned her into a *pegaz*, and now demons were speaking in her mind.

She had never killed a human in her life, but she would kill that magician now if she had the chance. And she would not let him or any other man ruin her alliance with the Raj ir Adham.

In a rage, she circled back toward the tree, locking onto their scent. As she flew past the trio of demons, she lashed out her head and grabbed one with her teeth.

My queen, it cried in her mind. *I've longed for you, my queen.*

She crushed its skull between her teeth and tossed it to the grass below, without mercy, ignoring the taste of blood and brains. Ruthlessly, she circled its corpse to ensure it was dead. It was.

"Are there more?" Prince Tahir asked.

She nickered and he understood.

"Fly by that tree again, and I'll try for another," Prince Tahir said.

Banking with her left wing, Shahrazad turned, thrilling in the speed and power of her new form. Her wings swooped through the air, covering a mighty distance. The cool breeze caressed her mane, sending it fluttering over her withers.

On her back, Prince Tahir swung blindly at a cluster of dates in the tree, but her nose had no trouble finding a demon. Again, she grabbed one between her teeth and crushed it. The satisfying taste of success overrode the coppery tang of blood on her tongue.

Prince Tahir's sword snagged a third demon, knocking it to a lower branch. Bathed in blood, she could see the thing, and she watched it gnash its sharp teeth. Shahrazad whipped her wings through the morning air to turn. Tahir skewered it on their third flight past the tree with a mighty slash of his sword.

Her nose told her they were all dead, and she breathed a sigh of relief.

"Did we kill all of them?" Prince Tahir asked.

Again, she nickered. She had to return home. It had taken a full day to reach this oasis, and it would take that long to fly back home, but if the demons were overrunning the palace, her father would need help. And she could help, she realized. No longer the helpless girl she'd been yesterday, she could crush and stomp. She could kill the demons. Thrilling power coursed through her veins. She'd never imagined physical strength would satisfy her.

She flew south, toward her home, without Prince Tahir's leave.

"Did I hear you say that this turban belonged to your father?" Prince Tahir asked. He rode her well, not disrupting her balance at all, not even when he spoke.

She nickered, hoping he would take that as an affirmative. That dazzling ruby set in the center of a sea of spotless white silk could only belong to the Sultan.

"Have they attacked your palace?" Prince Tahir asked. "This isn't a promising sign."

Agreeing, she extended her neck and poured all her strength into her wings, flying as fast as she could. Perhaps her ability to fly had improved with yesterday's practice. Perhaps she'd arrive home in time to aid her father. The mountains beneath her seemed as vast and endless as the dunes.

"Slow down, Princess," Prince Tahir called. But he didn't rein her in, and his seat remained sure. "There's a note in here," he explained. "It's pinned inside a fold, but I can't read it with all this wind."

Reluctantly Shahrazad tilted her wings inward, letting the wind beat against them, slowing them. But before she plummeted to the ground like a rock, she extended her wings, stretching the golden feathers as far as they could go. The tickle in her stomach delighted her as they glided like birds through the desert sky. She'd never imagined such joy, not even when she galloped her father's fastest stallion across the sands.

"I'm going to read this now," Prince Tahir said, and she bobbed her head, letting him know she was listening.

She snorted again impatiently. What did it say?

She heard the unfolding of paper as she banked her wings again and let the breeze float quietly over them. "The note says: *Daughter, you have spent the night alone, unchaperoned. If you come home, I will behead you. I have no choice. Perhaps you should seek the refuge of Badr the Bad who lives in the Cavern of the Sixty Thieves in the easternmost segment of the Amr Mountains."* Prince Tahir paused, and she felt him shake his head. "There's a signature beneath it," he continued, "which I assume belongs to your father."

For a moment, she wondered if the demons had done something to her. She couldn't breathe. Fire raced through her veins. How were her wings transporting them?

Her home had just been forbidden to her. She'd never see her father again . . . or her nieces or her nephews, or her brothers and sisters. She'd never enjoy Duha's warm embrace. She'd never—

"I'm sorry," Prince Tahir said, weaving his fingers through her mane. "I'm very sorry."

But suddenly, she didn't believe the note. The Sultan wouldn't behead her. He couldn't. He loved her, and even if he didn't, he needed the Raj if he were going to put any force together whatsoever. Besides, would he really have given the note to the demons to deliver?

She snorted and shook her equine head. So what did the note mean? Was the magician trying to trick her into polluting herself? Was her father trying to save her from some danger within the palace walls? Had someone else altogether sent this insidious message?

Suddenly this seemed very much like the magician's brand of ilk. But there was only one way to find out.

She was going home. Now.

With a deliberate swoop of her wings, she continued over the mountain range, thrilled with the sense of freedom and power her new wings gave her. But as the sun rose to its peak and began to slide down again, she realized her liberty was simply an illusion. She could no more fly away from this situation than she could turn herself into a cactus.

"We should land within walking distance of your palace," Prince Tahir said once the air cooled around them. "If the soldiers see us flying above them, they might shoot us."

She looked at the sun. If she landed now, they could walk, reaching her home just at sunset—just as she regained her true form. She adjusted her wings and headed toward the ground.

The sand grabbed her ankles as she landed, threatening to trip her, but her powerful legs prevailed. Cantering through the shifting sands in equine form was so much easier than running in human form.

Prince Tahir slid off immediately as she stopped. With the magician's cape billowing around his neck he took several steps away from her, presumably so he wouldn't accidentally touch her. That he continued to honor her wishes even after reading the note from her father made her soften toward him just a shade more.

Within heartbeats, the flesh of her ankles began to tingle, and she now recognized this as the sensation of her transformation. Standing still as the mountains behind them, magic tendrils wrapped around her feet and curled up her legs. Fetlocks, stifles, and gaskins became calves, thighs, and hips.

She opened herself to the flow of the energy swirling around her. The nerves in her breasts and at her wrists hummed in pleasure, leaving her weak with desire. The heady sensation spread throughout her being. Her thighs ached; her hips loosened. The length of her neck craved a lover's hot kiss. Her knees actually shook with the lust rushing her veins.

As the enchantment swirled around her, she caught a glimpse of Prince Tahir. His dark eyes were locked upon her, and what she saw in his expression made her heart throb. Magic wrapped around her breasts and made her nipples tingle. His desire for her, his lust, radiated from his gaze.

But her pleasure was short lived. *Come to me,* she heard a

distant *shitani* call. But as her hooves vanished, the cackled words faded. *Come to me . . .*

Her mane gave way to hair, and she became fully human. As the transformation completed itself, the sun's orb now completely below the horizon, Tahir looked away, giving her what privacy he could offer on these open dunes.

"Sand," Tahir said, looking at a mogul near her. "I hope you're listening. I'd rather speak with that smoldering princess in the purple silk, but alas, I am not permitted."

The way he addressed the sand struck her as flirtatious. After all, they'd spoken directly in the heat of battle. Now, Shahrazad shook her head, holding back a laugh that surprised her. Did he really think she was smoldering? She hooked her veil closed to hide her smile.

"If I were permitted to speak to the lovely Princess Shahrazad, I'd ask if she knew where her father's men would be holding Badr the Bad. If she knew, maybe she'd throw a handful of you, Sand—hopefully not at me."

Even knowing she'd already broken all the rules, even knowing she could use her voice, Shahrazad couldn't resist this new game. She picked up some sand and tossed it. She aimed at his feet, but somehow the well-defined muscles of his thighs caught her attention, and the tiny pebbles went high—too high.

"Sand!" he said in mock pain. "How have I offended you? Why do you dance in my eyes and make me cry?" He wiped his face. "No, I apologize. It is not you that brings tears to my eyes; it's the sight of this dark-haired beauty with whom I'm forbidden to speak, certainly forbidden to touch."

She flashed a quick glance at him. The strength of his profile nearly wiped away the fear generated by her father's purported note, her dread of remaining unwed. The aquiline curve of his nose, the defined planes of his cheeks . . . they perfectly suited his lanky form. He seemed very centered, like he could handle anything that came his way.

"I wish you'd tell Prince Tahir that political prisoners are generally held within the north wing on the top floor. I wish you'd tell him that he cannot enter the main gate with me, or my name will be ruined. They will behead me." Of course, her name might be ruined anyway.

"Please tell Princess Shahrazad that I'd never jeopardize her. I will accompany her, but no one will see me."

How would that be possible? she wondered. But then again he had the magician's cape. And the *shitani* themselves had been invisible. Anything seemed possible.

"I am certain," he said, rubbing his temples, "that the magician is alive—and in your palace. It is almost as if he summons me."

Something about those words struck her as familiar. "When I am in *pegaz* form, I believe I hear *shitani* voices in my head."

"Seems like similar magic," Prince Tahir noted.

The last of the sun's rays were nearly gone, she noted as they walked in silence, and they still had a third of a league to go. As if reading her mind, Prince Tahir pulled a lantern from the cape, already lit. A huge moon rose over the horizon, adding its golden light to theirs.

She stepped forward, toward the walls of her home. What would she find there? Demons in the throne room? Her Duha's eviscerated body? Would the Sultan still be alive—and ruling? The shifting sand grabbed her feet, and she stumbled to her hands and knees.

Prince Tahir rushed to her side, probably to help her, but she stopped him, holding up her palm. As she stood, she found she'd discovered something new about herself. She didn't care if her fate were written on the moon above them and in the sand below. She didn't care if every augury between here and the place where the desert gave way to jungles said her fate was doomed; she didn't care if demons swarmed her home. She would fight it. She would save her land at all costs.

And she would let no man touch her—not even this delicious, powerful, delightful man with the aquiline nose. The augury had warned against it, and she wouldn't gamble the land that depended on her father—and her.

"Sand," Prince Tahir's voice interrupted her dark thoughts. "Please ask the princess to wait a moment."

Shahrazad stopped as he fumbled not with the magician's cloak but with something in the pocket of his riding breeches.

"I would like to tell the princess I have a bottle of demon saliva that will render me invisible. Would you be so kind as to whisper that in her ear?"

As the full moon rose higher in the night sky a shiver went through her. His words held an intimacy she'd never heard. Forget the disturbing notion of using demon saliva, the way he spoke to her made her skin vibrate with anticipation.

"Would you please ask the princess to turn away from me? I must rub this strange potion over my bare skin for it to work." Then his voice took a roguish tenor, and he said, "Unless it pleases her to see me without clothing . . ."

She quickly turned away from him, but she couldn't help imagine how his dark skin would shine in the desert moon, how the moonbeams would play over the muscle of his chest and arms, over his thighs. Embarrassment and maybe even shame made her stand motionless in the moonlit sand, but it had an unfortunate effect—she could hear the sound of him undressing. She listened as buttons left holes and couldn't help but wonder which holes they'd left. She heard the sound of cloth kissing sand and couldn't help but wonder which part of his body now gleamed in the night.

"Would you please tell the princess that I'm finished," he finally said. "Naked, but invisible."

With her heart pounding, her mouth dry, Shahrazad turned

and looked. A strange brown spot floated in the air where he should have been standing. Thick gardenia scent filled the night air, and she realized that this was how the demons had done it. They'd covered themselves in their own flower-scented saliva and become invisible.

"Is the prince supposed to be invisible?" Her voice sounded faint and breathless, at least to her.

"I am." She heard alarm in his voice, and the strange brown spot twisted as the sand beneath his feet churned. "The princess cannot see me, can she?"

"Please tell him he's missed a small spot. Perhaps in the middle of his back?"

"Let her know I thank her." A small brown jar floated from his pile of clothing sitting in the sand. It turned upside down and jumped. She understood then that he was emptying out the last of the oil.

"I can't—" She heard his voice strain. "I can't reach this spot." He paused a moment, then said, "Can the princess still see me?"

"Yes."

Silence filled the desert night as he paused. But then the jar soundlessly floated over to her and floated above her palm. She understood. To save herself and her land, she and Prince Tahir needed to find the magician. That task would be made easier with his invisibility.

Therefore, she must help Prince Tahir become invisible. Even if that meant touching him.

In that heartbeat, she knew what she had to do. "Please tell him I can help." She dreaded it. She delighted in it. Holding out her hand, she said, "If Prince Tahir would be so kind as to give me the amphora . . ."

The small drops of ointment in her hands looked just like olive oil. She set the amphora in the sand and rubbed her hands together, prolonging the moment until she had to touch him.

Until she was permitted to touch him. Until she touched him to save her land.

Tentatively, she permitted her fingertips to skim his flesh. The heat of his skin surprised her so that she nearly lost her nerve, but then she realized the heat came from her hands, born of her desire. She flattened her palm over his broad back.

Relaxing to her task, she felt his muscles dance beneath her touch. Her hands slid over the planes of his back, and the scent delighted her nose. If she caressed him a moment longer than strictly necessary, not even he would know it. She hoped.

He certainly didn't have to know how the heat of his muscled back made liquid silk flow between her thighs.

"You're completely invisible now," she said. With a momentary regret, she stepped away from him. Glancing down, she saw the saliva had rendered her palms invisible, and she wiped them on the sand.

"Thank you," he said, his voice sounding huskier than she remembered.

"You're welcome."

The magician's cape began to fold itself around the other items—Prince Tahir's breeches and white linen shirt, his boots and belt—and then they floated in the air. Only then did she realize that Prince Tahir must be retrieving his clothing and carrying them.

"Prince Tahir," she said. If he lived, her father would behead her and she'd deserve it. "What do you plan to do with your items? Surely you cannot carry them . . ."

"I'll hide them near the gate," he said.

"You might give them to me. You'll want your clothing and weapons sooner or later."

"Ah, I cannot have you risk yourself for my mere clothing."

"I'll take them to the fountain and leave them there. No one will find them."

His clothes and sword floated over to her then, and she took them, savoring their warmth, savoring the sandalwood scent of his skin even as gardenia swirled through the night. "But I won't leave your side."

Alarm raced through her. Even invisible, the guards and soldiers would be sure to detect him. His scent. An accidental noise. "My father wouldn't harm me," she reassured him. "He loves me. The magician sent that note somehow."

"Perhaps you're correct, but maybe he truly was warning you away."

"He couldn't have been." But maybe Prince Tahir was right. Somehow she had the feeling her father was in trouble. "Please don't risk yourself—your land and family—on my behalf. I will be safe."

"No matter. Together we'll find the magician and instill in him a need to lift your curse and restore my sister."

"My father might not want to—"

But bright torches from atop the gate suddenly burned brighter. "Who approaches?" a deep voice called, one of her father's soldiers, and each was handpicked for his ability to wield a sword and bow with equal proficiency.

Relief rushed through her. Whatever the turban meant, at least her palace seemed to be safe, still guarded by soldiers.

"It is I," she called in her most imperious voice, before she could see their faces—before she could be said to be speaking with men. "It is I, Princess Shahrazad. I must meet with my father, the Sultan, and I must do so now." Would they behead her here on the spot? Would they tell her he was dead?

"That is impossible," the deep voice called, and she heard boots stomping down the stairwell. "Princess Shahrazad turned into a *pegaz* and flew away, before my own sight, leaving her bridegroom standing alone, deserted under his wedding canopy."

She knew in that moment they believed her. She knew they had no immediate order to behead her. Otherwise why would they be talking to her at all?

6

At the point of their spears, two soldiers marched Shahrazad to her father's study. They shoved her through the door into the sprawling room, and the Sultan's dark eyes lit with happiness.

Relief surged through her veins, negating the pain from the sharp ends of the weapons digging into her shoulder blades, negating the pain of the note in his supposed turban. She'd been so afraid he'd been killed by *shitani*—or that he'd kill her on sight.

And his white turban of leadership sat on his head, exactly where it belonged. Perhaps she could convince him to lead, to help thwart the *shitani* in this land and in that of Prince Tahir.

"Daughter," he said, standing from his blue velvet pillow and placing warm kisses on both her cheeks. He did it again, and again, until she wept with joy. The rich smell of his tobacco surrounded her as his *huqqa* bubbled next to his cushion. Never had his spare face seemed more dear to her than in this moment.

"I have returned, father, ever your humble servant."

"May God hold you in his eyes, you live!"

And you're not a horse. He didn't say the words, but she

heard them nonetheless—and they tightened her resolve to find Badr, make him lift this curse.

"I live, father," she said, "and never has a daughter been happier to see her father."

"Praise God and his eyes that you live!" the Sultan said. "The Raj will be most relieved—nearly as relieved as I!"

"That is my most fervent hope."

But when she thought of the Raj ir Adham, it was his passionless eyes that came to her mind. Of course, that assessment wasn't precise. He had passion—passion to defeat the *shitani*, passion to form an alliance with her father. His eyes held abundant passion—just not for her. Unlike Prince Tahir.

"And what of your night alone?" he said, emphasizing the last word.

Again, she heard the words he didn't say: *Can this marriage still take place?* And so many pitfalls riddled this question, an adequate answer escaped her.

She flicked a quick glance at the soldiers, who stood in the doorway. She doubted their stoic expressions reflected their actual state. The words they overheard would be traded for tobacco and *heit* to the gossipmongers by night's end.

"Begone," the Sultan ordered them, following her gaze. They left, closing the door behind them.

"Thank you, father."

"Daughter," the Sultan said, holding her shoulders as he kissed her cheeks once again. "The Raj is eager for this alliance. When you were stolen—when you flew away—he informed me that if you've remained untouched and if the wedding ceremony can proceed uninterrupted as ruled by the *klerin*, he'll go through with the marriage, despite the . . . disruption."

Shahrazad thought of the magician's touch slithering over the small of her back during the first day of her wedding ceremony. She thought of his masculine voice. Clearly, a man had touched her, but that wasn't what concerned her father.

"I spent the night in an oasis, untouched by any man."

"And what of that magician's assistant? Where is he? I'll send my soldiers after him so his head can join the others on the Pike Wall."

"He thought to save me from Badr," Shahrazad said, suddenly smelling gardenias. She knew then that Prince Tahir was here in this room, perhaps thinking to protect her against her father or his enemies. "And I believe he actually did save me— and I am restored to you."

"That man touched a princess."

"In horse form," she said, stifling her impatience. The *shitani* lived and threatened everything humans held dear—and her father worried about purity. "The magician's assistant saved that princess. He sought to save me from the magician, and he did save me from the *shitani*." Of course, she'd killed as many of the demons as he had—more, but she saw no reason to bring that point into discussion.

"I've missed your mother since the day she died," he said, apparently changing the subject. "But never have I missed her more than this moment. Women know how to speak to each other. But for a father to talk about these matters with a daughter . . ." He shrugged his narrow shoulders. "God's eyes."

Shahrazad took his fine fingers in her hand and brought them to her cheek. "I am ever your humble servant in all that I do, and I obey all of your wishes, even those that have not yet occurred to you."

"But?" he asked, knowing her well. "What do you request of me?"

"Perhaps beheading the magician's assistant wouldn't best express our gratitude. He saved me from the magician."

"And perhaps destroyed your reputation."

"If you behead him, everyone will believe me ruined—and he did not ruin me." When she oiled his back though, she might have ruined herself.

The Sultan looked at her a moment, his eyes boring into her. Shahrazad worried for a heartbeat that she'd defended Prince Tahir too vigorously, that her father himself doubted her purity. She knew then that to ask her father's help in extracting Queen Kalila from the magician's grasp was too much, at least for now.

"Do you love this boy?" he asked finally.

"How could I?" she asked, exhaling to get the scent of gardenias from her nose. "I barely know him. But I am grateful for my life."

"Did he touch you?" *Not: Did you touch him.*

"Not while I was in human form."

"Did he speak with you?"

"He spoke to the trees in the oasis. He spoke to the sand in the desert. He spoke to himself. And those words, I overheard." She straightened the purple riding outfit bestowed upon her by the magician. "I too spoke to the sand and rock."

The Sultan said nothing for a moment, then he sighed. "Let us not discuss this way of not-speaking with the *klerin*—or the Raj. While it doesn't directly violate their rules . . ."

They wouldn't like it. More unsaid words. "Yes, father."

"Do you know his name? His family? Where is he now?"

"The boy is apparently well born of a powerful House in the Land of the Sun," she said. If not now, then at some time in the near future, she needed to broach the topic of the *shitani.* But Shahrazad decided to sidestep that issue with the most startling of her news. "We have a larger problem brewing on the horizon, I believe."

He looked at her with raised eyebrows, like he couldn't imagine a bigger issue than that facing them now. Like she was a foolish girl to even dream things could get worse. "And what is it, my daughter, that troubles you so?"

"I live safe and unsullied," she said, eyes downcast. "But when the sun rises in the dawn sky, I will once again transform into a *pegaz.*"

"What?" he demanded. "But how can this be?"

"Badr the Bad laid this curse upon me—upon us."

"My most beloved of daughters. Is this news true?" His color had turned an ashen gray.

"It is."

"Then what of the wedding? If the Raj is to wed you, the Flower Taking should happen tonight—shortly. Now." He ran his hand over his face, knocking his white turban askew. Its huge red ruby glittered in the firelight, and Shahrazad knew the turban dropped by the *shitani* was fake, completely fake. What was the magician trying to do to her? "The wedding must take place," he said.

"The Flower Taking should take place tonight," she agreed. She'd lived her life impeccably, seeking to avoid trouble with every decision in her life. And now this. Shahrazad hated this new weakness, this need to accommodate the unasked-for changes in her life.

The Sultan cleared his throat, almost nervously. "Well," he said, "we must get Badr to lift this curse, of course. I hold him in my prison, surrounded by many guards."

Just as Tahir had said. "I'm glad to hear that he is alive," she said. "I believe he's the only one who can lift the curse." And perhaps she could persuade him to release Prince Tahir's sister as well, even if she didn't dare ask her father for help.

"And if he's reluctant to aid you with this *pegaz* issue," the Sultan said, "I have soldiers who will help convince him." His words held strength, but his tone suggested fear.

"Now, father?" she asked. "Can we see him now? I don't want to be a *pegaz*, and I doubt the Raj wants to marry one."

His gaze shifted sideways, away from her, making her nervous. Her father was holding something back. "Perhaps we should first inform the Raj that you've been recovered from the desert," he said, "tell him you're willing to meet the Flower Taker and go through with the marriage."

Shahrazad suspected she knew what her father wasn't saying. Unwilling to ruin the meter of the wedding ceremony, he wanted her to visit the Flower Taker now, and then worry about the curse.

"When will we meet with Badr?" she asked.

"After the Flower Taker, you have my word." He paused for a moment and drew a long breath from the *huqqa*. He blew out his breath and said, "This wedding must stay on schedule!"

Startled by his vehemence, Shahrazad looked at her father. "Has something . . . changed?"

"Yes, but it is not suited for the ears of a princess."

"This humble servant of yours would like to bring something to your attention."

"And what is that?"

"I ceased being a simple princess when I was enchanted and kidnapped. I think I deserve to hear the information that you're not sharing." *Especially since you made me ride that* pegaz.

"Daughter," he began. But the Sultan held up a finger, its fat ruby winking in the candlelight of the room, as he drew in another breath from the *huqqa*. Again he exhaled and examined her. "Perhaps, since it involves you, I should tell you." He scanned her face, maybe seeking proof of her strength. Then he sighed. "We think the *shitani* have entered the palace."

"*Shitani in the palace!*" She couldn't keep the horror from her voice. When she'd seen everyone unruffled by demons here, she'd thought they were unscathed, that the demons were still only in the wilderness.

"Yes." He set the *huqqa* to the side and added, "One of my top soldiers disappeared from his post inside the palace walls."

"Perhaps he deserted?"

"That would be most out of his character. And we found shredded clothing where he'd last been seen. According to ancient texts, *shitani* shred clothing before they make a person into one of their slaves."

But they hadn't been going for *her* clothing; they'd gone for her face. They'd licked her just before she shifted into *pegaz* form. "Has the missing soldier become the *shitani*'s creature?" she asked. "Isn't that what the texts say?"

"Perhaps. The Raj ir Adham believes it—and he also believes he knows how to combat them." But her father looked neither happy nor relieved at this news.

"He'll only aid us with a formal alliance?" she said. "Is that why you're worried?"

"According to him, his augury implored him to accept nothing less."

The auguries were motivating all the major houses, Shahrazad realized. Her own Duha had read a dire warning. Prince Tahir's augury foretold doom regarding the *shitani*, and now this—Raj ir Adham's augury read something similar.

"I feel it also," the Sultan said, looking directly into her eyes, "that thing that makes you shiver."

"What do you mean, father?" she asked, careful to keep her gaze on her feet.

"That the world is on the brink of some important change and that it could go either way: the world could fall to the demon *shitani* or the world could go to us."

Badra had meditated until *prana* oozed from her hands. In the early days, when she'd reached this stage of control, every demon obeyed her merest suggestion.

Those days were gone.

Cupping the energy, the *prana*, in her numb hands, she reached for the *shitani. My pretties?* she asked. *Did you find the princess?*

She tried not to sound anxious, but she was. If her once abundant energy still brought the demons to heel, she'd simply vanish from this cell and go home. But now, she couldn't afford to gamble. Going home took *prana*, and she didn't want to use hers until she knew that the princess awaited her there. *My pretties,* she called into the silence. *Where are you?*

Once she had the princess ensconced in her cave, she'd ask

the girl if she'd like to try her hand at prolonged mortality. If the girl agreed, she could leave this hardened Sultan to his life. And if he changed his mind? So much the easier.

My pretties, she called again.

Instead of demon voice, she heard the distinctive fall of footsteps on the flagstone hall. The Sultan. Again.

"Badr," the Sultan shouted. His voice echoed off the prison brickwork. "Badr."

They killed us, our queen! she heard her pets cry. Finally.

What do you mean they killed you? Her *shitani* had teeth and claws. They could mesmerize and make themselves invisible. *How did a pampered princess who's never been out of her father's sight kill you?*

She used hooves and teeth and feet. The man with the pointy sword killed us, too. He jabbed us and we bled. We want—

Did you give her the turban? she asked. *Did the princess take the turban?*

Yes! The man with the sword took it. We did everything you asked, but she killed us.

I'm sorry, my pretties. But if you gave her the turban, all is well. She'll be heading to my cave now, frightened and alone. We can show her how much we love her.

She'll make a good replacement for you, the *shitani* told her. *And Prince Tahir, he would be good, too. But don't forget the Sult—*

The Sultan approached. "I wanted to thank you," the Sultan said. "You returned my daughter."

What?

She allowed one of Badr's black eyebrows to rise. "Does that mean you'll behead me now rather than later?" Her words were cool, but her mind was racing. Shahrazad had returned here? This wasn't as planned. Not at all. Was it a trick?

"I won't kill you," the Sultan said. "But if you don't lift the curse from her, I'll most certainly torture you."

"Lift the curse from her?" Apparently, her words infuriated the Sultan, although she hadn't meant them to do so. Her faltering control on even her speech indicated how quickly her power was fading.

"Don't pretend to be naïve, man—woman—whatever you are." The Sultan eyed her, caution in his gaze. "Princess Shahrazad is heading to the Flower Taker," he said. "And when she is finished with that step of the marriage to the Raj, she will visit you."

"Visit me?" Badra asked.

"You've made it clear I should fear you," the Sultan said, "and I do. But there is that I fear more—the demise of my land. I will not permit you to sow our ruin. This marriage will take place, whether you will it or not."

Was there hope for this man still? He'd make a magnificent magician. "What would happen if you took my place and ruled the *shitani?*"

"I do not trust you," the Sultan snarled. "You contradict the augury, and the augury never fails." He spat on the ground in disgust. "You, on the other hand, steal. You take false forms. You manipulate."

"I will ask your daughter then," Badra said, losing her patience. "She may rule in my stead."

"You will not." Again the Sultan spat. "You will lift that curse from her or I'll hang you from these very rafters from your absurdly stupid mustache."

Badra curbed a chuckle. "What makes you think you can compel me to obey?" she asked.

But the Sultan had no answer for that. "Guards," he said as he left. "Double the number of soldiers by this cell. He is not to leave. Not under any circumstances. Not unless I myself command it."

For a moment, the magician concentrated her *prana*. She would have to get to the Princess Shahrazad before the Sultan did. Badra herself would need to find the Flower Taker's chambers.

And for that, she needed magic.

7

For a moment, the Flower Taker's beauty left Shahrazad unable to speak, and she must permit this woman to touch her, to take her virginity. Was she truly prepared to take this step toward irrevocable adulthood?

"Congratulations," the Flower Taker said to her. The woman lay in the oversized bed with all the confidence of a desert cat. A fitted top of ruby beads held her breasts, pushed them high and offered them like succulent fruit. Shahrazad wasn't at all certain she was ready to accept this gift.

"Thank you," she said finally.

"Are you prepared to change your view of the world?"

The question was appropriate, but it held a threat. The view from the Pike Wall was different. "I'm prepared," she lied.

"You will be a delight between the sheets."

"Thank you," she said again, years of court training taking over where courage might falter. "The marriage is a well-planned alliance. The Raj and his army will help us defeat the *shitani*."

The Flower Taker laughed, a rich and delightful sound that

seemed to ring with approval. "Congratulations for that, too, but it is not what I meant, little hawk."

"What did you mean, then?" For a wild moment, she thought the other woman congratulated her on surviving her night in the desert and fighting demons in the morning.

"I'm simply congratulating you on your courage and quick mind."

Shahrazad swallowed. What did this woman know—and how did she know it?

"Don't look so nervous, little hawk," the woman laughed. "Some of my clients stand at that hall door for ages, afraid to take the initiative, afraid to knock or open it." The Flower Taker rolled to her stomach and stood. Her luscious gold hair fell past her shoulders in graceful waves.

"Oh." Of course, this woman wasn't talking about her night with Prince Tahir.

"And the women who get that far generally choose the lighted hallway over the dark one," the Flower Taker added.

"And where does the lighted hall take them?"

"Not to me," the woman said with a lazy smile. The Flower Taker ran a long fingertip over the top of her breast, her eyes locked on Shahrazad's, challenging her to accept her sexuality.

"Their loss."

The Flower Taker laughed again. "Your husband-to-be will be a lucky man."

And Prince Tahir, Shahrazad wondered to herself. Who would make him a lucky man? She pushed the thought away. "Will you make me a lucky woman?"

The Flower Taker's laugh rewarded her, and Shahrazad wondered if she'd spent too much of her life being polite. "You are a delightful girl," the woman said. "And I will help you become an even more delightful woman."

A *huqqa* stood on a side table, smoke coiling from the topmost dish. The Flower Taker strode over like a tiger and placed green herbs in the *huqqa*'s marble top. Then she added a burning ember. Soon the unfamiliar scent she'd noticed in the entryway filled the room.

"When you say he's lucky, you're not referring to the benefits of our alliance with the Raj, are you?" Shahrazad asked.

"I'm not speaking of politics. I'm speaking of flesh." The Flower Taker slid a mouthpiece onto the *huqqa*'s long, silk-covered tube. "He's lucky because you're a bold woman, and you have a quick wit. That cannot be trained or untrained in a bed partner—only embraced."

"Or rejected."

"Only a fool rejects a quick wit."

"The world is filled with fools." She couldn't imagine her father seeing the value of a witty woman, for example.

"I don't believe your husband-to-be is one of those."

Did the Flower Taker know this, or was she trying to placate a nervous client? "What makes you say so?"

"I have many clients, little hawk."

"You . . . know the Raj ir Adham?"

The Flower Taker chuckled. "I've known many people in my life."

"And you think he might allow a wife to be more than a mother?"

"I think he'd be very happy to have a clever wife."

"In what sort of capacity would he value me?"

"That is too political of a thought for this evening." The woman inhaled from the tube and the sound of bubbling water filled the room. "Let us discuss flesh instead." She grinned. "Then we shall do more than discuss."

"Perhaps I'm not ready."

"Trust me," the Flower Taker said. "You're ready. You just haven't realized it quite yet." She let her fingers drift seductively across her midriff, just above her pubic triangle. "You're a succulent peach begging to be picked."

Shahrazad looked at the woman's midriff. With surprise, she realized that the Flower Taker's flesh tempted her. Her time with Prince Tahir must have opened something in her, made her crave things she'd never craved. "As you wish, Flower Taker," she said, her compliant words masking a burgeoning desire.

"It will be as you wish, too," the Flower Taker said with a wicked grin. She stepped toward Shahrazad and caressed her breasts.

With sharp intake of breath, Shahrazad stepped back, but the Flower Taker closed the distance between them. "I will pluck these peaches," she said, fingertips dancing under the brassiere's seam. "I will pluck them and suck them and taste them until you can think of nothing but satisfaction."

Shahrazad blushed, knowing it made her look as naïve as a child but unable to stop.

"Your *oraz* is lovely," the Flower Taker said, ignoring her embarrasment "The color brings out the warmth of your skin."

"Thank you," Shahrazad said, her voice thick. "But I hear a 'however' in your tone."

"You are very direct for a princess."

"Directness is not the point," she said. The Flower Taker's bold words, her touch, left her preoccupied. To her left, the air stirred, and she caught that gardenia scent. That wasn't Prince Tahir, was it? Surely he wouldn't have come to her Flower Taking. He didn't need to guard her here—a safer place didn't exist in the entire palace.

At least as far as Shahrazad knew.

The woman held up her elegant hand. "My point is this only, I would like you to wear a *bedlah*."

"For dancing?" Shahrazad recognized the stupidity of her words, but her thoughts seemed . . . abstracted. Visions of curves and breasts and lips haunted her mind.

"Yes. I have one for you." The woman's long fingers gestured toward a neatly folded pile of silk sitting on the table opposite of the *huqqa*.

Shahrazad touched the plum-colored mound. "It's lovely."

"You may change behind that screen," the Flower Taker instructed, indicating a latticed structure. A lantern had been lit behind the filmy parchment, and it flickered invitingly.

Shahrazad looked at it, observing the backlighting and its implication. "You plan to watch me, don't you?"

"I'll watch your shadow," the woman corrected. "And your husband will always watch you. With a beauty like yours, he'll be unable to help himself." The Flower Taker ran a warm palm over her arm. "Let me show you how much fun can be had between the sheets. You must leave modesty behind with your maidenhead."

Her mouth suddenly dry with nervous anticipation, Shahrazad stepped behind the parchment and paused, frozen with anxiety.

"You do want to please your husband, don't you?" The tone was gentle.

"Of course."

"Perhaps you'd rather please Prince Tahir?"

At first she thought the huqqa smoke had gone to her head. She couldn't have heard those words correctly. "What did you say?"

"I've heard you were alone with the handsome prince. Did you like him? Did you like the freedom?"

"Freedom of the sort I believe you're suggesting does not exist." Haughtily, Shahrazad stretched her arms over her head, and turned, knowing the movement would accentuate the long line of her torso and then the curve of her breast. Slowly she extended her fingertips and bent her wrist. Her dance instructor would have been pleased.

"Even the illusion of freedom can tantalize," the Flower Taker observed in her husky voice.

"That may be," she answered the woman who must be her father's spy. "But the land must come first."

"I believe you'll come first," the Flower Taker chuckled. "Do not stop undressing. I'm very much enjoying my view."

"And if I've lost that desire?"

The Flower Taker chuckled, but it wasn't a derisive sound. "You're angry with me because I've touched you where you're the most vulnerable. But you mustn't be that way."

"Why not?" She stood still frozen in place.

"Because to truly enjoy the pleasures of the flesh you must make yourself vulnerable. You feel insecure. You wonder how much I know about you and the prince. You wonder how much I know about your secret fears and desires. And yet you crave me. Don't you see? No one can resist such a duality between the sheets. Flames and ice. Truth and lies. Virgin and whore."

"As the virgin, my vulnerability is clear," Shahrazad said. "But what have you done to make yourself vulnerable?"

The Flower Taker laughed aloud then, no sultry chuckling now. "Why, you are a true delight!" she said.

"But you've not answered me."

"Perhaps I need no vulnerability," she said, and Shahrazad heard hedging. "I am to teach you."

"Then teach by example. Tell me something that makes you vulnerable to me. Open yourself. Expose yourself."

"You challenge me, then."

"I suppose I do."

"Continue to remove that *oraz*, and I will consider."

She inexorably turned, twining her wrists . . . crossing her elbows. In one succinct movement, she shed her *oraz* and stood naked. "Have you thought of something?"

"I have a secret, which you might guess if you are clever enough."

"If you do not distract me with pleasure enough."

"I shall endeavor to distract you beyond all thoughts and

words," the Flower Taker promised. "But still . . . if you are clever, you might discover something that would bring my downfall."

Had the woman discovered Shahrazad's secret? Did she know that the magician had marked her? Did she know she secretly craved Prince Tahir?

"Then I shall endeavor to ascertain your secret while enjoying my time in your hands." She put more confidence in her words than she truly felt.

"Your nerves do not show, little hawk."

Shahrazad struggled to keep the lines of her arms long and elegant while slipping into the plum-colored brassiere. As her fingers and hands trembled, she knew the Flower Taker lied herself. "I am nervous," she said. "I'm sure you know that."

"I have the solution, and so will your husband-to-be."

"What is that?" Shahrazad asked, looking down at her new clothing. The skirt fitted perfectly, low and snug on her hips. The triangle formed by the gold beads fit right over her pubic mound. What would Prince Tahir have thought of this?

"Quit hiding behind that screen, and I'll show you."

With a deep breath, Shahrazad stepped out. The place where the magician had touched her back stung, exposed by the low-slung skirt and her bared midriff. Surely, the Flower Taker would notice. Would she recognize it? Would she negate the marriage after all this effort?

"I had this made just for you, in anticipation of this night," the Flower Taker said. With heavy-lidded eyes, the woman drew another deep breath through the stiff tube of the *huqqa*. Her pupils were huge. With neat efficiency, she passed Shahrazad a small box wrapped in bright green silk. "I hope you like it."

Careful to keep her back away from the woman, Shahrazad took the box and unwrapped it, letting the silk covering flutter to her feet. Inside she found a mouthpiece for the *huqqa*. It was an adult's gift, and Shahrazad admired the intricately carved pattern of diamond shapes and curlicues. "It's lovely. Does it have anything to do with your darkest secret?"

"No." Shaking her head with an enigmatic smile, the Flower Taker gestured to a second silk-covered tube attached to the *huqqa*. "But you may thank me by trying it."

Shahrazad walked over to the *huqqa*, careful to turn her body so the burning flesh from the magician's touch wouldn't show. She slid the mouthpiece onto the tube. "The herb smells intoxicating."

"It should. It's *khansari*, the herb of seduction from the land of the most sensual people in all nine Lands." The Flower Taker gently passed the smoking tube in her direction.

"I'd wager you were Khansari," Shahrazad teased. Inhaling deeply, she let the smoke fill her lungs, and she held it there for a moment. She slowly let the smoke drift, then said, "I didn't realize there was a drug of seduction."

"There's much you don't know, little hawk."

"And you will teach me."

"Another inhalation?" The Flower Taker pointed at the *huqqa*. Her tapered fingernails glowed in the candlelight. Shahrazad wondered in a lazy way if the Flower Taker were Khansari. Perhaps that was her secret. But how did that make her vulnerable?

"I will," Shahrazad said, struck by the woman's voice. It wasn't the tenor of her words . . . it was her pronunciation that struck a chord. The Flower Taker spoke with a slight lilt, something she'd heard recently. One of the Raj's relatives? Not Prince Tahir. But the smoke in her thoughts impeded her rational self, and the identity escaped her.

As she inhaled, an odd somnolence filled her. She watched the Flower Taker wrap her ruby lips around the tube and suck in a deep breath. What else might those lips caress? And where was Prince Tahir? He should be seeking the magician, but the sexual part of her wanted him here. He'd said he wouldn't leave her side. Maybe he was here . . .

"I've heard . . ." Shahrazad tried to remember, but the thought that'd been so clear just heartbeats before flipped away like a fish in a pond. Then her eyes caught the glittering of the woman's lips. "I've heard you have penis-shaped toys." The words came from her lips with a surprising slowness, as if the herb had somehow wrapped around the sands of time and choked them until they flowed at a mere trickle.

"Ah." The woman shifted her shoulder so her hair fell straight down her back in a sunshine-colored sheath. "I have such delightful toys, and we'll play with them."

The Flower Taker walked over to a screened panel, her hips undulating in a way Shahrazad had seen only in professional dancers.

But they weren't as beautiful as the one small spot she'd seen of Prince Tahir's back. She realized that her thighs ached for him. She turned her head and inhaled deeply, trying to catch his scent. But she detected only *khansari*. Of course she couldn't smell him. Accompanying her here would be more than a venial transgression.

"Little hawk," the woman said, her voice shimmering through the air as if conducted by magic. Shahrazad embraced the sultriness of her voice, letting it wash over her like cool water squeezed from a sponge. Rich colors—oranges, reds, and purples—danced behind her closed eyes.

"Little hawk, are you listening to me?"

"Yes." The word fell so slowly from her lips.

"I won't hurt you."

She'd heard those words before—from her prince.

Cool lips grazed her forehead. Prince Tahir! Shahrazad opened her eyes aching for him to appear before her. But she met only velvety black pupils nearly obscuring the woman's irises, which were a shocking violet. Not Tahir. Of course, not Tahir. Just the *khansari* smoke twisting around her thoughts.

"Your eyes are beautiful," Shahrazad said. "Like jewels. Amethysts. Tanzanite."

"And yours are the color of amber, gold as honey, so beautiful against your skin."

The Flower Taker sat next to Shahrazad's head and slowly wrapped a braid around her index finger as seductive drumbeats filled the chamber. Enraptured with the colors, the textures, Shahrazad watched the black braid coil around the pale finger until only the gold bead and red fingernail showed.

"I understand you dance well, little hawk." As slowly as the dawn sun creeping over the sands, the Flower Taker stood from the bed. And it was as if the drumbeats were somehow tied to her hips. With each accented beat, the woman's hip undulated, her red-beaded belt glittering in the dim candlelight. Her breasts and torso remained still as her hips invited, beckoned.

Even with the drug wrapped around her mind, Shahrazad saw she lay in the presence of a master dancer. The drum began a more complicated tattoo, and the Flower Taker's arms slithered through the air as gracefully as a snake charmer's serpents. Her hips and breasts swiveled and summoned. Her arms and fingers tantalized.

"Dance with me. Imagine your . . . husband. Dance for him and he will desire you above all others."

As if lifted by the drumbeat instead of her own will, Shahrazad found herself on her feet, her own hips undulating. She closed her eyes as she danced, letting the rhythm pour over her, through her.

And then the drums quickened. The music poured crazily over her, like a wild spring rain that sends the desert into riotous bloom. Her long black braids floated around her shoulders as her feet spun madly over the floor.

She slowed, picking up every fourth beat instead of every third. Her arms snaked through the air, but she could easily imagine holding the Flower Taker or a lover—her lover. She reached her fingertips toward her teacher. Hoping.

"Yes," the Flower Taker breathed, and this time Shahrazad opened her eyes. The woman danced in front of her, a small step away.

Shahrazad's hips flowed like water, and the Flower Taker's followed. Like they were bound together with an invisible tie, everything Shahrazad's hips did, the Flower Taker's tracked. Watching the other woman, Shahrazad couldn't help but imagine Prince Tahir. He looked like he'd dance, like he could match his hips to hers.

For a moment, she could feel him dancing behind her. His cock pressed hard between her legs, and his sandalwood scent teased her nose. She could feel the heat of his chest against her back. Lost in the *khansari* fantasy of him, she leaned back as she danced and imagined his hands gliding over her waist, skimming her stomach. His cock throbbed against her ass, hard and insistent with his desire for her.

The fantasy seemed so real for a moment she knew he was there, dancing behind her. She twirled and reached for him but caught only air.

"I'm here, little hawk." The voice was feminine, and ruby-covered breasts shimmied so close to Shahrazad's plum-covered ones that one misstep would bring a soft collision. The woman moved her breasts to the wild beat of the drum, and the purple of her areola peaked over the top of her brassiere.

The Flower Taker spun again, bringing her breasts so close to Shahrazad's own that she could feel the heat pouring off the woman's body. Inside her plum-colored brassiere, her own nipples hardened until they ached.

"Go ahead, little hawk," the woman purred. "For tonight, your desire gets full rein, full freedom."

Craving that freedom, Shahrazad's hands reached out, skimmed the Flower Taker's breasts. She pressed her hips against the Flower Taker's, and as their hips together circled to the drumbeat in a delicious dance, Shahrazad slid a fingertip over the woman's areola.

Like lightning over the night dunes, the effect electrified her. She did it again, dipping her finger into the woman's brassiere. The tiny nub of her nipple was as hard as a pebble.

"You may taste if you desire," the Flower Taker invited, arching her back to present a breast to Shahrazad even as her hips followed the drumbeat.

Shahrazad didn't need a second invitation. She dipped her lips to the woman's breast and licked. The woman tasted of warm sunblossom just picked from a sun-soaked orchard. She licked again. And then again, her hips rocking against the other woman's, no longer needing the guiding pressure of the Flower Taker's hands.

If Prince Tahir licked her nipples . . .

The drumming slowed to a stop, but it didn't break the spell. The Flower Taker captured Shahrazad's hand and led her to the bed, her hips still swiveling to a rhythm only she heard. Gently, the woman laid her in the piles of silk.

Shahrazad hummed in pleasure. "I should have realized . . ."

"Should have realized what, little hawk?" The Flower Taker caressed the grooves of her ribs, just beneath her breasts, and Shahrazad hummed again, squirming.

"What your secret is, of course. As you said, all the clues lay before me."

"Oh, really?" The blond woman's hand ran over Shahrazad's bared midriff as her fingers delighted her nipples. She wanted out of her brassiere.

"Oh, yes."

"Is it that I've lusted after you since the heartbeat I laid eyes on you?"

"That's not it."

"Is it that I've lusted after your Duha since the heartbeat I laid eyes on her?" Her lips followed her fingers.

Shahrazad laughed. "No. But that feels delightful."

"I give up then."

"I doubt that."

The Flower Taker's fingertips flowed exactly where the burning was—exactly where the magician had touched her. "You have a delightful birthmark here." She leaned over and kissed the burning spot. Her hot lips cooled the pain. "Unusual."

"I think it's unusual," Shahrazad said. "But I doubt it surprises you. I suspect you've seen others like it. It tells me your identity."

"Your birthmark tells you my identity?"

"That is no birthmark." She rolled to her back and looked the supposed Flower Taker in the eye. "You're the magician, and you put it there—on the first day of my wedding ceremony."

Badra had been stroking the girl's back, preparing to induct her into the most pleasurable of human experiences—when the girl's words stopped her still. The girl had guessed. What a delight this princess was. She would indeed rule well as the magician.

"How?" Badra asked. "How did you discover my secret?"

"Your accent," the girl said. "I recognize it from when you snuck up behind me at the wedding. From when you touched me."

"Very clever." And Badra meant it. Her accent was unusual since the people who spoke her dialect had been gone for centuries. She tried to keep it modern so she could blend in with local populations as necessary, but apparently she hadn't been completely successful.

"Your gender fooled me for a while," Shahrazad said. "Everyone knows Badr the Bad is a man." She shrugged, a delightful movement that shimmied her full breasts. "But of course, you're a magician. You changed me into a *pegaz*. Why should you limit yourself to one form?"

"Why indeed?" Badra asked in admiration. "Would you like to take—" She shut her mouth before she could finish the sentence.

Truly, her age was catching up on her. After the way the Sultan had responded with a direct request to replace her, what did she think the princess would do? Agree? Preposterous.

"Would I like to take what, magician?" the princess asked.

In that moment, Badra knew what she had to do to ensure the compliance of Princess Shahrazad, to convince her to take her position—to make her believe she had no other choice. She needed to unmask the second secret she harbored this evening.

"Would you like to take full freedom tonight? Would you like to truly run wild?" she asked, laying the lightest kiss on the girl's full, delicious lips. "I can grant your heart's desire."

Badra felt the girl freeze beneath her, even as she deepened her kiss. "What do you know about my heart's desire?" the princess asked.

"I know he's standing next to you, thinking he's invisible." Badra had lured him to her, planting the suggestion in his mind that he'd find the magician with the princess, planting the suggestion that he should watch . . . protect the princess. Having him close let her observe him without draining her powers overmuch.

"What?" The girl's raised eyebrows bespoke her alarm even if her controlled voice masked it.

"Prince Tahir, you may speak," she said, using her most compelling magician's voice, wasting more precious *prana*.

"What?" Shahrazad sat, pushing Badra firmly away. "Prince Tahir is here? Did you trick him? Trap him?"

Badra let a sultry wisdom fill her voice, amused that

the prince was standing as still as one of the walls. Did he truly believe she, the greatest magician in five hundred years, couldn't see through demon spit? "I suspect he thought to protect you from me."

"I tracked you here," he said, finally stepping forward, the scent of gardenias wafting around him. "From the prison. Badra, I need my sister, and I need her now.

"Then why are you watching?"

"I wanted to make certain you didn't . . ." He didn't sound certain, and indeed he wasn't. His actions had been suggested—strongly suggested—by the magician.

"Didn't what?" she asked, provoking him. "Hurt the princess?"

"Virgins can be fragile," he said.

"Ah, you speak from great experience."

Princess Shahrazad stood, her knees visibly wobbling, no doubt from the herb they'd smoked. "I don't know how most women's Flower Taking's progress, but I doubt this particular set of scenarios is acceptable. I need to find the Sultan."

"And tell him that Prince Tahir has seen you naked?" Badra scoffed. "Your head will join your cousin's. Pike Wall will be filled with beautiful young girls cut down in their prime."

"What are you suggesting then?" the princess demanded. "You wretched creature."

"He could be yours," she said, teasing the girl with her gentle fingertips over her stomach. "For tonight only, of course. You know you want him. You entered my chamber thick with desire for him."

"I cannot." Her tone held no hesitation. She didn't sound remotely tempted. What a fantastic magician she would make. "I cannot risk my land," Shahrazad said.

"I'm leaving you no choice."

"You can't make me succumb to him," the princess said.

"Oh, but I can," Badra said, laughing at the girl's innocence. Desire and duty could so easily be coalesced into one.

"You cannot make us lie together, magician," Prince Tahir said. "I will not take her against her will, and her will is clear."

"This is why you two will fuck. You," she turned to the princess, "must leave this chamber without your maidenhead. The only way to do that is with him."

"You can't—" the princess began to say.

"You have two choices: enjoy the pleasure of the flesh with the man of your dreams or don't."

And with those words, Badra the Bad vanished, releasing her hold on these two. She needed to give free will a chance to work its magic.

8

"Badr!" Tahir howled, launching himself toward the golden-haired woman. "You'll come with me now. Give me my sister."

But she was gone. Of course she was. He'd waited too long.

"Your land," Princess Shahrazad said, calmly wrapping a blanket around herself. Her huge pupils obscured the honey color of her eyes. "How will we find her now?"

Her words calmed him—because he knew the answer. "I'm not doomed, at least my land isn't. The magician's in my head," he said, touching his temples. "She called me here."

"Is she talking to you? Telepathically?"

"No, I *feel* her. I'm linked to her somehow." He looked at her as he sifted through his thoughts, trying to make sense of them. "I said I'd serve the magician—Badr the Bad—for a month and a day. When I spoke those words, he—I mean, she—took hold of some part of my mind."

"For a month and a day?"

"I hope not a heartbeat longer. Even this is too long."

"And you can detect her, find her?" she asked, rising from the bed. "Or can she only call to you?"

He paused for a moment, concentrating. Even while in the oasis far from here, he'd sensed the magician's lifepulse. Focusing on that pulse, he realized he could track it even now. "I think I can find her," he said. "I believe she's still in the palace." He paused again. "I believe she's several floors down from here . . . in a room filled with books. The library?"

"Yes," she said.

He nodded. "That feels right. She's . . ." he paused again. "Looking for something, something on the shelves."

"Tracking her at will could be very useful," the princess said, "even if she can vanish so easily."

"Yes."

Princess Shahrazad walked past him, wrapped demurely in her blanket. "I shall dress myself then, and we shall retrieve your sister. Or we shall attempt to."

"And when you arrive in your marriage bed as a virgin?"

"The marriage will be annulled. The Raj will reject me. The *shitani* will invade."

"We cannot allow that."

"But you know where the magician is, what she's doing. We must find her and restore your sister."

"I can always find the magician. I can find her after we meet your needs."

A desire to wrap her in his arms surged through him. He could hold her and protect her from her father and her husband-to-be. He could love her, show her the Way of Pleasure. Keep her for his own.

But the smell of *khansari* tobacco burning in the *huqqa* filled the air, bringing him back to himself. "I—" Tahir reached for her, but stopped himself. "My desire for you burns my skin. I ache for you. I fear my desire to aid you is completely self serving."

She smiled shyly, her eyes cast on her feet. "It would serve me as well." She stepped toward him and said, "Show me my tattoo, if you please."

And Prince Tahir couldn't disobey a direct order from a woman. Could he?

He could not. "Your birthmark looks like this," he said, pushing the edge of the saffron blanket aside with gentle fingers. He placed a lingering kiss on the base of Shahrazad's spine, his fingers tracing the silk-covered line of the princess's thigh.

He thought his bold touch might make her flee like a hunted deer, but instead she stood trembling under his hand. She moaned in pleasure as he placed kiss above kiss, climbing the princess's back.

"Its tongue is right here," he said, flicking his own tongue over Shahrazad's right hip.

"Oh." She drew the syllable into one long moan of pleasure. The scent of her desire filled the room, making him ache for her.

"And what if this delicious snake slithered over here?" he asked as he rolled Shahrazad onto her back, keeping his tongue on the skin right above the *bedlah* skirt.

"Tattoos don't slither," Shahrazad answered, her voice nearly as husky as his. The way her hips moved told Tahir exactly how much desire burned her veins; desire burned in his veins. "Tattoos don't move."

"But what if it did?" He traced the gold-beaded triangle with his finger, and the princess caught her breath. "I'd crawl right here, if I were that snake." The vee plunged from the curve of her hips down over her pubic hair, and as he traced the edging, the princess's nipples pebbled beneath the plum-colored top. Her nipples were as hard as any of the gold beads, as hard as his cock.

"Are you a snake to crawl over me so?"

"For you, I will be. I'll crawl all over each of your curves. I'll lick every bit of you that craves me."

And when his red lips traveled the same line his fingers had traced, Tahir felt the princess surrender. In the smoke-filled room, he imagined the heat between her thighs turning to molten silk. He longed to swim in her river.

"Does my invisibility distract you?" he asked.

"Perhaps it makes me bold."

"Let us see how bold." Spying a perfect accoutrement to pleasure, he retrieved a small glass jar from the end table. It was inlaid with the same blue gems as the *huqqa* sitting on the small table by the bed, and he suspected it contained massage oil. When he uncorked it, the pop sounded ethereal, like it came from a distant plane. Tahir knew then that the smoke had stoned him too.

"I'm going to give you a massage." He warmed the oil in his palms.

"Mm-hmm."

He slid his hands lingeringly over the princess's stomach, her hips, her navel. Then he moved higher, coating her shoulders and arms with the warm oil. His fingers teased at the edge of her brassiere, just where the swell of her breasts began.

He craved her full lips, imagined them wrapped around him, sliding and sucking. He knew he shouldn't think of her this way, destined as she was for another man, but still . . . he wanted her. He imagined her writhing beneath him, calling his name. He imagined sucking her breast, tasting her kiss. Did he dare?

"Your husband will like it if you do this to him," he said, rubbing oiled hands over her midriff.

"And you?" she asked. "Would you like it?"

"I crave your touch," he said as the princess took the jar from him. He knew she was about to touch him in ways he'd been touched before, by many women. But the fact that it was she—Princess Shahrazad, who was shy and bold in equal measure, who was braver than any of his mother's Warqueen Abbesses when fighting the demons . . . Never had he ached like this. "Today," his voice sounded just like a croaking toad's, "you may practice on me."

"I might like such an opportunity." Her words were solemn, but her fingers were tracing his hip.

"Where are you, my prince?"

"If you want me, you should find me."

"You doubt my desire?"

He laughed, a low, seductive sound. "I don't doubt. Not you."

"Then where are you?"

The bed shifted. A caress delighted her arm. "Find me."

Slowly, Shahrazad closed her eyes and used her intuition to find the man. She caressed his flat stomach. At first she used only fingertips. But he hummed in pleasure, giving Shahrazad a sense of boldness. The curve of his chest invited the whole flat of her palm.

And the delight that raced through Shahrazad's hands as she skimmed the surface of his stomach and chest and arms left her sizzling with a new hunger.

"You may press harder, you know."

Tahir's voice was barely recognizable, but Shahrazad obeyed, letting the texture of his skin speak to her breasts, her thighs.

"Now it is my turn," he said. She felt him move. Was he sitting now?

When he began sliding warm fingers over her shoulders in a deliberate way, Shahrazad didn't object. Even as she looked down and saw her breasts shining in the candlelight, she didn't want to object. She longed for . . . something. For something she didn't know how to describe.

Warm and seductive flesh touched her cheek, slid across it tenderly. He was kissing her, she realized. His lips stroked her cheek and then her chin, teasing her. With half-closed eyes, Shahrazad parted her lips, inviting his attention.

She wanted to be devoured; she wanted to devour. A primal

hunger was upon her, and she didn't want to wait another moment.

He molded his hands over her breasts, running his fingernails lightly over her nipples. The friction sent a crack of electricity through her.

Writhing from the sensation, Shahrazad felt her very core soften and yield. She parted her legs to reduce the throbbing, but the texture of her silk skirt against her thighs did little to soothe.

Then he slid a finger just under the edge of Shahrazad's *bedlah* skirt. His rough fingertip glided over the bone of her hip, danced just above her pubic line. Rubbing one hand lightly over her nipple, his hand swept over her mound, pressing, pitching the hunger to a fever heat.

And when his finger caressed her nerve-filled nub, her breath hitched in surprised pleasure. The delight between her thighs hovered right on the line of exquisite pleasure.

Each time he neared her throbbing nub she thought she'd explode from the pleasure of near release. "In God's eyes," Shahrazad moaned, grasping the silk blanket in tight fingers. "Please. I need—" But she didn't know what she needed.

Prince Tahir did.

He nudged her with the tip of his experienced tongue. Shahrazad jerked in response to the searing lash of delight that burst over her.

Between butterfly-light strokes of his tongue, he sucked. Then, while he stroked, he slid his thumb heavily over her nub, gliding just barely inside her opening.

Shahrazad arched toward her lover, seeking release from this excruciating torture, but he pulled back. She sensed a smile on his invisible face.

"Do you know what you want?" he asked.

"Yes—" Shahrazad said. "I want . . ." She wanted him. She wanted him now.

"You must be able to tell me what you want," he said without recrimination. "You must be able to tell your husband."

In answer, she grabbed his hand and slid it between her thighs.

Again, she sensed amusement, but not a cruel sort. Something patient and kind.

"What do you want, Princess Shahrazad?"

"I want you," she said, finally answering the question. "Please, slake this fire."

"Are you burning for me? Do you ache for the Way of Pleasure?"

"I—" She couldn't help herself. She pushed his fingers where she wanted them to be. "I ache. Help me. Please."

"Yes," he said. Then the bed shifted, and she felt his lips touch hers, kissing her lips gently. "Do you want this?" He flicked his tongue just inside Shahrazad's mouth, tracing the line of her lips.

She opened herself to the kiss—and wasn't disappointed. His tongue twined around hers, teasing and promising—pulling a groan of pleasure from her.

"Do you?" he asked again, flicking the tip of his tongue over Shahrazad's top lip.

"Yes."

"Yes," her teacher breathed. His breath tasted of cloves and cinnamon, and his lips burned a path from her neck to her breast. Tiny kisses covered each nipple, leaving her breathless. She'd never imagined a touch could feel so . . . erotic.

When he softly sucked a nipple, it felt as natural as breathing. He applied the gentlest pressure, as lightly as a feathered sun-chaser landing on a flower, and Shahrazad blossomed.

With a groan of pure longing, she rolled her head back and gave herself to the pleasure, to the delight. Whatever he wanted to do to her, she'd allow it. He could have her mouth, her breasts. He could have her thighs and what lay between them.

Spreading her thighs, she caressed her own breasts and pushed them up, offering them. Tahir sucked harder, grazing her nipple with careful teeth. Shahrazad pressed toward him, moaning, and he ran his thumb over the other nipple, pressing harder as he circled.

Pleasure left her malleable as wet oasis clay, even as she gave her mouth and breasts and tongue to him.

An ivory item floated from the end table—he carried it, she knew—and her fear did more than whisper. The item—the imitation penis—glowed like bone in the dim light, and Shahrazad wondered what it would look like stained with her blood.

"You like that?" he asked, tracing his fingers over the curve of her stomach.

"Oh," she breathed. "I like it."

And as he sucked the sensitive skin on her neck, she longed to show him exactly how much she liked it. He traced the low line of Shahrazad's pubic hair, sending delicious shivers of anticipation through her.

When the ivory penis lightly glided over Shahrazad's inner thigh, liquid fire lit through her blood. He slid it between her legs, over her nub, and she gasped. *Open your legs*, he silently demanded, and she wanted nothing more than to obey.

"You're beautiful," Tahir breathed. And Shahrazad believed him. She felt him shift around her, the bed moving. Then she felt the heat of his breath between her legs. As he placed a gentle kiss on her nub, teasing her thighs with the ivory penis, hot anticipation thrummed through her veins.

His tongue danced over Shahrazad's nub, his thumb stroking her nipple. He sucked and stroked until Shahrazad couldn't tell where his skin ended and her own began.

And as the ivory penis, warm from his palm, slipped just inside her, her need for satisfaction burst through her.

She pushed her pelvis toward him in hopes that she would

ease her hunger, that he would lick and suckle between her thighs, that he would fill her—that he would end this beautiful yearning.

Lying on his stomach between her legs, he spread her with deft fingertips. She felt his hot breath as he nuzzled his face into her. Lightly at first, he trailed his tongue, swirling around the tip.

Every muscle in her body was tightened in throbbing ecstasy. If he didn't stop sucking, flicking, gliding, she knew she'd lose her mind.

But the sizzling flicks of delight unrelentingly swarmed her body. Then, while he stroked, her lover slid the toy more fully into Shahrazad.

Squeezing her eyes shut against the sudden rush of pleasure, she screamed as he slid the toy to just the right spot. The pain was fleeting, but the pleasure encompassed her very soul. She didn't care what he thought as she shrieked. She didn't care if her voice bounced off the palace walls and woke every member of the household.

For several moments, she was unable to move, unable to take any but the most shallow of breaths. Tahir stroked her cheek and caressed her neck. The soothing touch offered the counterpoint to her beating heart.

Slowly, she opened her eyes. The room spun.

"Princess Shahrazad?" he said, sliding the ivory toy from her.

"Mmmm."

"Welcome to the Way of Pleasure."

She stretched just then, arching her back and extending her arms above her head. God's eyes, he thought, eyeing the long line of her waist, the curve of her lush breasts. She was beautiful. Her *bedlah* skirt hid her thighs in shadows, but the gem in her belly button shined in the lantern light. It shined like her eyes.

Just then, he saw her fingers surreptitiously exploring, looking for him. Even after she was sated, she wanted him. That knowledge did something to his heart. And to his cock. He rolled toward her and nipped her ear. He'd used the ivory toy on her. Now it was time for flesh.

Tahir touched her breasts and pushed them together. Flicking his tongue first over one hard nipple and then over the other made Shahrazad writhe, ecstasy clear on her face. He edged off the side of the bed, planning on pleasuring her with his tongue, his mouth.

Suddenly a huge soldier ran right into him. Both the soldier and Tahir tumbled to the ground.

Tahir leaped quickly out of the way, hoping the guard didn't figure out he'd just tackled a naked, invisible man.

"What the fuck," the guard said under his breath. He struggled to his feet as Tahir silently stole the guard's dagger.

"What is the meaning of this?" Princess Shahrazad asked in an arrogant voice. Tahir heard no fear.

"My ladies," the soldier said in a breathless voice, his bulk filling the chamber.

The princess sat and deliberately wrapped a silk around herself with all the elegance of a queen. "Fool," she said. Then she turned toward the wall and said, "This man had better have the ultimate excuse for bursting into this chamber—on this of all days—or I'll see his head decorating the Pike Wall."

"My ladies," he said, his breath mostly regained. "I—" He paused and looked around the chamber in confusion. "Where is the Flower Taker?"

"This fool should realize that the Flower Taker is seeing to her business. What reason could this fool have for bursting into this chamber and attempting to speak directly to the princess?"

"I have news, and you—I mean, the Princess Shahrazad— must come with me this very moment." The princess did not move, her eyes dilated with *khansari*. He added with impatience, "Come, come! We'll retrieve the Flower Taker later."

"The princess will not be going anywhere, not alone with a foolish soldier," she said. She looked distressed, but Tahir couldn't rescue her yet. Not until he understood the situation better.

"It's Badr the Bad, the magician," the soldier said finally, sweat beaded in the russet hair of his brow. "He's escaped his cell. He's loose in the palace." Suddenly the soldier stopped and sniffed the air. "What's that scent?" he asked. "It smells like . . ." He paused, perhaps following the thought to its logical conclusion. "There's a man in here with you," he said to the princess, turning toward her, his spear at the ready.

Tahir brought the soldier to his knees with a blow to the side of his neck, and all nine hells broke lose—beginning with the Flower Taker's shouted warning, in his head.

Shitani! he heard in his brain, the magician's voice—her feminine one—said.

And then she appeared in Shahrazad's bed. In the flesh.

9

For a moment, Shahrazad failed to understand what her eyes registered. Something invisible pummeled her father's guard. She blinked, trying to make sense of that, and the Flower Taker appeared like magic.

But then the Flower Taker—no, she remembered—the magician—leaped from the bed opposite the guard, grabbed Shahrazad's hand, and jerked her to the floor.

"Make no sound," Badra whispered. "Come with me now."

"What—" Shahrazad started to say, but the other woman shoved her under the bed.

"Move!"

"I don't understand. What's—"

"Go!" Badra hissed. She shoved her farther under the bed. Were they hiding? How absurd! This didn't strike her as a child's game.

"What do you think you're doi—"

But the blond woman gave a mighty thrust, and Shahrazad screamed as she fell. She fell, farther than should have been possible under the bed. Her fingernails scraped walls.

She hit the floor before she understood what was happening, the landing knocking her breath completely from her lungs. As Shahrazad battled the pain in her struggle to breathe, the magician landed on top of her, her elbow hitting her stomach.

"We can't just leave Prince—" Shahrazad managed to gasp.

"Shh!" the other woman said, standing. Shahrazad heard her slide something above her head, and then she heard a click.

"There," Badra said. "It's locked." The magician had a frightening knowledge of the palace Shahrazad had always considered her home, her safe home.

Shahrazad carefully stood in the pitch-black chamber. She rubbed her stomach, aching from the elbow. Then she rubbed her head. She must have hit that on something too. "Where are we?"

"Nowhere safe," the magician answered. She sounded angry, or perhaps frustrated. "We must hurry. Please, hold my waist."

Extending her hand in the darkness, Shahrazad accidentally found the other woman's breasts.

"Not those," Badra said with a deep chuckle. "Although I appreciate the enthusiasm. Try here." The woman slid Shahrazad's hands lower.

"Is the prince safe?" Shahrazad asked. "What's happening?"

"Your father will kill you when he hears you were with Prince Tahir at your Flower Taking." Badra began to walk—exactly like she knew where they were going in this utter darkness. "I need to remove you from his grasp."

A zip of fear raced through her. Her father *would* kill her when the soldier reported back, empty handed. Shahrazad heard the sound of another sliding panel, and the small chamber they'd been in gave way to a hall lit with the smallest lanterns Shahrazad had ever seen. The flagstone floor lay at a sharp incline.

"What just happened?" Shahrazad asked, still confused. "Were you expecting trouble?" Shahrazad pointed to the lanterns.

"Everyone's expecting trouble, everyone across all the lands. Auguries in all of the cities and palaces and villages are warning about *shitani*."

"*Shitani*." Shahrazad said this remembering the green monsters she and Tahir had battled.

Badra did not look behind her as she sped down the hallway. "I've read your destiny—fate has deemed you worthy. Therefore, I am saving you."

"Me? Worthy of what?" They'd stopped in front of a paneled wall. The magician slid another wooden panel aside, pushed Shahrazad through it, and latched it. Shahrazad saw they were in the lighted hall near the entryway.

"The way I see it," the golden-haired woman said, closing the panel behind them, "it's like this. It's within your power to rein in the demons, but should you fail . . ." The magician was running now, pulling Shahrazad by her arm.

"Should I fail, what—" Shahrazad ran to keep up with the other woman, but a horrible screeching on the other side of the thin panel stopped her words.

It sounded like the cry of some wounded animal, and it was attacking the wooden panel as if it would die if it failed. It sounded like a dervish of claws and teeth, and another shriek filled the air. Was it human? Was it masculine? The scent of human sweat filled the chamber, accompanied by the odor of gardenias.

"Is that the demons?" she asked Badra, alarm breaking through the haze of the *khansari* tobacco and the physical pleasure to which she'd been introduced. "Is Tahir battling a *shitani*?"

"Don't distract me." The magician turned left around a corner.

"We must help Tahir. He cannot conquer a demon and a soldier."

"He will win the night," the magician said. "That I can assure you."

The sound of fighting echoed down the dark hallways, and

it didn't inspire confidence. "But we must help him," Shahrazad insisted.

"I am helping you instead—because I need your help." The blond woman threw a glance over her shoulder, and she began to pull Shahrazad down the hall, toward the main gate. More wood splintered within the chamber's heart, and Shahrazad heard the sound of shattering glass.

The woman didn't pause; she continued to drag Shahrazad behind her, pulling her toward the door. Cold dread coiled through her stomach as an additional—and horrifying—thought occurred to her. If the magician was truly a woman, did that mean that the burning touch on the first day of her wedding had come from a woman—not a man? Was her embrace with Tahir the first time a man had touched her?

Her eyes locked on the woman as horror roiled through her veins. She tried to step back toward the direction from which they'd come, but the magician wouldn't let her.

"Princess," she said.

"Are you a man or a woman?"

"Why do you care?" She dragged Shahrazad a few more steps.

"If I let a man touch me, *shitani* invade. My land will fall."

"Why do you say that?"

"I don't—the augury does." She yanked her arm hard, but still the magician dragged her toward the main gate. Had she been safe from the augury's warning until just now, until she'd dallied with Tahir at the magician's suggestion?

"Princess Shahrazad," the magician said. "You think this is your fate, to doom your land?"

She nodded. "I fear it," she said.

"Then fight it."

"What do you mean?"

"Run. Or fly. Do not remain here."

Shahrazad tried to pry the other woman's fingers from her

arms, tried kicking her legs. The smoke addled her brain. "I won't go with you, Badra. You need to lift the curse from me. You need to restore Tahir's sister to the throne."

"If you stay here, you'll die. Your head will go on the Pike Wall or the *shitani* will destroy you."

Shahrazad wanted to scream and cry and run away from this insanity. But the death grip on her arm prohibited her, and it forced a cold logic into her heart.

"Which do you choose?" the magician asked.

"I will not run from my duties, and my duties are to my land."

The magician stopped and looked at her, easing the grip on her arm. "Your father won't believe that. Come with me. I'll keep you safe. You can flee this land and its fundamentalist rules. You can live as you will, love as you will."

"No, Badra." Her voice was calm. "I won't go with you. I won't run from this."

The violet eyes of the blond woman met hers for a moment. "Fool." She shook her head, but she released her arm altogether. "Your father will find exactly the evidence he needs to behead you, and you'll have no choice but to run to me."

And then the air around Badra began to shimmer.

Shahrazad lunged at it. She couldn't let the magician vanish, not until the *pegaz* curse was lifted. Not until Queen Kalila was returned.

But the other woman was too fast.

"You'll run to me," Badra said as the air coalesced around her. "Come to me."

"I'll never run to you," she said to the fading magician. "Never."

"Before you decide with such certainty, go to the library and search for what has been hidden from those who seek to stop me. Read what you find there." The words hung in the smoke even after the magician was gone. "And then choose your fate."

Shahrazad stood alone in the hall for a moment, stunned.

What in the thirteen paradises had just happened? She looked up the hall and saw nothing. She saw no one behind her either.

Which was a good thing, because in that moment she realized she was half naked in her father's palace. Her very suggestive *bedlah* skirt snugged her hips, but she had no brassiere. In the heartbeat she found a guard, she was dead.

Then she remembered her father's soldier, the tale he'd tell the Sultan. She might very well die tonight.

Taking a deep breath, she crossed her arms again over her breasts and walked calmly to the black door. She put her hand on the brass knob, and paused, wanting her clothing. *God, if you hold me in your eyes in even the smallest way, please let this door open.*

And before she could turn the knob, the door swung toward her with a gentle squeak.

"Who's there?" she asked, releasing the knob like it was a snake. "Hello?"

"Shahrazad," she heard. The voice was deep and masculine. "I'm so pleased to see you. I worried for your safety."

"Prince Tahir?" The scent of gardenia rolled over her. "You are safe. I'd thought—" She stopped, remembering the sound of the gnashing demon teeth. "Where are you?"

"I'm here, directly in front of you. I opened the door." Unlike her own voice, his sounded steady, and he was closer now. "I'm very happy to have found you."

The kindness of his words, the familiarity of his voice, these undid her. Tears fell and she couldn't wipe them away, not without baring her breasts. She turned to dry them with her skirt.

"By the six winds," she said, swallowing her tears. "I let the magician escape. I couldn't stop her—"

"Shh," he said. "Everything is fine. You know I can find her." Warm arms wrapped around her, protected her, completed her.

Shahrazad closed her eyes, envisioning Tahir where she could not see him. She imagined his muscular arms around her waist. She imagined the kind look in his eyes. Beneath her naked breasts, his chest felt strong and powerful. He could ward off any evil.

And he smelled better than anything she'd ever smelled— like sandalwood and tobacco. Like gardenias. He pulled her against him, stroking her shoulders. She relaxed into his embrace.

"In God's eye," she blasphemed. "This feels right."

"Mmm." His very masculine cheek rested against hers. Was she dooming her land by ignoring Duha's foretelling, letting a man touch her? She didn't care. When that magician slid a finger across the small of her back, her world had been doomed. In Tahir's embrace she'd find only solace, no damnation. The world might burn to ash around them, but she'd have him, and that seemed like the first sane thought she'd had since before her wedding.

"Tahir?" she asked, using his informal name for the first time.

"Mmmm?"

"Don't stop holding me." She swallowed back tears. "At least for another heartbeat or so."

He didn't answer. Instead he wrapped his arms more tightly around her.

"What happened in the Flower Taker's chambers?" she asked finally, her voice calmer now.

"*Shitani* came. The soldier and I killed them. I don't need to tell you it was messy."

"And the soldier? Did he live?"

"Yes." He pulled her more snugly against him, burying his nose in the hair behind her ear. Her bare nipples suddenly hardened, and she became achingly aware of the friction from his naked chest. "But he's tied in the bedsheets. I took his swords, but when I looked up, I couldn't find you—I had to find you."

She ignored the warm emotion his words elicited—at least for now. "I need my clothes."

"And we need the magician." The door opened wider, and she understood he was inviting her into the chamber. "I believe she's left the palace—but she hasn't gone far."

"I think we need to go to the library." She walked through the hall, down the same path she'd trod in what seemed a lifetime ago.

"Why?"

"The magician said she needs my help with the *shitani*. She said something is hidden there that I need to see before I choose."

"Why would she have hidden it? She could have given it to you?"

"She didn't say she'd hidden it—only that it *was* hidden."

"But why didn't she simply give it to you?"

"I don't know—I don't trust her. Maybe we should hunt her down and return your sister to the throne before we look at old musty tomes."

"We have a month to find my sister. And if the ancient texts in your library are anything like the ones in mine, educating ourselves will be a good use of our time."

"Education is fine, but I'd like my clothes." They approached the door to the Flower Taker's bedchamber. "Is it safe to go in here?"

"Your father's man won't have escaped; I promise you that." She watched the door open via his invisible hand, his blood-soaked dagger floating in front of them. "But let me go first."

Shahrazad entered the bedchamber following the faint sound of Tahir's footsteps. When she entered the room, she saw no sign of her father's man.

"He escaped," Tahir said. "We need to leave."

"I need clothing." She walked toward her tangerine-colored *oraz*, which was hanging just where she'd left it, on the intricate lattice where she'd changed.

Just as she stepped forward to retrieve it, two soldiers came through the opposite doorway. "Princess Shahrazad," the foremost man said. "Are you she?"

"Yes," she replied, to his feet. How could she deny it? How dare he speak directly to her?

"Princess Shahrazad." His tone was officious now. "We're here to arrest you."

"You're here to arrest me?"

"We are, you whore," the second soldier said.

"But why?" She needed her *oraz*, and she needed it now.

"You know why, slut."

She turned toward the feet of the second soldier. "Who gave you this ridiculous command?"

"Your father, the Sultan of the Land of the Moon."

10

As the first soldier walked toward her, his worn shoes clacking on the flagstone, the time-marking bell rang from deep within the palace. The hour was exactly between midnight and dawn, and for the first time since the magician vanished, she realized how little time she had left. She was going to turn into a *pegaz* in four short hours. And she was being arrested. And she had this burning snake tattoo across her back.

God hold her in his eyes, the Raj would never wed her.

"Just come with us, Princess Shahrazad," the second of the two soldiers said. "We'll take you to the Sultan."

Ridiculous. If her father killed her, he'd have no pawns left with which to build an alliance. Had her father lost his mind? The armed guards closing in on her suggested he truly had.

"Stop," she said to their feet.

They did. Maybe this arrest was part of the wedding ceremony? Maybe it was a test.

Increasingly aware of Tahir looming behind her, she held up her hand, keeping her eyes on her feet as trained. Her other arm covered both breasts. "You're not going to touch me," she said in the soldiers' direction. "I forbid it."

"You can't forbid anything, whore." The russet-haired soldier said that. She saw his worn sandals move closer.

"Wait," the second soldier said. "She hasn't been convicted yet. Don't touch her." He waved a spear vaguely in her direction. "But don't try to flee, princess. We have orders to bring you in regardless of the cost."

"I need to dress."

"You need to come with us now."

That was not going to happen. "You don't want to deliver me naked to my father, do you?" She boldly met the second soldier's eyes as she asked this, daring him to defy her.

"Very well," he muttered, looking away before she did. He gestured to the lattice where her garment hung.

Keeping her hands over her breasts, she went behind the lattice and turned out the lantern. She'd throw herself from a minaret before she gave these camelbrains a show.

"You will turn away, please."

"We're watching, whore princess."

But that was not to be. She heard the sound of a fist hitting flesh—not hard but with authority. "Turn," the second soldier hissed at the first.

"But she—"

"Turn away or face the lieutenant."

"You can't punch me."

"I just did. Now turn."

Shahrazad's mind raced as she removed the *bedlah* skirt and slid into her wedding *oraz*.

Struggling with the many tiny buttons, she realized she didn't have time to argue with the Sultan. If her father actually was trying to arrest her, she was in trouble. Not until she read what the magician wanted her to read, not until she helped Tahir rescue his sister could she cope with the Sultan—because she had the distinct feeling there was more at play here than random bad auguries, disappearing magicians, and the promise of a *shitani* invasion. They were all related.

"Hurry, princess," one of the soldiers goaded. "We don't want to keep the Sultan waiting."

She didn't dignify that with an answer.

With no more pressure than a sunchaser's wing beat, a silent fingertip glided across her cheek. *I'll stay directly behind you. I won't let them touch you or hurt you.* Tahir's touch whispered as clearly as his voice would have.

Then he whispered in a voice so low she struggled to hear. "Just stay calm," he said. "When the sun comes up, you'll turn into a *pegaz* and we'll escape this fiasco."

Odd. The magician had made the same suggestion—only now the threat truly existed. Now her father likely wanted her head to decorate the Pike Wall.

The feeling that they were being manipulated grew in her.

"We need to get to the library first—before we meet my father." The magician had also suggested that, and Shahrazad resisted the urge to balk.

One of the soldiers approached the lattice structure. "To whom are you talking?"

"I'm praying that God holds me in his eyes, and you would too if you knew the magnitude of your transgressions."

"I'm going to—" She heard feet stomp toward her, and a brief struggle.

"Hurry, Princess," the nicer soldier said. "We'll not wait much longer."

"I'll hurry her," the first soldier said.

"I'm putting on my slippers." With a sigh, she stepped out and toward them, completely dressed.

"You ready?" the second soldier asked.

"I'm prepared now." She straightened her shoulders and covered her face with the golden veil. "Lead the way."

With their spears at her back, she let them herd her through the narrow, darkened hall toward the door.

As they entered the hall that led to the foyer, Tahir acted. Not that she saw him, but when one soldier grunted and fell to the floor unconscious, she figured that was Tahir's work.

"What the fuck?" the remaining soldier said. And as she looked on, the man doubled over as if someone had punched him in the stomach, then he too crumpled to the floor.

An invisible hand grabbed hers and pulled her to the door.

"Now," Tahir said in his normal voice. "Where is this library?"

"Perhaps we should forgo the games and seek the magician directly in her cave," Tahir suggested as he followed Shahrazad through the hall. This second death threat from her father made it difficult for him to trust the Sultan. "We can fly there at dawn." Get her to safety. Find his sister. Lift her curse.

"The problem with the magician is that she vanishes before we can compel her to do anything, and we need her too badly to be chasing her vanishing shadow over the dunes for the rest of our lives."

Tahir knew she was right, but the sway of her hips below her long, thick braids didn't make it easy. Neither did her luscious scent . . . citrus and sexual excitement.

"I think we should get you away from the palace, away from your father who seems intent on chopping off your head."

"But that's just what the magician wants. She's driving me from my home. Only I won't go. I can't go."

"The library doesn't seem like a good refuge."

"If I can show my father how Badr—Badra—is manipulating us, he won't behead me. He needs me. And I remember books from my childhood. They had information about the magician . . ."

And ovulation, the Impregnator in him noted. She smelled of ovulation. The *shitani* would notice that, too, if the woman posing as the magician's assistant was to be believed. He tightened his grip on the dagger. "I'm not sure some arcane book will convince your father to accept you as you are."

"That may be." She shrugged. "But the issue at hand is bigger than his acceptance. It's larger than my life."

"You mean the safety of your land?"

"Yes, and I have this vague memory that the magician is an immortal. I remember something about the *shitani*, too. If we can show my father how to control them—"

"Or control her."

"Exactly. If we can show him these things, the Land of the Moon won't fall to the demons," she said.

"Perhaps."

"You sound doubtful."

"The demons outnumber sands in the desert," Tahir said. "How can anyone control them?"

"The magician seems to."

"Or she lies."

"She lies, but the demons have not attacked for years."

He nodded. "Perhaps they can be controlled."

"There is another advantage of seeking the library," Shahrazad said.

"And what is that?"

"I think making the magician wait for us may be beneficial."

"Rather than ineffectually chasing her from place to place?"

"Exactly. It's this way," she said, the gold tips of her braids clacking as she looked over her shoulder—missing him completely.

"Where are you?" She stopped suddenly and held out her hand, palm up.

He took it, luxuriating in its warmth. "Here."

"You need to know this about me. I should have been married years ago. My father should have used me to solidify the marriage with the Raj long before he used—tried to use— Haniyyah, who is merely his niece."

"Why didn't he? Are you trying to tell me you're secretly a camel?" The woman had no flaws as far as he could tell.

"I love books. I love to argue."

He paused, trying to find the sense in this. "And that means . . . ?"

"In my land, intelligence is not fostered in wives. In fact, many fathers refuse to teach their daughters how to read and write. Apparently, knowledge makes them less compliant."

She was telling him this as if his opinion of her mattered, and what that did for his ego he'd never be able to put into words. "Let me introduce you to my mother," he said finally. "Her power rivals that of your father."

"So . . . you don't mind?"

He wrapped his arms around her. "You amaze me."

Suddenly, the hall went dark, and she froze in his embrace.

"Is this hall usually lit?" Tahir whispered, but he smelled the answer. Someone—or something—had recently extinguished the torches.

Badra sat in the small garden, letting the sound of the fountain soothe her nerves. If she meditated, perhaps she could regain some control of the demons. They weren't supposed to have attacked Prince Tahir. They weren't supposed to show the guards that she'd left her cell. But when they'd sensed Tahir's imminent penetration of the princess's virginal flesh with his cock . . . it had overwhelmed their limited self-control, stupid creatures.

Turning her face to the moonlight, she tried to control her emotions, but the task proved difficult. She took a deep breath of the cool night air, held it, then exhaled. Still her mind brooded.

The *shitani* didn't require a virgin queen as their ruler; she herself certainly hadn't been one. But still, they wanted Princess Shahrazad all for themselves.

She took another deep breath, and paused this time, focusing on the space between the inhalation and exhalation. That was where her power resided. A fragile calm settled upon her.

My pretties, she called to them. *My pretties, where are you?*

They didn't answer.

Badra let them go for a moment, considering other options. When the Sultan's soldiers came for Shahrazad, Badra had thought the girl might flee, right to her. But, no. Shahrazad had not appeared through the gates or any of the doors. Nothing was easy. No doubt, the girl was taking her advice and heading toward the library—exactly the opposite of what she'd thought the girl would do.

My pretties, where are you?

Go away. We don't listen to you. We won't obey.

Her disconcertment nearly derailed her concentration. Why was nothing easy anymore? The demons hated her. The Sultan flatly refused her. Tahir's sister was nearly useless, and the Princess Shahrazad was slow to bend to her will.

Try Prince Tahir, the demons suggested. *He might do.*

Badra wanted to strangle the demons. *I can't try anything if you refuse to obey,* she said, but to herself she mulled over the idea of Tahir. He wasn't a ruler in his own land, but that didn't mean he couldn't rule . . .

Badra regained control of herself. *Inhale.* The breath calmed her. *Exhale.* She released her anger. *Inhale.* She allowed peace to enter. *Exhale.*

She reached out toward her assistant, Tahir.

Unease filled Tahir as the princess confirmed his doubts. "I have never been here at this hour," she breathed, "but yes. The torches have always been lit." He could barely hear her whispered voice.

"Are we far from the library?"

"It's just around that corner," she whispered, pointing to an intersection not three steps away. The door to the chamber was painted blue for learning. "But . . ."

"But what?"

"Something feels . . . not right."

Tahir knew what she meant. The atmosphere felt ominous, like the hallway waited for something. He'd felt this before . . . in the desert, when the red-haired woman let the demon capture her. He knew exactly what this feeling was. Suddenly a voice burned through his mind. The magician, the bitch. *Keep her safe.* He heard Badra's sultry voice as clear as if she stood directly behind him. *The demons wait for you here.*

"*Shitani,*" he whispered to Shahrazad. "They're here. Badra just . . . told me."

Shahrazad stepped backward on silent feet, her shoulders rigid with fear. Slipping his arm over her shoulder, he could feel her heart pounding, but her expression remained implacable.

Tahir's own pulse raced. He had only one small dagger and the element of surprise with which to protect the princess.

"Run!" he whispered. When they came after her, he'd go after them. "Just get through that door!"

And she did, not questioning him. She flew over the flagstone like her life depended on it, and he stayed right behind her, ready to leap on the demons if they attacked her.

"Here!" she screamed. "It's here!"

Her hand was on the knob when he saw a *shitani.* Its skin was a patchwork of visibility. He saw the floor, the walls, through mottled green pieces, like a child's puzzle—and the pieces were scuttling quickly toward the princess. The creature was losing its invisibility, but its haunches gathered beneath it as it prepared to jump.

The princess opened the door. Tahir raced toward the *shitani* and punted it, kicking it hard in its face. The solid feel of it beneath the naked ball of his foot told him more than his eye, which saw a confused jumble of patchwork fly down the hall. The *shitani* slammed against the brick wall and landed on the floor with a catlike mewl.

"Are you safe?" the princess asked, pausing in the doorframe.

But he didn't answer. He shoved her into the chamber and slammed the door behind them.

"No one comes in here," a soldier said, stepping in front of the princess. In the small foyer, a second soldier stood taciturn next to the inner door.

"If I deigned to speak to a man," she said, "I would point out that this is merely a library, and I am the princess."

"The Sultan said—" the first soldier began, breaking the rule Tahir knew to be sacred to the royal women of this land.

"Soldier," Tahir commanded, opening the only door standing between them and the *shitani*. "You have something more important to worry about than the Sultan." Tahir shoved the soldier into the hall, hoping he'd see the *shitani* before it regained its senses and saw him.

The soldier wildly looked around for the speaker, for the source of the push. "Who—"

"Soldier," Tahir interrupted, maximizing the effect of his invisibility. "A *shitani* is catching its breath seven steps from you. Kill it now. I must keep the Princess Shahrazad safe. You must keep the palace safe."

"Who's speaking?" The first soldier's deep voice sounded commanding, but it quavered, belying his fear, and he'd drawn his dagger.

"It is I, Prince Tahir of House Kulwanti from the Land of the Sun, who speaks. Now go! The demon must be stopped."

"I know of no such prince," the soldier said, but already the princess was moving away from the blue door, fear etched on her face, her arms crossed.

"You'd better kill that *shitani* quickly," Tahir said.

"I'll kill you," the man said, but Tahir ignored him. The princess had opened the inner door and was already walking toward the interior chamber. He walked after her, seeing the wall of books ahead of them.

"God's balls," Tahir heard the first soldier curse, the cry echoing through the sanctum walls. "Lutfi, get your ass this way."

Snarling and squealing filled the air, but when Tahir went to protect the princess he saw she'd vanished. Looking around, he saw a flash of orange from her *oraz*. She was already at the end of the hall.

"Where are you going?" he asked her. She only shook her head in reply.

He stood undecided, halfway between the princess and the fighting soldiers. She needed to read books, and she was willing to do it on her own—even if he couldn't protect her.

"God's holy mother!" one of the soldiers swore, his voice pitched high with fear. And then the man called, "God's eyes, Lutfi, help me now!"

The scream that followed decided it for Tahir. If the *shitani* defeated the soldiers, keeping the princess safe would be that much more difficult. After a quick glance at the retreating princess, he grabbed a torch from a sconce near the door and ran back toward the darkened hallway.

The first sight greeting him was confusing. One of the soldiers appeared to be sleeping, curled up in a small ball on the floor. Even while Tahir realized that couldn't be right, he saw the second soldier grappling desperately with something on his back.

The soldier twisted his arms behind him, and he slammed his back as hard as he could into the brick wall. Each time he did it, a wretched squeal erupted from behind him.

And then Tahir saw a flash of teeth and the small brass hook embedded in the soldier's nose. The small hook curled into a nostril and poked out the other side. Blood dripped off the man's face and onto the floor, forming a copious puddle. More blood from the man's scalp made the puddle bigger.

Tahir squinted and saw the *shitani* on the soldier's back—the odd patchwork of visible demon flesh. Spurred talons as large as any fighting cock's jabbed into the man's neck, and the creature sank teeth into the man's head while it jerked the ropes connected to the hooks.

After slamming the torch into a sconce, Tahir raced toward the sleeping soldier. Planning on slitting the demon's throat, he ran toward the beleaguered soldier who'd nearly given up his attempt at pulling the *shitani* from his back. The man stood in a stupor, staring blankly ahead as the demon buried another hook in the opposite nostril.

With a murderous cry, Tahir threw back his dagger hand to strike the demon, to bury the blade in its neck, but as his weight shifted he slipped in the blood and landed hard on his knees. As pain raced to his brain, the dagger skittered across the slick floor.

He lunged madly for the weapon, but the thing skidded off his fingertips. A crazed chuckle filled the air, but Tahir paid it no attention. Instead, he lunged again for the dagger, smearing his chest with blood with his effort.

But this time, he grabbed it, its warm handle fitting perfectly into his palm. "Ha!" he roared.

As he scrambled to his feet the demon looked down at him—the demon saw him. Tahir realized this even as he knew it was impossible, even as he looked at his arms and thighs and saw his invisibility firmly in place. He shut his mouth and vowed to keep it that way—no more warrior cries.

But it was too late.

One orange *shitani* eye was only half visible—the soldier's gray-clad back showed through the other half. The demon's second eye was completely missing, shielded from view by a layer of demon spit. But still, Tahir felt its heavy gaze weighing on his face. The goat-shaped pupil met his eye and refused to yield.

Even as Tahir silently moved toward the wall, the demon licked its mottled lips. Tahir could see the slate wall through most of the tongue, but he could feel the gaze completely.

Somehow, Tahir had lost his ability to remain invisible to the demon; he'd lost his element of surprise.

Come get us if you can, Tahir heard in his head.

Or was it his imagination?

Oh, we're very real, Tahir heard as if in response. *Your imagination isn't as wild as we are.*

I'll kill you, Tahir thought, perhaps to himself.

We repeat, he heard in reply, *come get us if you can.*

Tahir jumped to his feet and lunged toward the stunned soldier. The man reeled, but the demon on his back cackled like a mad hen. Then it leaped—right toward Tahir's face.

How was the abortion of God seeing him, he wondered as he ducked.

But he didn't have time to think as the demon leaped toward him a second time. It launched itself through the air, giving Tahir a glance at razor-sharp fangs behind a half-formed grin. *We'll get you,* it said in his mind.

Try, Tahir replied as he ducked, slashing with his dagger as the creature flew toward him.

He whooshed the blade through the air just as the demon tried to land on his back. His arm jerked, and the thing's warm blood sprayed over him, over his hands and arms and face.

You'll kill! it screamed. *You'll kill those you love the most! You'll kill the princess and your sister and your mother. You'll wish you were dead!*

Ignoring its hysteria, Tahir whirled around looking for his prey. And just as his eyes found the *shitani,* it leaped again—but this time not at him. This time it jumped toward the torch.

Before Tahir could stop it, the demon extinguished the flame—the only source of light in the dark hall—with the flesh of its inhuman hands. The scent of burned meat filled the hall as the *shitani* screamed again.

"God's balls," Tahir said as darkness pervaded the space. Only faint light from a torch around the corner made it to this corridor.

You'll suffer! it screamed in Tahir's mind. *You'll bleed and kill everything you love!* And it jumped toward him, leaping with all the strength of a horse jumping a nest of snakes.

Tahir slashed again, but the move was too defensive, and the blood-covered dagger slipped from his hand. It clanged to the floor and skittered across the flagstones into the shadows. In the nearly complete darkness, he couldn't see the weapon or the *shitani*—but he could see himself.

The blood from the floor and the demon coated large portions of his skin. He was now as much of a patchwork as was the demon, and no artful lunge would save him this time.

With the stealth of a cat, the *shitani* slunk along the wall. Its mélange of visibility worked with the wan, flickering light to trick his eye.

Still, Tahir moved toward the soldier who stood in a trance. He wouldn't let it escape now. It would attack the princess if he did. And she would be helpless—just as the magician craved.

He moved slowly, hoping his blood-splattered self was as difficult to see in this light as was the partially visible demon. Never had he wanted a weapon as badly as he wanted one now.

His hand, coated in a glove of blood, reached toward the enchanted soldier's dagger. His fingertips slid over the hilt, then the handle. The demon leaped—but too soon for Tahir, coming at his head with the speed of a crossbow bolt.

He didn't have time to dodge. He shot out his fist and slammed the thing as it flew toward his face. But the creature didn't fly across the room as Tahir desired. Instead, the demon slithered down his arm. It landed on his bare foot and looked up at him, almost beseechingly.

Tahir stepped back, ready to punt it again, kick it off the walls until it died. As he drew his foot back, the diamond-shaped pupils of the demon met his. A small mewling sound came from the *shitani*'s mouth. *You're ours*, it said. *You're ours. You belong to us.*

"No," Tahir roared, pulling his foot back to kick. But the demon smiled, its orange eyes boring into him as its fingers wrapped around his calf. Instead of kicking, an overwhelming lethargy filled him. He wanted to curl into a ball next to the soldier on the floor. His blood pumped through him like sludge.

You're ours, the demon said again.

Tahir put his foot down on the solid flagstones. He didn't need to kick anything. The Sultan could take care of the demon. This wasn't even his palace. It wasn't even his land. The Princess Shahrazad—

The Princess Shahrazad! he thought, his mind locking on the memory of her face, the curve of her smile, the intelligence of her expression. He had to kill the demon!

Squeezing the last bit of energy from his body, Tahir reached down for the creature.

Still, he fought. He had to save the princess. Tahir mustered all his will to close his palm around the *shitani*'s throat, to strangle the thing.

But his grip refused to tighten. His fingers didn't want to close.

You'll be ours, Tahir heard in his head as his fingers stroked the slimy skin of the *shitani*. His traitorous hand stroked the thing like it was a cherished pet, a hawk just returned with a prized hare. *You'll be ours*, the demon said. *All ours.*

"I . . . won't."

We'll have so much fun . . . especially with the Princess Shahrazad. She's going to bear the next shitani *queen.*

"No," he managed to gasp. "No. She won't."

Come, our little prince, the demon said, slithering up his naked thigh. Froglike fingers began to stroke his cock. *Let me climb upon your back, and we'll go find the darling girl.*

"Not . . . her."

But her cunt is waiting for our seed—our royal seed! Our old queen is tired. We can't hear her voice. And our land is waiting for its new queen, the child that will come from her loins.

"Abom . . . in . . . ation." His voice croaked.

Or perhaps you'd like to be our new king. You can fuck us. Your child will be ours.

"Never."

The princess will like us! She'll love us. The demon chuckled, climbing higher up Tahir's thigh to balance on his hip. *Do you smell her desire, little prince? Do you smell how she loves to fuck?*

"No."

She will spawn a royal hybrid, a demon suited to rule human and shitani *alike.*

As the demon crawled up his arm, Tahir waited for the truth of those words to give rise to horror and horror to give rise to action.

But nothing happened. His fingers continued to caress the *shitani*'s neck as if he were stroking Shahrazad's silky stomach, her breasts, her neck. Even as the *shitani* shimmied up his side, he stroked the creature.

Maybe you'll be ours instead, the creature cackled. *The belly of your demon consort will swell with your cum. That hybrid will rule instead of the princess's.*

Dragging Tahir's palm with it, the creature scampered back down to his hip. It flashed him a sharp-toothed grin and again stroked his cock, which hardened, filling him with hatred for the weakness of his desires.

"Stop." He tried to pull his hand off the *shitani*'s skull but could not. He tried to wrap his thumb and fingers more tightly around its throat and couldn't do that either.

You're ours now! the creature said, and Tahir knew it was true.

"Release . . . me."

Not today, the thing laughed, flicking its tongue over Tahir's cock. The traitorous organ throbbed—and became invisible. He hated himself even as he longed for the demon to wrap its entire tongue around his cock. Even as he longed to fuck the creature.

A sudden urge to rage against the creatures roared through him. Now! Now, was the time to lose that control and kill that demon. But no matter how he struggled against the hold they had on his mind, he couldn't move. His fingers wouldn't obey. His hands remained in the demon's control. Even his feet refused to kick.

Violent thoughts had no effect. His mother was right, he told himself as the demon stroked his thigh—men are nothing but violent apes, a hair's breadth away from losing all self-control.

But the ridiculousness of that thought hit him. He was fighting for his life. He was fighting for the life of the princess. As the *shitani* sucked his cock his fingers refused to tighten. He had no control to lose.

In desperation, Tahir embraced his innate violent nature, the nature he constantly coated in civility. It occurred to him that death should be dealt coldly, rationally—not in red-eyed anger.

Human flesh, the *shitani* said. *It's so salty and tasty.*

Tahir tried a different tactic. He put violence and anger aside and concentrated on specifics. He thought of his fingers. He thought of his bones and his knuckles, and his fingernails and the dusting of hairs. He imagined those fingers closing around the creature's neck. And—

Nothing happened.

Then he imagined taking Shahrazad's hand in his own. He envisioned his fingers opening to accept her outstretched hand. He remembered the heat of her palm in his, the warmth in her gaze when she looked at him. And—

And his grip incrementally tightened.

Ignoring the welling hope, he honed his focus; he imagined his index finger curling toward hers. He saw the thick silver ring he wore there moving closer to her palm. He envisioned his entire hand around Shahrazad's delicate hand.

Only the flesh in his palm didn't belong to the princess—it belonged to the demon. It was the demon's neck.

No, my princeling, the *shitani* said in his grip. *That's no way to behave. You love us. You want to obey us.* It sucked harder on Tahir's cock to make its point.

For a heartbeat his hand relaxed, falling out of his control. His knees began to buckle, to lower him to the floor.

But Tahir's mind rebelled. He wanted to kill this thing! But, no. He ignored the words, words he'd heard from the women of his land, words he heard now from this demon. He didn't want death; he wanted control of his own body . . . of his own destiny. Once again, he brought a picture of his fingers to mind.

And his hand began to obey his brain with more assurance. It obeyed his heart—not his mother's, not the demon's. His fingers squeezed the demon's neck.

Stop that, the creature said. *Stop that now. You're hurting us.*

"Which is the point," Tahir growled, struggling to regain his own control. "I will hurt you. I will—"

Suddenly, the blue door banged open. Tahir hadn't realized it had closed in the melee.

The creature took advantage, leaping from his grip toward the door.

"Tahir!" Shahrazad called. "Where are you?"

"No!" he shouted, racing toward her, fully free of the creature's thrall now.

"What—"

But he grabbed the thing's neck just as it scurried up her ankle. Slippery with blood, it squirmed out of his grasp, scuttling toward the darkened hall as it cackled. Tahir couldn't let this thing escape, not this time. With a warrior's cry, he launched himself after it, throwing himself on top of it and flattening it beneath his chest.

It gave a pitiful cry, almost like a baby's, but before the thing could trap his mind, he grabbed its neck and shook it. The violence he'd sought to quell had vanished and he found the thing's stunned silence satisfied him. He had no need to rage against it—or kill it.

"You're safe, Princess," he said, his words ragged as he stood, careful of the puddles of blood. "I've got the demon, and it can't escape."

She blinked. "That's you, isn't it, splattered with blood and holding that—that thing like it's a market chicken?"

"It is," he said, tightening his grip on the demon's neck.

She paused and said in a less-than-steady voice, "Is that your blood covering you?"

"No." He stepped away from her, remembering the demon's words, its plans for the princess. "The blood belongs to the soldier standing by the wall—and to the demon itself."

"Is it dead? Are you safe?"

The soldiers around him were beginning to stir. Apparently his grip on the creature allowed the other men to break their trances.

"Please, answer me. You're wearing a terrible amount of blood."

He looked down at the *shitani* in his hand, not completely trusting himself, not trusting his ability to control the demon. The demon appeared to be breathing, but its eyes were closed.

Perhaps because it was nearly asphyxiated? "The *shitani* isn't dead," he said finally. "And neither am I."

"Kill it," said the solider who'd been curled up in a ball. He stretched his legs as he spoke, then he stood, drawing his sword. "Kill it now."

"Yes," said the standing soldier, turning to him while he drew his sword. His words were strong, but his eyes were blank. "Kill it now."

"What's wrong with those soldiers?" the princess asked, stepping away from the two approaching men and their swords. "There is something odd about them. Look at their faces!"

And she was right. Despite the vehemence of their words, their faces had no expression. They seemed to be in a trace—a demonic thrall.

Tahir tightened his grip around the *shitani*'s neck, cutting off all but the slightest ability to breathe. Its goat eyes opened as its slanted pupils rolled back in its head, and in his hand, Tahir felt the thing's muscles relax.

And the soldiers fell back, both collapsing on the floor as if unconscious.

"Interesting," he said. "It seems our little friend would rather be dead by these soldiers' swords than captured alive by me."

"It might be the only idea on which both it and I agree," Princess Shahrazad said, examining the demon with distaste. "Don't you think you should kill it?"

"A few heartbeats ago, I would have agreed with you. As I fought the thing, I wanted nothing more than its death."

"But?"

"But its desire to the contrary makes me think we should keep it alive."

"Alive or dead makes no difference to me," the princess said. "But you need to come with me."

11

Aware of the heat of his body, Shahrazad led Prince Tahir toward the library. And even though she knew now was not the time for this, the memory of his tongue and fingers left her limp with need.

"I found the book—a book," she said, trying to focus her mind. "The one regarding the demons."

"What does it say?"

"I haven't read it yet." She didn't want to admit it, but the book unnerved her. And Tahir gave her courage.

Whatever had occurred in that hallway had been life threatening—but he'd saved her. When that demon had crawled up her leg like a rat, she'd thought it was her day to die.

Even coated in blood, partially invisible and holding a gasping demon, Tahir looked more powerful than any of the men she'd seen in her sheltered life. In his own land, he must be an honored ruler.

"It's in here," she said, as they approached the door. She was amazed at how simple it was to drop a lifelong aversion to speaking to men. She could certainly lose her aversion to touching them—at least this one.

She led him into a lavish chamber. Leather-bound books filled shelves to the ceiling, and well-crafted ladders set on wheels made accessing the high books easier. Long tables with stuffed chairs invited scholars.

She pointed to a book she'd laid on the table. "That one was hidden—although librarians might have thought it misplaced." Misplaced behind a huge stack of books regarding ancient treaties on boundaries of lands that no longer existed.

"It's not small, is it?"

She laughed. It was thicker than her father's thigh. "Not so small."

"I meant the book," he teased.

She felt blood rush to her face, suddenly uncertain of their familiarity. "This book is about demons," she said quickly, to cover her embarrassment.

He stood next to her, his blood-covered hand resting on the antiquated pages. "Look," he said, pointing to a paragraph at the bottom of the page.

She read the words aloud. "As described in the *Thaumutugicon*, only the magician can keep the *shitani* from overrunning the Land."

"Is this the *Thaumutugicon*?" he asked, tapping the book.

"No. This is the *Kitabu a Shitani*. I looked for the *Thaumutugicon* first—it isn't where it belongs. It should be with the ancient history books, where the resident thaumaturge shelved it."

"You mean you have a magician living in your palace?"

"No. Three generations ago my great-grandfather tossed him into the desert, and we haven't had one since. But that magician created the current shelving system. No one has changed it in all those years."

"So maybe the magician is particularly focused on hurting your lineage—since your great-grandfather tossed him out."

"Maybe. But why she's interested in me doesn't concern me as much as what to do about it. What I'd like to know is how to control her. How do we stop her from vanishing every time we find her?"

"Why would she direct you to books that would give you that information?"

"Why does she do anything? Maybe she thought I'd do the opposite of what she suggested."

Holding the silent demon in one hand, Tahir thumbed the great tome sitting on the table. "So do you want to read this book on demons or look for the one on thaumaturges?"

"You read, please," she said. "I'll look. It might be difficult for you to climb one-handed, and I don't want to hold the *shitani*."

He sat in the chair as she climbed the ladder. "How do you know where to look?"

"I don't." As she climbed the ladder, she looked at the window, seeing nothing but darkness. But dawn would be coming soon. Her eyes burned with fatigue, and for a moment she wanted nothing more than to crawl back to her bed—preferably with Tahir.

But she couldn't give up now, she thought, looking behind a row of religious texts. She didn't have time—a *pegaz* might not be able to peruse these shelves.

After the religious texts came a collection regarding animal husbandry: camels, goats, zebu, horses. If she remembered correctly, the *Thaumutugicon* had a glossy cover the color of oasis grass. But the only books she saw in this row were tan and brown.

"God's eyes," Tahir said, breaking her reverie. "This is it. This tells us everything we need to know about *shitani*." He shook the creature in his grip to make his point.

"Does it tell us how to defeat them without allying my father's armies and the Raj's?" she asked. "Can we defeat them without your sister?"

But he ignored her, his fingers pressed so hard against the page she could see his tendons through the sheen of blood. "It says here that the demons wake and attack when the magician needs a replacement."

"A replacement? What does that mean?"

"Maybe she can no longer control them. Maybe she's too old."

She thought about that for a moment. "Do the *shitani* go to sleep if we find someone for her? Will they leave our lands alone?"

"The magician talks telepathically with them, it says here." His voice vibrated with excitement. "And the magician can control them to some extent. She can direct one or two to do particular things—"

"Like attack us outside the library?"

"Exactly." He paused for a moment and added, "But I think they were acting on their own."

That stopped her. "Why?"

"She warned me."

"Maybe to mislead you."

"True." She saw his bloody head nod. "But the demon said something while attacking me." She heard his body shift and felt his eyes on her. "I think the magician wants you to herself."

"Me?" she asked. "For herself?" Even to her own ears, she sounded afraid.

"I will not leave your side," he said.

She shoved her fear aside, not so much because of his words but because fear didn't help, not here. "Maybe she thinks I'll replace her," she said, remembering the magician's words. The magician had said Shahrazad could rule the demons. "Would that stop the *shitani*?"

She felt his eyes on her as his blood-splattered face turned away from the book. "You wouldn't actually consider that, would you?"

"If it saved my land, perhaps. If the price wasn't exorbitant."

"You'd rule the *shitani*?"

"To save your land, wouldn't you?" she asked. He didn't answer, perhaps considering the question, so she added, "I'd need more information. The *Thaumutugicon* might permit an educated decision." Which is what the magician suggested. Which meant she shouldn't trust it. Didn't it?

"What if the magician herself wrote it?" he said, echoing her own doubts.

"The book's been here for years."

"The magician is by definition magic. Maybe the words in the book have changed over time," he said, sounding angry. "Besides, if the magician needs a replacement, why doesn't she just zap someone into her cave?"

She heard protectiveness in his voice, and male rule was something she understood. But perhaps she'd outgrown her need to obey it blindly. "I don't know," she said. "She's old and tired?" Regardless, this wasn't a discussion for this moment. She shrugged and said, "What else does the book say?"

She saw his head tilt down. "Once the *shitani* wake in earnest," he said, "they must be fought, battled to the death. The magician can't control them any longer."

"So we have to kill them," she said.

"Unless we get her to put them back to bed right now."

"I think we'd have to find her to do that."

"I can find her." He looked up. "In fact, I can sense her. She's meditating . . . next to a fountain outside."

"I think we should ignore her for now."

"We are."

"We must discover how to keep her from vanishing." The frustration she'd been feeling since the magician first slithered her finger across her back threatened to explode. "Where is that book?"

"I could ask her," he suggested, looking startled at the thought.

146 / *Lucinda Betts*

"Would we trust where she sent us?"

"No." He paused. "You keep looking. I'll keep reading."

Her eyes scanned the next shelf—all red books. She even looked behind them and found nothing. Rubbing her eyes, she climbed the rungs to the next shelf.

"It says here the *shitani* die by normal means," he said. "We've killed enough of them to know that's true. If you cut them, they bleed."

"What else does it say?" Brown books here, and two black editions. Maybe they *should* ask the magician.

"The saliva can be used to produce invisibility . . ." he read.

"We knew that."

"And they can mesmerize you if they touch you, or if you meet their eye."

"We didn't know that—at least I didn't."

"No, I didn't either. I mean, I knew they could mesmerize, I just didn't know how." But he seemed distracted as he scanned down the page.

"What is it?" she asked.

"I'm just reading here what they do to their victims after they mesmerize them." She heard him swallow. "It's gruesome."

"Tell me."

"I don't think you need to know."

"You know very well that isn't true. You'll tell me now, please."

He sighed. "The demons are only the size of large cats . . ."

"That doesn't sound too daunting, but we've seen them in action. They're very fierce cats."

"And they leap on their victim's head or shoulders, it says here."

"While the person is enthralled?"

"Either way."

"And then what?"

"They have brass hooks they insert into eyebrows or eyelids or lips or nostrils, and the hooks have ropes."

"So they ride you like a horse?"

"Yes." She saw his blood-splattered head nod. "I think that's what they were doing to the soldiers."

"And to you?"

"They were trying to." He nodded, then looked back at the book. "They turn people into steeds while they keep control of their minds. And if a person is particularly recalcitrant, the *shitani* slice off fingers or ears. They might even put the hooks in . . . more tender places."

Shahrazad swallowed. She didn't want to know which more tender places. It sounded like once a person fell under a demon's thrall, he lost any grip on their personal fate. She went back to scan the book spines.

"God's eyes," he said again.

"What is it?" The demon in his grip cackled, making them both jump. "What is it?" she asked again more softly.

"As a group, the *shitani* won't stop fighting unless we kill them all—every single one of them—or . . ." He still hadn't torn his gaze from the book.

"Or what?"

"Or unless they find their black mother, the human woman who'll birth their next lord." The *shitani* suddenly opened its eyes and caught her gaze in its own. It seemed to Shahrazad that it grinned at her. She could almost imagine it leaping to her shoulder and dropping brass hooks into her lips.

Never, my queen, she heard in her head. *We'll never sink hooks into your soft flesh. We love you.*

"God's eyes." Her knees felt suddenly wobbly. "God's eyes. That's why I hear them in my head." She started climbing down the ladder, wondering if she'd fall before she reached the ground.

"But that's only in *pegaz* form, isn't it?" he asked. Then he looked at her face and raced toward her. "Here, beloved. Let me help you."

She took his hand, not caring that it was smeared in demon blood. "Thank you." He'd called her beloved. Tahir helped her sit in one of the padded chairs. "Thank you," she said again.

"Wait." He went to a back table where writing implements and a few flasks stood. He poured water into a short crystal glass and gave it to her. "Drink this."

She took a deep breath and drank. "What else did the book say?"

"I don't think—"

"Prince Tahir, you will not hold the truth back from me. I've been cosseted my entire life, and it has done me no good at all."

"Very well." He nodded. "The voices should get louder and more insistent as more *shitani* wake."

That made her consider a different point. "If *you* heard them, does that mean you can rule them? Can they have a black father?"

He froze, and she could almost hear his mind racing. "I don't know," he said finally, walking back toward the book. He scanned the pages for a moment.

"Does it say anything about black fathers?" she asked.

"God's eyes, it does," he said. "You're correct."

"So, you can sire a hybrid with one of the demon females."

She watched his blood-splattered head nod. "The human ruler doesn't need to be a black mother. A black father will do."

She thought about this for a moment, loathing the feeling that the fates had chosen her for this hateful task. "They're deciding between us, then. One of us may rule them."

He didn't deny it. Instead he fell to his knees, wiping his eyes with his palms until at least that part of his face was visible.

"Princess Shahrazad," he said to her. "I make you this promise: I'll do everything in my power to protect you. I'll give my life if necessary. I won't let them hurt you. I won't let the Raj hurt you. I won't let your father hurt you. No *shitani* shall take you in their thrall, not while I live."

"Tahir." It was all she could think to say, and even that one simple word came out thick and husky, like she'd just inhaled *huqqa* smoke. "Thank you. Please stand. I don't know what to do with you on your knees before me."

A roguish grin crossed his face as he stood. "That might be a lesson for another day."

Perhaps seeing the blush cover her cheeks, he quickly changed the subject. "If the choice is between you or me as the next magician, I will serve gladly rather than force you to that fate."

But was it his decision to make for her? She swallowed the cool water. "Maybe it isn't such a terrible thing, hearing their voices, being chosen."

His partially invisible eyes blinked and she heard surprise in his voice. "Why do you say that?"

"We'll have a warning." She stood, setting the glass firmly on the table. "We'll know when the demons are coming. We'll know what they're thinking." She walked toward the shelves.

"What are you doing?"

"I'm looking for the *Thaumutugicon*. We're running out of time." She headed toward the ladder, resolve strengthening her knees. "We must discover what responsibilities come with the magician's role, and should those prove untenable, we must find a way to thwart the magician."

"Let me look—you read."

"Thank you." She smiled. "But you don't know what the missing book looks like. I can find it faster."

"But—"

"We don't have time to argue. Dawn is coming."

"If you faint, we'll be equally out of time."

"If I feel lightheaded, I'll stop. I promise."

"Fine. We'll both look. I've read everything of interest in that book."

"I'll let you take the ladder then," she said, feeling stronger now but still too nauseated to want to climb. "Look for a vibrant green book that's about half the size of the *Kitabu a Shitani*."

"Very well." He climbed the ladder, knocking the demon's skull against the ladder's runners. She walked to the bottommost shelves on the opposite side of the room. A row of fat blue books lined the shelf, and a thick layer of dust across the top indicated that they hadn't been moved in a long time.

She started to walk away. Obviously, no one had touched these in ages. Except . . . no other books in the library were dusty, and why should they be? The palace drudges cleaned every nook and cranny on a regular basis.

With a quick step back, she tore the books off the shelf and let them tumble to the floor with a resounding series of thumps.

"What is it?" Tahir asked from his perch.

"I think I've found something."

"What?" He began climbing down the ladder.

"Dust," she said.

"Dust? I don't understand."

"These are the only dusty books I've seen tonight," she said. "The *Thaumutugicon* must be hidden here."

"I don't understand this magician's motives," Tahir said, allowing the demon's head to hit the shelf as he climbed. "Why would she go to so much trouble to hide books she wants us to find?"

She moved a dust-covered book to the side. "Maybe she wanted them hidden from other eyes—perhaps the librarians, or even my father."

"I don't think much is hidden from your father," Tahir said. "But that's not the point. The magician could have used magic to put the books in our hands. Why make this difficult?"

"If her power is waning," Shahrazad said, pushing brown books, red books, yellow books out of her way, "perhaps teleporting the books into our hands is too costly."

"Waning?" He stopped.

"She's old. She's tired. She needs a replacement. Maybe she doesn't have power to spare."

"Perhaps you're right," he said after a moment. "Maybe that's why the *shitani* attacked us. Maybe she's losing control."

"But maybe it was a trap," she said, shoving a faded green book to the floor. The *Thaumutugicon* was shiny. "Maybe she told us to go to the library not because she wanted us to read anything, but because she wanted the *shitani* to attack us."

"They could have attacked us anywhere," Tahir countered.

"I mean—" But she paused midsentence as the last of the blue books fell to the floor. "God's eyes," she said, peering toward the back.

"What?"

"I found it." She pulled the green book, less glossy than she remembered, from the back of the shelf. "This is it." She carried it to the table, and she set it gently next to the *Kitabu a Shitani*.

"Well done," he said, glancing at the window. "Let's see if we can unravel this mystery before sunrise."

She flipped open the front cover. "What's this?" she asked.

He walked toward her. "What is what?"

She looked at the strange coil lying between the pages. "I believe that it's hair."

The glowing mass lay coiled on the book. Prince Tahir walked toward it and fingered the silky strands with his free hand. It was as red as henna paste but iridescent as the throat of a sunchaser.

He picked up the braid. As the shorn tress left the page and floated between his fingers—invisible save the splattering of blood—the hair turned black. "I don't understand."

"I don't either," she said. "Not exactly. But hold the tress near the light and watch what happens."

The hair turned as yellow as gold in the torchlight, glittering in an oblique way. "How very odd," Tahir said. "This hair turns colors." He held it near her orange *oraz*, and the hair turned brown.

"Let's see what the book says about magician," she said, sitting on the bench. "Perhaps an explanation for the hair lies in these pages as well."

"You read," he said, setting the braid onto the table. "I'm going to wash."

As she read the opening paragraph to herself, her heart began to pound. The answers were here! "Listen to this," she said.

"I'm listening." His blood-splattered body stopped mid stride.

"Once accepting the magician's mantle," she said, her finger following the words on the page, "the human—man or woman— accepts immortality. She or he may not be killed, not by any traditional means, although the immortal corpus will experience pain should such be inflicted. This person also accepts full responsibility for the demons, which may be controlled as described in these pages."

"So we can't kill her," Tahir said. "But can we catch her?"

She ignored his question and continued reading. "A magician's powers will last for five to six hundred years, at which time he or she should find a replacement. That replacement should be found while the magician still has his or her powers, otherwise Faruq the Great's binding spell on the demons will unravel, and the *shitani* will transform into intractable forces, impossible to harness or control. They will bring an end to mankind."

"She waited too long," Tahir said. "She needed a replacement, and now she's desperate."

"Maybe," she answered, looking up at him. "I wonder why?"

"What else does it say? What does the magician do?"

She found her place then read to him, "As the magician considers various candidates for replacement, several points are imperative. The replacement must have enough intelligence to understand not only this text, and the *Kitabu a Shitani*, but also the spellbook."

"What spellbook?" Tahir asked.

"I've no idea," she said. "I've never seen it. But listen to this."

"I'm listening."

"The replacement must willingly accept the magician's mantle. No coercion is permitted. Free will is of the utmost importance. Otherwise, the *shitani* will break through Faruq the Great's magical working." She looked up from her book. "So she can't just 'zap us into her shoes,' as you said."

"Perhaps she needs our free will," he said, obviously angry now, "but it appears that she's doing all she can to give you— us—nowhere to run . . . except to her."

But she wasn't interested in the injustice of the magician's motives, not in this moment. The next words in the book had her attention. "Listen," she said, "This book contains only one spell, and it is to be used in only the most dire of situations—if a magician has not found an appropriate replacement while still in control of his or her full powers." She paused, reading the text in silence for a moment.

"What's the spell?"

"It lets the magician—or the spell user—see potential replacements—people who are intelligent, potentially willing, and . . . moral enough to take on the magician's mantle." She looked at him, seeing only the bloody outline of him. "Apparently the spell will work for non-magicians too."

"Why?"

"In case the magician becomes incapacitated somehow."

"But I thought this paragon was immortal."

"Maybe she has no desire to use the last of her energy in casting this spell." She shrugged. "Maybe she cast it, and already knows the result. She desires that we see the result for some reason? I don't know." She flashed him a grin and added,

"But I do want to see who might replace Badra. Our lives might become easier if we knew."

"Shahrazad, maybe—" he started to say, but she ignored him. Gently pushing the ancient tome away from her, she placed the coiled braid in the center of the table. She held her hands above the hair and began to stumble through the words written in the *Thaumutugicon*.

"*Kuku mgeni hakosi kamba mguuni*," she said. "*Mkuki kwa nguruwe, kwa binaadamu mchungu*."

Immediately, the hair began to glow, and then it floated from the table, hovering between the wood and her hands. Gently, she moved her hands away, but the hair remained floating.

"God's eyes," Tahir said. "I've never seen such a thing."

But the spell wasn't complete, not yet. The shafts of the braid began to spread, forming something that reminded her of a spider web, a very complicated spider web. When it formed a sphere, it began to spin, first slowly, then quicker and quicker. Inside the spinning fibers, a face appeared, nebulous at first, but then it began to take shape.

"My sister!" Tahir gasped. Shahrazad saw the Queen Kalila resembled Tahir with her arching brow and strong nose, but her lips were fuller, her skin a shade lighter.

Then the face morphed. The softness of the cheeks gave way to something masculine, and the flesh aged. Cheeks sagged to jowls, and light skin gave way to darker flesh. The piercing eyes were familiar, but when the white turban appeared atop the white hair, she knew. "My father?" she said. "He could be the magician?"

"Apparently, so," Tahir said.

But the spinning ball wasn't finished. The flesh slowly regained its youth, although the dark tone remained. A broad face appeared, crowned by blond hair. "That's the Raj ir Adham," she said. "Amazing."

"It is," Tahir agreed. "I thought those people . . ."

He didn't finish the sentence, but she thought she knew what he meant. She barely knew the Raj, but the Sultan hadn't seemed particularly trustworthy in these last few hours. But perhaps that was the magician's manipulations, her attempts at tricking good people into abandoning their lands to take over her mantle?

"The spinning is slowing," Tahir noted, breaking her musing.

Raj's face was melting away, and the amorphous oval where his face had been gave way to Tahir's—and then quickly to hers.

"You and I are viable replacements, apparently," Tahir said. "I suppose we knew that."

Individual hairs could now be seen floating above the table. She pushed the braid back toward the page, idly forming it into a circle. The hairs still glowed with residual magic.

"God's eyes!" Tahir exclaimed. "Did you see that?"

She looked up at him, alarmed. "What?"

He pointed at the circle of hair. "Badra," he said. "I just saw her face in there."

She looked down and saw what he meant. Long blond hair floated down her back and a sultry violet eye winked at her. As they watched, her face morphed into a handsome man, a young man. His eyes were violet.

"Is she disguised as a man, then?" Tahir asked.

"She's done that before." The image faded away, leaving the room bereft of magic. "His—no, her—touch created the snake tattoo on my back," Shahrazad said. "She touched me, yes. But her words frightened me almost more than that. She said—"

"*I can grant your heart's desire.*" His words fell right on top of hers.

"She said the same to me," Tahir said.

Something in his voice sounded tight. Shahrazad knew more was going on here than he was telling her.

"I think we're ready to hunt down the magician," Shahrazad said.

Tahir paused, apparently concentrating. "She's here. In a chamber above us. And . . . she's waiting for us. She also says . . ."

"What?"

"My clothes are here in the library, in a drawer."

"Badra told you that?"

"Yes." His arms reappeared as he washed, as did his jaw.

"I'll look." Shahrazad opened a small drawer that normally held parchments, ink, and quills. It held parchments, ink and quills. Then she opened the neighboring drawer, one that normally held the catalog of all the books. She found that list, and something else.

"These may fit you," she said. "Perhaps they look familiar?"

"What?"

She pulled out clothing, then a sword—his—and two daggers. "These are yours, too," she said.

"God holds me in his eye," he said. "Thank you."

Holding the demon away from him, he poured the last of the water from the pitcher over his head, then he dried it with the inadequate towel.

And just then the pre-dawn bell began to sound throughout the palace. The sun would be rising very soon.

"We are being manipulated again," Tahir said. "We are being pushed to the Raj's chambers."

She knew he was right. "And yet," she said, "what choice do we have but to go?"

"None at all." In his hand, the *shitani* began to chuckle.

"At least this time we know how to stop her from vanishing," she said.

"We do?" Tahir asked, his dark eyes visible now, to her delight. "How's that?"

"I tell her I'll take her place."

12

When they reached the guest chamber of the Raj ir Adham—his door painted magenta in celebration—Tahir slid his palm over the knob and turned it silently. "I wish we were both invisible," he whispered.

She looked at the demon, raising her eyebrows in question.

"We don't have time," he said. He opened the door and padded quietly into the room.

Through the door, she noted the layout of his chamber was much the same as the Flower Taker's: a small foyer giving way to two halls. The same intricate table covered with suggestive carvings graced the dividing wall. All of the figures on his table were male, however, and each of them sucked another's cock. She wondered if the *klerin* would remove the table—or even arrest the Raj—if they discovered it.

"This way," Prince Tahir whispered, interrupting her thoughts. "We'll take the back passage." He entered the left hallway.

The scent of male sweat filled her nose as the hallway narrowed, and it wasn't from Tahir. The pungent odor belonged to someone else. The Raj?

Prince Tahir fiddled with a wooden panel at knee height for a moment, and the wall slid open. Before she could fully wonder how he'd known the secret of the latches, they'd entered an antechamber. And the sound filling the room distracted her from any other thoughts.

The sound came from a man—no, men—and they were grunting. Prince Tahir shot a quick glance at her. *Does this upset you?* his gaze seemed to ask. But she just shrugged her shoulders, confused. Why the men were grunting was no concern of hers. She wanted the magician, and she wanted her now. She peeked through the panel.

But there was no woman in the Raj's bed.

She recognized her betrothed immediately, despite the fact she'd never seen him in anything less than the most formal of occasions. Now, he wore nothing. His long blond braid fell between his shoulder blades, and his heavy-lidded eyes were closed. His lips were parted as moans fell from them.

A slim man was on his hands and knees before the Raj, and the Raj had him from behind, his cock buried to its hilt.

A bolt of horror rushed through Shahrazad. Men were not permitted to love each other, not like women. Even the word for male lovers, *rakeb*, was dire. It also meant dead. On the rare occasion when men were discovered pleasuring each other, their heads always ended up on the Pike Wall—unless their neighbors stoned them first.

But disgust wasn't the emotion Shahrazad felt while she watched her betrothed and his lover. She felt . . . fear for them. And appreciation of their beauty.

A fine sheen of sweat covered both men, making their skin shine like velvet in the pale torchlight. The Raj's strong fingers gripped the slender man's hips like his partner could save him— but from what menace, Shahrazad couldn't begin to guess.

Will this get them killed? That was Shahrazad's first thought. But then she saw their expressions.

Raj was slamming into the other man in a way that looked painful, but the expression of ecstasy on the slim man's face made Shahrazad realize she was wrong. His eyes were rolled back in pleasure, and he wore a half smile of rapture. One of Raj's hands stroked the slim man's waist, and he curled into that caress the way a cat does. He yielded his body completely to the Raj, and something in that yielding caught Shahrazad's heart.

As an orgasm grabbed hold of the Raj, his broad face screwed into something unrecognizable. His thick blond braid fell over his shoulder and around to his face. Both men were howling now, and the noise was so loud that anyone passing in the hall would've been able to hear it, despite the thickness of the walls.

Shahrazad wanted to shush them, warn them of the danger, but within heartbeats the Raj collapsed onto the slim man, spent. The slim man collapsed onto the bed beneath him, and silence filled the room.

Their wild passion, the exhausted bliss on both of their faces, filled Shahrazad with longing.

She looked closely at the Raj's face now, more closely than she'd ever looked. His broad features were relaxed, something she'd never seen before now. And as his fingers lazily traced the line of the other man's ribs and hips, devotion filled his eyes. Would he have that look if he enjoyed the Way of Pleasure with her? Could a *rakeb* even enjoy the Way of Pleasure with a woman?

As the Raj ran his lips over the slim man's shoulder, Shahrazad saw an emotion deeper than affection. With a start, she realized her betrothed loved the man with whom he lay.

Oblivious to her thoughts, to her presence, the Raj hitched himself up to one elbow, the dim torchlight making his blond eyebrows gleam. He'd been caressing the other man with his lips, slowly and deliberately. But now that caress turned into something hungrier. He started kissing the other man. He nipped the other man's shoulder and side, making him laugh. Even as Shahrazad realized the nips tickled, she recognized the voice.

It was the Flower Taker's, the magician. The Raj ir Adham loved Badra.

With determination, she stepped forward toward the men, but Tahir held her back. "She wants us to wait," he whispered.

She looked at the two lovers for a heartbeat, trying to decide if they should obey the magician. Raj flipped his partner onto his back and began nipping his chest, and the torchlight silhouetted the man's throbbing cock, and Shahrazad realized that this version of the magician possessed no female traits—none at all.

"We'll wait," she agreed.

She didn't need to worry about the men hearing the sound. The Raj and his partner were caught up in their own world of delight. Her betrothed's fingers slithered between the magician's thighs and curled around his cock. In the faint light, Shahrazad could see a glistening around the tip.

"Harder," the magician directed. "Slower."

And Shahrazad was surprised to see her betrothed obey. His thick fingers traveled up the magician's shaft more deliberately, and the slender man groaned his appreciation. In her world, the Raj was the man giving the orders, not taking them. What spell had Badra used?

Whatever it was, the Raj was enthralled. Between his teeth, he tugged the magician's nipple. The slender man arched into the bite, pulling the Raj's head closer. The Raj stretched the magician's cock back, and Shahrazad saw her betrothed tremble with desire in exactly the same way the Flower Taker had made her tremble.

"God's eyes, I love you," the Raj said, flicking his tongue over the magician's nipple. His hand was working the other man's cock more vigorously now. "You're magic, you know. You've ensorcelled me."

"This is a natural magic, my love," the magician answered. "Though my cock doesn't believe it for the way it aches for you."

"Let it ache no more," the Raj said, trailing his tongue across the magician's chest, over his stomach and lower. The magician wore a gold stud in the foreskin of his cock, and it glittered in the torchlight. The Raj ran his tongue around it, making the other man lift his hips in pleasure. Then her betrothed inhaled the magician's cock, sucking until his cheeks were hollowed.

The magician moaned now, and his cries sounded so much like the Flower Taker's, Shahrazad found herself wet with a need of her own. Oh, what had that woman wakened in her? The untroubled bliss of her childhood seemed as distant as a faded dream.

Suddenly aware of Prince Tahir's sweet breath over her shoulder, her desire blossomed. No, it expanded like some monster from a storybook. Longing started to grow, and it wouldn't stop, no matter how she bade it to leave. Yearning saturated her heart, her veins, her blood. It pulsed through her like it had a life of its own.

Helpless, she leaned back; she leaned into him, once again breaking the rules of her land, shredding them like an unwanted note and throwing them into the east winds. Her desire left her weak, besotted, and no amount of shame could strengthen her resolve to behave in a manner befitting a good woman of her land.

Tahir didn't appear to care. Like the men tumbling in the bed before her, his cock was hard, throbbing against her ass. Gentle fingertips caressed her neck and teased her shoulders.

She couldn't squander this gift. She couldn't swim in this desire and fail to acknowledge it.

Snaking her arm behind her, she took Tahir's cock in her

palm, marveling at her boldness. She—who'd never broken a single rule before her wedding day—grabbed the cock of a man not her husband, of a man who could never be her husband. And the single thought rolling through her mind revolved around how solid such a cock could be, how very solid and how very hot.

Behind her, Tahir slowly shifted her *oraz* from her shoulder. The slide of it over her bare collarbone was sensual, delicious, and a shiver of delight ran through her. She leaned her head against his shoulder. Tahir ran his teeth over the line of Shahrazad's shoulder. The tip of his tongue teased her skin.

In the bed before them, the magician gave himself to the Way of Pleasure, arching toward his lover as the Raj ran his mouth up and over the magician's cock. Knowing Tahir's eyes were locked on the men, she ran her hand up and over Tahir's cock, the material of the cavalry trousers feeling suddenly very rough beneath her fingers.

Behind her, Tahir reached beneath her silk and ran his hand possessively around her bared stomach. His fingers danced over the curves of her waist, along the plain of her midriff. He didn't touch her breasts, but oh, she wanted him to. She wanted him to bury his face there and bite and suck. She wanted to feel nothing but him, think of nothing but pleasure.

Her betrothed could open his eyes and see them. He'd see her eyes half closed in pleasure as her lover's hands skated over her like he owned her. Her betrothed could open his eyes and see her watching, and she would die, her head festooning Pike Wall like any common criminal.

But Tahir's touch felt so good, and she wasn't doing anything now she hadn't done in the Flower Taker's chambers.

When his fingers looped through her pubic hair, she didn't stop him. She couldn't. Instead she shifted her stance, opening her thighs.

In the bed, the magician rocked his hips in tandem with the Raj's mouth. The magician's fingers were wrapped in the silk sheets so tightly that his knuckles were white. The desperation in his grasp made Shahrazad see how close he was to losing control.

As Tahir's fingers slid over her nub and edged inside her, she thought she knew something about control. One more glide and she'd lose it.

Through the trouser linen, Tahir's cock felt so hot. His moisture dampened her fingers despite the fabric's weight, but her fingers couldn't be as wet as his as he glided over her nub. She soaked him. As he dipped inside, she gasped with the pleasure of it.

"Yes," she breathed, not caring one bit if her betrothed and his lover heard. Let them hear.

Wanting to awaken the same desire in him as he had in her, Shahrazad slid her hand inside Tahir's trousers and felt the velvet of his cock for the first time. His muffled groan filled her ear, and his teeth bit more insistently at her neck.

In the bed before them, the Raj quit sucking. He lay atop the magician and slithered up toward his face. As Tahir slid his fingertip just barely inside her, she saw the Raj's cock press hard against the magician's. Her betrothed wrapped his hands through his lover's short hair, and his thumbs caressed the magician's face.

"I've said it before, and I'll say it again," the Raj said, his voice throaty with desire. His gaze was locked on the magician's, their lips so close that they almost touched. "I love you more than life itself."

"Raj," the magician chided. "Don't say such things."

"But my words are true," the Raj said, running his lips over the magician's. "I've never been so fervent in my desire, and I plan to prove it."

"Would you give up your land for me?" the magician asked.

"For this fleeting moment of pleasure would you risk your life, even if you never saw me again? Even if you never fucked me again?"

"You know the answer to that." The Raj kissed the magician then, their tongues tangling as their cocks rubbed against each other.

Even as she wondered how the magician was maneuvering the Raj, and her, and Tahir, Shahrazad leaned against the strength of Tahir's shoulder, trusting him to support her knees, which grew ever weaker beneath his touch. She still had the strength to slide her thumb over the wet tip of Tahir's cock.

The caress seemed to undo something in Tahir. He buried a finger deep inside her core, making her gasp in surprised delight. He caressed her nub with his thumb. The Flower Takers in his land must be very talented to teach their men such tricks.

A slow, intense shudder was building in her blood, in her core—and she knew nothing could stop it. Her hand embracing Tahir's cock froze with the impending pleasure, but he didn't seem to mind. His finger slid deeper; his thumb pressed harder. He kissed her neck more deliberately, sucking and biting until she couldn't tell where her skin ended and his mouth began.

And as the Raj abandoned the magician's mouth in favor of his cock, the magician's cries grew louder. His hands were wrapped around the Raj's long braid, and he held it as if it tied them together.

Tahir pulled her more tightly against him, and his cock pressed against her ass. Her fingers—frozen with pleasure—woke now, sliding over his shaft. Following the Raj's lead, she quickened her caress, and another groan escaped Tahir.

Suddenly, stars exploded behind her eyes. She was coming with an intensity she hadn't believed possible. With her free hand, she pushed Tahir's hand against her nub, making his fingers plumb deeper, making his thumb press harder. Her body quivered in delight, then buckled. The sensation became too much. Every nerve screamed in pleasure. She pulled his hand away and trembled in his embrace.

In the bed before them, the magician locked his legs around the Raj's neck, and the Raj sucked his cock as if enough suction would prove his intentions to the magician.

And perhaps it did.

Shahrazad moved her fingers harder and faster over Tahir's cock, and in the bed the magician shivered and came, his bellow of delight filling the chamber—and perhaps the palace hall.

The Raj's big hand went to the slim man's stomach and gently stroked, but he didn't remove his mouth. Instead, he stilled himself and rested his head against his lover's hip. To Shahrazad they looked like perfect lovers, content with their world, with their lives.

Neither looked afraid of the Pike Wall. Neither looked like the most evil being alive.

Behind her, pressing hard against her ass and hand, Tahir himself came. He came hard, bucking against her and gasping. His fingers possessively grasped her nub, and as he came, he brought her with him, caressing her nub with competent insistence. His orgasm continued as hers started.

And this time, their cries of pleasure weren't masked by those of the other men.

"Who's there?" the Raj ir Adham called, apparently surprising the enthralled Prince Tahir.

His fingers gripped her stomach almost painfully, but the demon in his other hand leaped forward with a cackle of glee. It landed on the bed with a crazed laugh, and it launched itself toward the magician with its razor-sharp teeth bared.

Shahrazad shouted a warning, but the magician's hand shot out and grabbed it—just as the creature ran an adoring tongue over the magician's cheek. It reminded her of a lost dog happy to see its master.

The magician didn't seem to care. His arm snapped up with

the speed of a snake, and before Shahrazad could step forward, the *shitani* dangled by its back leg from the slim man's hand. It hissed, almost sadly, then whined like a puppy, its eyes locked on the magician with what looked like adoration.

"I think this belongs to you," Shahrazad heard the Flower Taker say as she—no, he—held out the demon toward Tahir. The magician was almost laughing, but the *shitani*'s orange eyes seemed to reflect resignation at the handoff. "Thank you for coming."

"Is that a pun?" Tahir asked, not sounding particularly amused.

Badra had changed much since Shahrazad had last seen her. Lightly muscled chest muscles had replaced her small breasts, and the luxurious mane of blond hair was gone, replaced by close-cropped stubble. The voice was the only thing the man in front of her shared with the Flower Taker. That, and the purple eyes.

"I think this one likes you," the magician said to Tahir. "Would you like your pet back?"

"I've not come to replace you, if that's your true question," Tahir said, stepping forward as if nothing were amiss.

"Then perhaps the Raj will," the magician said as Tahir made to retrieve the demon. The Raj stopped him, knocking his hand aside with a snarl.

"What's going on here?" the Raj demanded, making Shahrazad cringe as the demon cackled and gnashed its teeth. It snapped at the Raj, although it couldn't get near her husband-to-be.

Shame washed over her. She shouldn't be here. She shouldn't see the Raj like this, naked and in the arms of a man. If her father knew . . .

But it wasn't his love for Badr that shocked her; it was the fact that he placed this love higher than his need to keep his land safe. He said he'd give up everything for the magician, and he proved it with his reckless affections. She shouldn't know how little he cared for everything she held dear. She didn't want to know.

A small voice in her mind called her a hypocrite. If she herself cared so much for her land, why had she let Tahir touch her? Being a pawn in this game didn't excuse her.

"I'm sorry, Raj ir Adham," she said quietly. "We shouldn't have intruded."

"You," the Raj said, perhaps only now recognizing his betrothed. "I'll have your head on a pike. What are you doing here?"

Before Shahrazad could answer, Tahir stepped closer, shielding her with his body. "Why, we're here at the behest of your true love," Tahir said in a cocky tone Shahrazad had never heard. "And we'll see whose head ends up on a pike."

With those words, the Raj roared and leaped off the bed, directly toward Prince Tahir.

13

"Stop!" Shahrazad called, but her words had no effect. "Stop, now!"

"I'll kill him," the Raj ir Adham roared as he flew across the bed clothed only in his rage. "And I'll kill you. Your father will kill you."

Prince Tahir stood unflinching, legs spread, an expression of defiance on his face. His arms remained at his side. "He'll need to get through me before he can touch her."

The Raj landed in front of Tahir, but still Tahir remained unruffled, despite the fact the other man's nose was so close to his.

"Men like you are the reason we castrate," Tahir said.

"Men like me," the Raj scoffed, grabbing Tahir's throat. "You know nothing of men like me."

That Tahir still didn't fight amazed Shahrazad. Instead he said to the Raj, "You're violent. That I know." She could see the Raj's fingers tightening inexorably around Tahir's throat.

"Stop!" Shahrazad called again. She didn't want anyone to

die, not for this. Everyone needed to work together if they
were to have any hope of defeating the *shitani*. "Stop!"

"Be quiet, wife-to-be," he snarled, his knuckles white with
effort. "You'll learn your place soon enough."

"Raj, stop," a calm voice said. The magician. "A man should
always treat his wife-to-be with respect, and the man you seem
intent on strangling is Prince Tahir."

"I've no interest in his name."

"But I did invite him to our chamber."

"You knew what he'd find?"

"Oh yes."

The Raj's thick blond braid flew as he turned to look at his
lover. "Why? You heard him—he hates men like us. Why would
you invite him?" Which was the exact question Shahrazad was
wondering.

Because he might make a good demon king, a voice said in
her head, a *shitani* voice. *She's testing him . . . and you.*

Tahir took advantage of the Raj's inattention, calmly extri-
cating himself from the man's grasp. "You know nothing, Raj ir
Adham." Prince Tahir took the *shitani* from the magician, grabbing its neck again.

"I'm going to stran—" the Raj began, stepping toward Tahir
again.

"Raj, please stop this," the magician said.

"Why? Because you ask it?"

"I believe," the magician said, standing from the bed, "that
you misunderstood Prince Tahir." The magician took a crimson robe from the floor and belted it around his slim waist. "If
your people weren't so insular, you'd know that his people
don't loathe love between men. It falls beneath the notice of the
ruling queens to care what men do amongst themselves. What
he loathes is violence."

Shahrazad looked at the Raj to see what he thought of this,

but the man just seemed confused. Shahrazad saw now that her betrothed was handsome in his own way, with green eyes and a strong jaw. Her sisters would have found him very attractive— at least before they'd married.

"What man loathes violence?" the Raj finally asked. He scratched his head with his brawny hand. "That's unnatural."

"He's from the Land of the Sun," the magician said, his voice taking on a strange tenor. Then the air around him seemed to flicker, bending the pale torchlight in a strange way. His hair glowed metallic red, then blond, then sorrel, then black as night. "Capture him. Give him to the Sultan for the Pike Wall. You will have the Sultan's alliance in hand then, even if he decapitates his daughter.... And he can grant your heart's desire."

There's no need to test anyone, she wanted to say, wanted to shout. But the hair on the back of her neck stood on end as he spoke, as she watched the strange glittering transformation.

The *shitani* in Tahir's hand broke the silence, cackling. The effervescent light around the magician's face vanished, and Shahrazad wondered if she'd imagined it.

Finally the Raj said, "But you're my heart's desire." He tried to run his hand through his braided hair. "I never knew my true nature. Until I met you, I didn't know why women . . ." He pointed toward his cock with a helpless gesture. "Why women . . ."

Shahrazad understood then just how profoundly his state of *rakeb* affected him. She longed to console him, to forgive him, to tell him that his secret was safe with her.

"You could turn him over to the Sultan," the magician said. "He has no right to be in this palace. He is a trespasser here—in many ways. Of course if you choose this path, he will die and so will she."

Again, that wave of strange magic washed over her, and she knew the magician used more than simple words to convince her betrothed. "The magician tests you," Shahrazad said to her husband-to-be, pleading with him to listen.

The Raj said nothing, gaping at his true love instead.

"Raj!" she said, "Listen to me."

"She speaks the truth," Tahir added.

The Raj's gaze shifted from the magician's to Tahir's face, a considering expression on his broad face. "He seeks to discover if you would make an adequate replacement," Shahrazad said. "Then he'll give you no choice but to accept his mantle."

The Raj looked at her finally, ignoring Tahir—and the magician. "What mantle?"

"The magician's mantle. He rules all the *shitani*. He keeps them from attacking cities and people."

"Ignore her drivel," the magician said with that knowing smirk—but Shahrazad felt no wave of enchantment. These words were simply words. "She's nothing but a weak and powerless girl. Bring the interloper to the Sultan . . ."

In frustration, Shahrazad turned toward the magician. "Badr, we cast the spell in the *Thaumutugicon*—we used the hair! We know the Raj will make an acceptable replacement. There's no need to torment him any longer."

"He's acceptable, yes. But is he willing?" Badr turned his narrow back on her. "Not yet."

"My love," Raj said, taking the magician's hands in his. "What does this mean?"

"This man," the magician gestured toward Tahir, "is an Impregnator."

The Raj, the magician, and Shahrazad all looked at Tahir, who flushed.

"My love," the Raj caressed the magician's arm. "I understand that this fact has some meaning to you, but I don't understand it at all."

Shahrazad didn't either, not in this context. But the awkward expression on Tahir's face told her that the concept meant something to him.

"You've been dreading this marriage, haven't you?" the magician asked the Raj. The words were kind, but she saw a cold machination in the magician's expression.

"You of all people know I have."

"Because of the final night."

The Raj nodded, his blond braid catching the light. "Yes. And because heirs . . ."

Shahrazad understood that if a man couldn't travel the Way of Pleasure with a woman, no children would come of the union. Was that to be her fate? No children? Suddenly, life seemed to be filled with worse things than turning into a flying horse by sunrise.

"But the Impregnator's function is to impregnate," Tahir said to her betrothed. "And the magician is suggesting I service your wife-to-be because you can't."

"Oh!" the Raj ir Adham said, understanding lightening his broad face. "That's a solution. I don't have to fuck the girl!" He straightened his braid. "And no one has to die."

Have to fuck the girl. That's how the Raj saw her, saw their union.

But on the other hand . . . Wasn't she freed? Was the magician suggesting a night of running wild? What she'd done with the Flower Taker was nothing compared with what she longed to do with Tahir, what she'd come so close to doing.

She looked at her lover—the strong line of his jaw, the breadth of his chest, his rangy limbs—and knew a word existed for what she felt: lust. But did that capture the entire complexity of her feelings?

And was she actually fool enough to fall into this deliciously baited trap?

No.

"The magician's powers are fading. The *shitani* need a new ruler."

"But still . . ." the slender man said with a flirtatious smile that lit his violet eyes. She heard that strange echo in his words, as if they held a special, hidden power. "I can grant your heart's desire."

"You don't know what my heart's desire is," she shot back, ignoring the pulsing magic.

"Oh, I don't?" the magician asked, the challenge clear as the air around him glistened. The hard line of his jaw softened, his lips grew fuller, and his hair grew out longer. The tight contour of his chest gave way to breasts, and his hips swelled. "I think I do, little hawk," she said, tracing a lascivious fingertip over Shahrazad's breast. "I know it exactly."

"God's eyes," the Raj moaned. "What kind of evil magic is this?"

"But I've granted your heart's desire," the woman—and she clearly was a woman now—said to him.

"What are you talking about?" the Raj groaned. "What have you done? Sleeping with a woman wasn't my heart's desire!" Beneath his tan, his face had gone white. His broad fingers crossed his face, and Shahrazad could see the white indents in his cheeks from his fingerprints.

"You wanted to sleep with a woman and enjoy it," the Flower Taker—no, Badra—purred. "And now you have."

"You don't know what you've done," the Raj moaned. "You don't know."

"I know exactly what I've done," Badra said, a satisfied smile curled around her lips. The *shitani* started to cackle, but it quieted midcall. Tahir must have tightened his grip.

"The augury," the Raj moaned, his face so buried in his hands that his words were muffled. "The augury! My land will fall now to the *shitani*."

"My darling boy," the magician said. "Run to my arms. Meet me in the Cavern of the Sixty Thieves. You don't need to fall with your land and your palace."

The air around her twisted and shimmered, and the magician vanished into nothing. Shahrazad blinked, but not even a tendril of smoke remained where Badra had been standing.

"Where is she?" the Raj called in a voice thick with rage. "I'll kill her!"

"One of you will replace me," an ephemeral voice said.

Shahrazad almost spoke. She almost cried the words that would seal her fate. *I'll replace you, Badra. I'll take your mantle. Leave these men be.* She wanted to say this, but her tongue was frozen, unmoving.

"Come to me, Raj," the fading voice said. "You don't have to fall to the *shitani.* Come to me, Shahrazad. You're head doesn't need to grace Pike Wall. Come to me, Tahir. Come join your sister."

"Where is that magician, that pox cunt whore?" the Raj roared in a voice loud enough to penetrate the walls. "Where is she?"

"Calm down, man," Tahir said, as Shahrazad scanned the room for the magician. "I can find her."

"Where is she?" the Raj roared again.

"Princess Shahrazad," the ephemeral voice said. "The Raj will betray you. He cannot help it. Come with me and I will save you."

She was going to agree. She opened her mouth to agree. But instead, she said, "How can I replace you? You, who have the ethics of an asp. You, who manipulates without a thought. You were too vain to find a replacement earlier, weren't you? Your vanity has endangered everything I hold dear."

"Your father will behead you."

"I must take that chance."

"And have you discovered that you're a Dark Mother, the

RUNNING WILD / 175

woman chosen above all others to fuck the *shitani* lord and bear his child?" she asked from somewhere—from everywhere.

"I've learned that Kalila, Tahir, the Sultan, the Raj or I can serve as the Dark Mother—or Dark Father."

"No one said you were a stupid girl—only foolish. Come with me and I will save you."

"Never." She looked at Tahir, hoping he could protect her, hoping she could protect herself.

"Where is she?" the Raj demanded, whirling around the room.

"Lift your curse from me, magician. I've no wish to be a *pegaz*. I've no wish to aid the *shitani*."

"As a *pegaz*, you will fly to me to take my place. I sense your acquiescence, young princess. You will come to me. You will be mine. Leave these fools behind."

"Don't do this, Badra," Tahir said. "She's done nothing to you."

A spectral laugh filled the chamber. "Will you take her place, Prince Tahir? Will you take mine? Your mother will not welcome you back, not after you ran your sister off. Certainly not after you defied her." Her voice seemed to be growing weaker.

"Badr!" the Raj bellowed. "You're the love of my heart, the light of my eyes! Come back. Drop your female guise and come back to me."

"Come to me, Raj," she said. "If you're man enough."

"You're not a woman! Don't use a cunt's voice!"

But the magician did not answer. She was gone.

Shahrazad turned to the Raj and Tahir. "That's what she wants more than anything."

"One of us," Tahir said.

"Yes." She shook her head. "At any cost."

"Do you suppose she's behind the auguries?" Raj sat on the bed as if exhausted.

"Maybe. They've spoken to all of us," Shahrazad said. "The augury told me that if I allowed a man to touch me, my land would fall—and then Badr touched me." She looked at her lover and added, "And Prince Tahir. He also touched me."

She looked at her husband-to-be, wondering if she'd see her death in his face. But the Raj simply looked at the ceiling and the walls and shrugged. "Nothing has fallen."

"Nothing's fallen," she agreed. But she turned and lifted her *oraz* in a most undignified fashion. He could see her back now, her new birthmark. "But things have changed."

The Raj looked at her back for a moment, confusion lining his forehead. "Does your father know you have a tattoo? I've never seen one of that quality. The scales on that snake actually look like they're moving."

"I beg your pardon, my Raj, but I don't have a tattoo," Shahrazad said, lowering her silk and turning back toward him, eyes modestly downcast. "This appeared in the place where the magician touched me—at the ceremony of the first day of our wedding. At the time I believed she was a man."

"Well," the Raj said, tightening the green sheet around his hips. "Nothing like that appeared on me."

The *shitani* in Prince Tahir's hand wheezed out a weak cackle and kicked its leg like a kangaroo rat trapped by a falcon. Its toes caught the Raj's green silk, and the sheet slithered to the Raj's knees.

"Fucking creature," the Raj said, grabbing the sheet. He wrapped it around his hips again and said, "What are you going to do with that thing—" He suddenly interrupted his question with a vicious scratching between his thighs. "God's eyes!" he said.

"What is it?" Tahir asked.

"God's eyes!" the Raj said again. "It stings. It hurts! What did that demon do to me?"

"It's the tattoo," Shahrazad said. "It's forming right now. Right where her skin touched yours."

"No," the Raj exclaimed, but he looked down, under the sheet. "God's eyes!" he cried, dropping the green silk. "What's happening to me?"

"Let me see," Tahir said, his voice still steady. But Shahrazad saw quite clearly what had happened to her betrothed. A snake tattoo covered his hip and his lower stomach. Its head—a beautiful collection of green and blue scales—had been magically tattooed on the head of his cock. Beady black eyes peered out, but they looked kindly rather than evil.

"It's lovely," Shahrazad said. "The diamonds of its scales are works of art."

The Raj bent to look more closely at his new tattoo, and his stomach muscle rippled, making the snake look like it actually slithered across his body.

"It looks very much like yours, Princess Shahrazad," Tahir said. "It even moves like yours."

The Raj looked up, startled. "Have you two—" He shook his head. "Have you—"

"Have we what?" Tahir's gaze was intense. "Enjoyed the Way of Pleasure together?"

"Well?" the Raj asked.

"We have not, my Raj," she said. "But I have kissed him and taken solace in his arms. I've allowed him to touch me in inappropriate ways, and I've touched him as well. My head belongs on a pike, my Raj, and I offer it to you freely."

"No." The Raj shook his broad head as he wrapped the sheet back around his hips. "I wasn't judging. I was simply appreciating the wisdom of the magician's suggestion."

"Were you?" she asked. She'd heard the magician's warning: the Raj would betray her. But did she believe it? Did that offset her fear of following the path so clearly laid out by the great deceiver herself?

"I defied the augury, and this tattoo appeared at her touch. You defied the augury, and the tattoo appeared at his touch. The magician is behind them. Her touch caused each of the tattoos."

"So, we're not to trust her. That seems quite clear." The Raj rubbed his broad face with his massive hands.

"The *shitani* threat is real." Tahir glanced at the demon in his grip. "The threat is real even if she's manipulating the auguries."

"My house cannot defeat the *shitani* without the help of the Sultan's armies." The Raj looked at both of them and added, "And I firmly believe the *shitani* will invade soon. We need this alliance, Princess Shahrazad."

"What if the alliance won't work?" she asked. "What if the only solution is to usurp the magician?" The Raj just looked at her blankly, and she snapped in frustration, "I've been cursed by the magician in a second manner—I change into a *pegaz* by day."

"I don't care if you change into a winged hippopotamus. I want this alliance, and I cannot enjoy the Way of Pleasure with you or any woman. It seems Badr—or Badra—has found a solution to my impossible dilemma."

"Hand Prince Tahir and me over to the Sultan?"

"What?" he asked. He seemed genuinely surprised. "And have you tell him about the magician and me?"

"I am weary to my bones of the Pike Wall and its threats. If I had my way not one more head would grace it—man or woman. But your word is my law. What are you suggesting, my Raj?" she asked.

"Follow the magician's suggestion. Let Prince Impregnator here impregnate you," he said, gesturing at Tahir. "You both like each other; there's no hardship. He can impregnate you on the appropriate wedding night—"

"Tonight," Shahrazad said, trying to ignore both the anticipation and the fear as they rolled over in her stomach. "The conception has been timed to take place tonight."

The *shitani* cackled, and Tahir shook it, but the Raj ignored it completely. "Let this man impregnate you tonight, and our alliance is sealed."

"I don't know what to say," Shahrazad began. "Will the *shitani* vanish simply because we wed—" And suddenly her ability to speak evaporated as her lips and limbs began to tingle. "It's dawn," she managed to gasp—just as wings sprouted from her back and a mane grew along her neck.

Tahir saw immediately what had happened to the princess. *God's eyes*, he thought, squeezing the demon's neck in frustration. But maybe it wasn't so . . . upsetting. The Raj didn't seem to mind, and if he didn't mind, the alliance could take place.

"I see she was serious about changing into a horse, wasn't she," the Raj said.

The *pegaz* snorted, her sand-colored mane rippling as she pinned her ears and shook her head. The jeweled reins of her bridle flopped around her neck but didn't drop.

"I'd take that as a yes if I were you," Tahir said.

"Did you get a snake tattoo, too?" asked the Raj.

"No, but the augury didn't forbid me to touch anyone or anything—I was told to restore my sister to her throne or my land would fall to demons."

"Well, fuck." The Raj walked across the chamber and retrieved his clothes.

"What is it?"

"The Sultan has one of these damned tattoos. It's on his arm, from his wrist to his shoulder. I wonder what that old bastard did to enrage the magician, may God refuse to look at him—or her."

"The Sultan has a tattoo? When did you see it?"

The Raj chuckled. "What? You think I fucked him, too?"

"That thought never occurred to me." And it hadn't.

"I was hunting with him last month, and his hawk shit all over his arm. He changed his shirt in front of me."

"He had the tattoo a month ago? Before Haniyyah was put to death? I don't understand—"

The Raj snorted an impatient sound. "Understand this, untattooed prince from the Land of the Sun. We might be doomed at this point—I touched a woman and she"—he waved his hand at the *pegaz*—"touched a man—or men. God only knows how the Sultan fucked his land. But I'm not giving up. Fuck the auguries. They've done nothing but ruin my life. I'll do what I need to to keep the land safe from the *shitani*."

The princess in *pegaz* form nickered, sounding exactly like she agreed with the sentiment.

"Including taking the magician's place?"

"Are you going to believe that camel shit? Has anything that—that creature"—he spit out the word—"has anything that fucking monster said been true?"

He didn't know.

"Princess Shahrazad and I found several ancient books in the palace's library."

"So?"

"They agreed with the magician's words."

"So?"

And Tahir had to agree with the Raj. He'd made the same point to Shahrazad when he'd heard she was considering accepting the role of magician. The truth and lies were so tangled in his mind he couldn't tell one from another. "So, what are your plans?" Tahir himself sat on the bed, suddenly exhausted. What was he going to do with a flying horse and a demon he didn't dare put down?

"I'm dressing myself like a decent man, and I'm waking the Sultan." He jerked up his brocade pants as if they were to blame for his problems. "And then I'm getting this marriage consummated tonight, even if we miss today's ceremony. I hope your cock is nice and hard at the thought of substituting for me."

Tahir looked at the princess's betrothed, considering. The torchlight caught the emeralds in her headstall and made them wink. "Unless you need a *pegaz* at the wedding and not the bride herself, I don't think you'll have the ceremony today."

"What are you talking about?"

"I don't think you'll marry a horse, even if it has remarkable wings."

"When does she change back into a woman?"

"Sunset."

"Good." The Raj pulled on his boots. "I'll postpone the ceremony until sunset." He shot a wary glance at the *pegaz* and said, "Just to be clear, you will impregnate her for me, won't you? And keep this just between us. I can't take the chance that fucking her will doom my land. I can't form an alliance between our Lands without a marriage—my people wouldn't have it and neither would the Sultan."

Tahir couldn't think of anything he'd rather do than act as the princess's Impregnator—but it wasn't enough. Even without the magician's taint hanging over this plan, it wasn't enough. Whatever the rules of this land were, in his own, a secret impregnation would be treason, especially if the queens hadn't given their approval. Beside that, what if she didn't want him?

And he should really inform his mother, but then . . . maybe not. Shahrazad was too good of a model to ignore. The time to buck his land's traditions was upon him. "I can't agree until the Princess Shahrazad agrees," he said finally.

The Raj looked at the winged mare again. "Can it understand us?" he asked, tugging on the stirrup of her exquisite saddle. She pinned her ears back in response.

"She can."

"Do you agree to this? Will you let him service you?" the Raj asked her. "I've no right to ask anything of you, but I assume you've been groomed to rule behind the throne-room door. Will you let Prince Tahir impregnate you tonight in my stead?"

The princess simply looked at him, her expression too equine to read, and Tahir's palms grew unaccountably damp.

"You can start now and yield to me in this," the Raj said to her.

Tahir looked at her, sympathy for her running through him. She could only answer *yes* or *no* as she had no voice. And she'd been trained since birth to yield in all things.

But the *pegaz*, her dark eyes shining in the torchlight, bobbed her head, keeping her nose near her knees. Only a quick swish of her tail indicated irritation. Was the Raj horseman enough to recognize the signal?

Was he man enough to care?

The Raj patted her shoulder as if she were a dog and tucked the stirrup leather into the iron so it wouldn't hit her side when she walked. "Good," he said to her. "We'll rule together. I should say, we'll rule well together."

And those words sent a pang of jealousy through Tahir, sharp as a spear. He might get to lay with the woman of his dreams, tumble her until she thought of no man but him—but he'd never get to rule with her at his side, forget this behind-the-throne-room-door nonsense.

The Raj strode out the magenta door with all the confidence of a man certain of his future, leaving Tahir alone in a chamber with a half-dead demon and an enchanted princess. When would he get it through his head that he was nothing but the stud horse in the stable?

14

Come to us . . . The plea echoed in her mind in a hateful way. She shook her head and snorted, her bejeweled reins falling to her feet. From Tahir's hand, the *shitani* looked at her with its orange eyes and cackled. *I'll have you*, it said.

Shahrazad turned away from the demon. She might be trapped in horse form, but she knew what needed to be done, even if Prince Tahir seemed stricken. They needed the magician—but not for Shahrazad's sake. As long as the Raj and the Sultan made their alliance, did it matter if she shifted into *pegaz* form by day?

Tahir on the other hand needed the loathsome thaumaturge. If she and Tahir saved his sister from the magician, maybe they could stop the *shitani* from invading the Land of the Sun—without serving in her stead.

After watching the magician's seductions and machinations, Shahrazad would never follow in her path. The *shitani* needed to be quelled, without a doubt, but not by destroying people, not by reducing them to their worst. She thought of the Raj and his pathetic love for a person who didn't exist. Shahrazad would not sacrifice her soul to rule the *shitani*, not if another way existed.

Be our queen. The words hissed in her head. *Be our Dark Queen and we'll love you. . . . Come to me . . . Come to us. We love you. We adore you.* The demon in Tahir's hand cackled.

She ignored the voices as she would a madman, and she stuck her nose in Tahir's pocket, seeking comfort. Oh, he smelled so good to her. Cleaned of the *shitani* spit, he smelled delicious.

"I can sense her, but I can't place her," Tahir said, perhaps thinking she was looking for the magician. "We need to find her."

She sniffed. The morning wind held a faint perfume that might belong to the magician. Could she smell as far as the Cavern of the Sixty Thieves?

"God's eyes," Tahir said as the magician's odor rolled through her nose and into her brain. She was too caught up in the sensation of the fragrance to see what had Tahir's attention. The odor was just so odd.

What a strange flavor the man—no, the woman—had. Yes, she smelled male essence. She smelled that clearly. But then that female scent wafted through it, too. And the perfume was more than just female scent—the magician had been ovulating. Or maybe just finished ovulating.

"Princess Shahrazad," Tahir said, interrupting her. "Do you see that?" Tahir asked. In the long shadows of the early morning light, her equine eyes had difficulty finding recognizable patterns. Dawn sunlight drenched the sand.

"She wants us to find her," he said. "She's probably in the Cavern of Sixty Thieves."

She nodded, making her forelock float through the air.

"Should we go?" he asked. She turned her face out the window, closed her eyes, and inhaled. She could smell the magician—and she was closer than the demons. She reared up so her hooves balanced on the brick sill and looked at Tahir, who needed no second invitation. He gathered the reins and mounted.

For a heartbeat, she looked out the window and doubted. What if she simply plummeted to the ground? But then she leaped . . . and soared. The momentary pleasure of the cool morning air beneath her wings permeated her every thought.

Her wings whispered through the morning air as they flew. "This may be a trap," he said.

Shahrazad huffed, wishing she could speak. If this were a trap—and it probably was—they could do no less than to go. They could do no less than let her marriage to the Raj continue. No matter what their fate was, she could no more lie down and let this terrible play roll out than she could spread her legs for the *shitani*.

The demon in his hand cackled. *We will have you, Princess Shahrazad. You will love us.*

Shahrazad tossed her head to clear the voices, but it didn't help. As they flew closer to the Amr Mountains, their voices grew louder and more insistent.

Come home to us, the *shitani* cackled in her head. *Come home now.*

"We're almost there." Tahir stroked her neck. "We're very close if she's in the cavern."

And he didn't need to say more, because the magician's scent filled the air around her, beckoning her. Almost without thought she tilted her wings, and the ground grew closer.

And in an instant, what she smelled changed dramatically.

For a moment she thought Tahir's scent had wrapped around the magician's—the fragrance smelled so much like his own. But then she realized that the scent truly resembled Tahir's, save it was feminine. How could his scent be in two places at once?

At first she thought the magician's evil thaumaturgy caused

the juxtaposition, but then she realized the scent belonged to his sister. His sister was below.

"Do you see that?" Tahir asked, pointing toward a rocky outcrop. In the long shadows of the morning light, her equine eyes had difficulty finding recognizable patterns. She saw several spiny cacti through the dawn light. Likewise, the isolated rocks made sense. But were those shadows simply caused by the edges of the boulders, or was something crawling over them?

She snorted in consternation.

"Can you see who it is?" Tahir asked, his voice thick with emotion.

She swooped toward the puzzling shadows—and smelled *shitani*, several of them. They were gathered around the woman—and it was a woman. And the thick gardenia scent told her they were licking their victim.

Plumes of sand poured into the morning air as she landed. Within two strides, she stood next to the captive, and the sight horrified her.

She was naked, her arms tied to stakes above her head and the legs spread, her ankles tied to more stakes. The magician's fragrance swirled around her, diffuse as the rare summer cloud. The captive's hair and skin were dark, but Shahrazad couldn't identify the colors with her equine eyes. She could smell desire, though—and gardenias. She looked closer.

One *shitani* licked the woman's bare toes, making them invisible, while a second demon lovingly ran its disgusting tongue over the woman's delicate wrist. Her hand was already gone, vanished in the coat of saliva.

Submit, our queen. We will love you. You are more lovely than this one. You are so fertile and ripe. The demon at the woman's wrist looked up at Shahrazad as the words floated through her mind. Its orange eyes glittered. *We will delight and cherish you. Look how pleased this queen is.*

Without thought, Shahrazad dove toward the closest *shitani* and lashed at it with her hooves. Her foot hit bone, and she heard a crunching noise, smelled blood. The thud it gave as it slammed against a boulder sent a surge of glad power through her veins. She leaped toward the second *shitani*, planning to slaughter it, to smash its blood into the powdery sand, but Tahir touched the reins for the first time.

"Stop," Tahir called, pulling her back but just slightly. "Princess, stop."

The unscathed demon skittered toward the shadows as she chased it—but she didn't pummel it, not yet. She'd been trained to obey, and obey she would.

"I know this work," Tahir growled from her back. "That woman is no innocent victim. She's not my sister—no matter what she looks like. The magician did this."

She wanted to ask how he knew this, but he leaped from her back and picked up a small jar sitting near the captive's wrists. He left a small scraper sitting in the sand. "Badra," he spat. "She's harvesting invisibility."

Shahrazad couldn't smell the magician any longer, not exactly. Delicate plumes of her perfume occasionally wafted toward her from the south, but she wasn't here. The fragrance that had been so thick moments ago was gone. With difficulty, Shahrazad focused her equine gaze on the woman. Her eyes were rolled back in pleasure, and she didn't seem to realize that Shahrazad herself had incapacitated one of the demons.

In fact, the free *shitani* crept back toward the woman's wrist, its tongue extended like a man dying of thirst in the desert. A strange cackling noise came from it as it approached the woman, its orange eyes locked on Shahrazad's.

We love you, Princess, it said. *Become one with us.*

Quick as a snake, Tahir lashed his fist out and caught the thing. Now he held two living demons in his fist. The *shitani* near the boulder chose that moment to start squirming, and Tahir retrieved that one as well.

Save us, beloved queen, she heard in her head. All three *shitani* in Tahir's hand pleaded with her. *Save us!*

She wanted to crush the awful things beneath her hooves, felt certain Tahir would feel the same if he knew what they said to her. But he was ignorant of the havoc they wreaked in her mind. Instead, he started shaking his sister's shoulder with his booted toe.

"Badra," he snarled to the bound woman. "Badra! Get up now, and quit the act."

Shahrazad finally understood that he thought the woman at their feet was the magician. That's why he didn't want to kill the demons. Maybe he thought she deserved them. Or that she still controlled them.

But her nose knew the truth—the magician wasn't near here. This woman was his sister.

As Tahir shook his sister more violently, Shahrazad gently took his shirt between her equine teeth and tugged.

We love you, she heard, her face so close to the demons she could smell their flowered breath. *Set us free and be our queen. Rule us! Bear our king!*

Without meaning to, she pulled too hard and Tahir flew toward her, his shirt ripping. "God's eyes," he said, anger thickening his voice. "Stop it. Whatever you think, that is not my sister—that's the magician. I've seen her do this trick before." He turned toward her, fury darkening his face. "In fact, that's how I met you."

Shahrazad couldn't say a word, and although she willed understanding into his head, he couldn't hear it. With his expression intent on his sister, he kicked the ropes that held her ankles. The bristly ties scraped across her bared flesh. The woman moaned again, although Shahrazad doubted it was in pleasure.

Closing her eyes against the demons' gaze, Shahrazad grabbed the fabric between Tahir's shoulders and pulled him away from the woman.

"That's not my sister," Tahir snapped, shoving her equine shoulder.

She wasn't big in *pegaz* form, but she was bigger than he was. Despite the vehemence of his push, she merely stumbled a few steps in the sand, but she was shocked at his loss of control. However, it wasn't her dismay that brought him to his senses. He did that on his own. With a horrified expression on his face, he said, "I beg your pardon, Princess Shahrazad. I—" The demon in his hand cackled, and it sounded just like laughter.

But the woman on the ground started to moan again, her pleasure obvious as a *shitani* lapped her breast, curving lovingly around a nipple. The warm scent of gardenias floated through the air, incongruously pretty given the ugliness of the *shitani* and what they were doing to Kalila.

But then Shahrazad realized that these were additional demons. Where had the *shitani* come from? How many more lurked in the shadows?

"Let it lick her," Tahir snarled at her. "We'll collect the saliva, use it ourselves."

Save us, our queen, the *shitani* in his hands beseeched her. *Save us!*

And suddenly, Shahrazad was tired of being told what to do. She didn't want to save the demons; she didn't want to wait and collect spit. This woman wasn't the magician, no matter how much Tahir protested otherwise, and she didn't deserve the punishment she was taking.

We'll make you so happy, our queen, the voices cackled. *We love you. We love all queens.*

"Stay away from her," Tahir warned her, perhaps sensing a change in her body language. "She's dangerous."

But she'd had enough. With an earsplitting equine shriek, she snaked her head toward Tahir and crushed a demon's skull between her powerful teeth. Brains and goo erupted over Tahir's hand, and its blood rushed over her tongue, making her want to gag—but she wasn't finished.

Ignoring Tahir's shouts and the pleas in her head from the demons, she reared onto her hind legs. Pointing her hooves like daggers, she pounced onto the *shitani* near the woman. It died instantly, crushed into a mound of bloody pulp in the sand. Overlong fingers twitched and quivered as the last of their life drained from them.

No! Our queen, no! The demons pleaded for mercy, but her heart was cold. Two more demons remained, throttled in Tahir's hand, and she lunged for them. She'd kill them!

But an earsplitting shriek from the woman at her feet stopped her.

Pulling herself up short, Shahrazad stopped, her hooves churning the sand. The *shitani* had dropped their thrall over Tahir's sister, and it looked like the woman thought Shahrazad was going to smash her.

Shahrazad stepped back, trying to alleviate the captive's fears, but as the woman continued to scream incoherently, Shahrazad saw that a large portion of the woman's body was now invisible. She writhed so much that her wrists began to bleed against the ties, the blood visible where the flesh was not.

"Badra," Tahir said to her, kicking the ropes again. "Stop. We're not fooled."

The sheer panic on the woman's face was more than Shahrazad could bear. No one should have to be as afraid as this woman.

She leaped behind Tahir and shoved him hard with her shoulder, right into his sister. Maybe he'd recognize her smell, even with his human nose.

His feet tangled in the ropes, and his face landed in the sand, a hand's breadth from the woman's. The demons in his hand screeched as their heads knocked together with an audible thump.

"What is wrong with you?" he demanded, and Shahrazad couldn't tell if he spoke to her or his sister.

God's eyes! What could she do to tell this man that this was most certainly his sister? She couldn't bear it any longer. The heartbeat she found that magician, she'd make her—

Dark Mother, she heard.

Damn them all, she thought. She threw herself into the air and bucked like a wildcat rode her back. She couldn't bear the saddle anymore. She belonged to no one. Not Tahir. Not Badra. Not her father. She bucked again and twisted. The saddle flew off, hitting a boulder with a thud.

We love you! Be ours! Rule us!

"Shahrazad!" Tahir called, finally leaving his sister's side. "What are you doing? Stop that."

But she wasn't finished. She wasn't going to be bound by one more rule, not a saddle, not a bridal. She'd let no man's hand rule her again.

With an angry squeal, she threw her head between her knees and rubbed the headstall off from behind her ears. It slithered to the sand like a dead snake.

As the bit fell from her mouth, the erotic tingling she associated with the change began. Her hooves went numb, and her legs vibrated with odd energy. She blinked and the world shifted from black and white. The deep brown of the surrounding boulders contrasted against the aching blue of the midmorning sky, and the overripe cacti blossoms climbing over their verdant flesh shocked her eyes.

"Prince Tahir," she said, anger making her voice quiver. "That is without a doubt your sister, and if you do one more hurtful thing to her, I will—"

"You're not a *pegaz*," he said, amazement etched on his features. "How'd you break the spell?"

"A fit of rage?" She had no patience for this. "I have no idea.

Now help that woman stand and get her cleaned. This is not right. What you're doing to her is not right."

She watched him look down at his sister, his shocked expression giving way to something more giving.

"Tahirdro," Kalila said, her eyes locked on his. Shahrazad watched her try to lower her arms, but the cruel ropes held them in place. "Tahirdro, is that you? Really?"

He jumped back as if he'd seen a snake. "Badra," he snarled, falling to his knees, "this is beneath even you."

"Don't be a fool, Tahir," Shahrazad said. "My *pegaz* nose doesn't lie. You smell exactly like each other. She is your sister."

"It's dark magic," he said. "Badra concocted the smell to trick you. Just like she concocted the words in those books. The magician spins nothing but lies."

"Fool—"

In that heartbeat, another *shitani* leaped off a boulder onto the woman's chest with its unearthly cackle. When its orange eyes met the woman's, she acquiesced, falling again into its hypnotic thrall.

Tahir didn't give the *shitani* any time to lick her flesh though. He lunged toward the woman and grabbed the demon. Then he gave Shahrazad a wicked-looking dagger.

"You've earned this. It's yours, Princess," he said. Then he dropped the demon at her feet.

I love you, my queen—it started to say. She barely had time to realize it spoke to her while she was in human form before she jumped at it, blade extended. It leaped away, but she was faster—or more determined.

My queen! it pleaded. *Do not hurt me!*

She wasted no time slicing it, ripping its abdomen until hot blood drenched the sand.

When she looked up, she saw that Tahir was finally untying his sister, helping her to her feet. The queen, apparently still dazed, remained speechless as Tahir rubbed her clean with his cloak. The muscles on his back slid deliciously as he took the shirt from his back and slid it gently over her.

"Tahirdro," the woman said. "Is it really you?"

"It is." He bowed to her. "I'm sorry I didn't believe you," he said, turning toward Shahrazad.

"Do you know the *pegaz*?" the queen asked, pulling the shirt down to her knees. She looked as regal wearing these soldier's rags as Shahrazad's aunts and cousins did in their wedding finery.

"Yes," Tahir said. "Queen Kalila, this is Princess Shahrazad, Daughter of the Sultan of the Land of the Moon." He bowed and gestured toward Shahrazad. "And Princess Shahrazad, this is my sister, Queen Kalila, co-ruler of House Kulwanti of the Land of the Sun."

"Please," the queen said to Shahrazad. "Call me Kalila."

"I'm pleased to meet you, Kalila."

"But why did you change from *pegaz* form?" the queen asked in a majestic voice. "Surely not on my account. Perhaps you fight better as a woman? Are you a Warqueen?"

"I—" But Shahrazad didn't know what to say. Killing the *shitani* was much easier in *pegaz* form.

"Princess Shahrazad is not a *pegaz* by her own choosing." Tahir turned toward her. "Badra cursed her. By day she's a winged horse—by night, she's a woman."

"But of course she has a choice," Kalila said.

Tahir looked at her a moment, as if he might disagree, but then he bowed and said, "As you say, my queen."

And it occurred to Shahrazad that she'd never once seen a woman generate subservient behavior from a man—not before this.

"Tahirdro," Queen Kalila said, "don't act like a camel's cock. I'm not pulling rank on you—I'm telling you your princess has a choice."

"I don't see how."

"It's day and she's in woman form—by her own choosing."

"I—" But Tahir looked confused and didn't finish his sentence.

"May I retrieve your bridle?" she asked, approaching Shahrazad with an outstretched hand. Shahrazad took her hand in response. Who could deny this woman?

"Of course, Kalila. But why?"

The queen gracefully retrieved the thing, handing the emerald-encrusted bridle back to her. "I would recommend that you not lose this. It gives you control."

"The bridle?" Tahir asked. "She removed the bridal and broke the curse?"

"I believe the curse still stands," Queen Kalila replied, her voice soft. "What I mean is that if you or I slipped this bit between our teeth, nothing would happen."

"But the bridle allows me to control it." The sense of wonder she felt made her words seem dreamy.

"You've been cursed." Kalila nodded, her lovely chestnut hair gleaming in the sunlight. She wore no crown, but Shahrazad could so easily imagine it. "Although maybe some would consider the freedom of this bridle a blessing." The expression on her face made Shahrazad see the other woman envied her wings.

"What do you mean?" Tahir asked. "She changes into a *pegaz*."

"At my will," Shahrazad clarified, looking at the mountains. Then she laughed, remembering the moment the magician touched her, how she wished for exactly this freedom. "The magician was correct, you realize," she said to Tahir. "When she said she'd grant our hearts' desire."

"What do you mean?"

"You wanted your sister." Shahrazad gestured to the woman. "I wanted freedom." She held up the bridle. "And what of you, my queen?" she asked. "Has your wish been granted?"

"I wanted to see what the world had to offer before I settled in to rule next to my mother," the woman said, without apology. "My mother's a difficult person to satisfy, and I wasn't certain I wanted to try."

A week ago, Shahrazad would have had no sympathy for such a selfish wish, but now . . . now, she saw that being forced to rule was just as imprisoning as being forbidden.

"Somehow," Tahir said, "I think we've all been granted what we wanted, but . . ."

"But our heart's aren't contented," Kalila finished.

"And each of these granted wishes have come at a terrible cost that we've yet to pay. Furthermore, we have larger problems on the horizon," Shahrazad told them.

"*Shitani*," Tahir said.

Shahrazad nodded. "Thousands of them, coming this direction."

"But the augury said if we restored my sister within a month and day, the *shitani* wouldn't invade the Land of the Sun."

"A trap. Another machination," Shahrazad said. "But again, do we have a choice? We should fly her to your land and see if that doesn't break the spell."

"I doubt very much it will," Queen Kalila said. "Badra uses her dark thaumaturgy to manipulate omens and augurs—it's one of the many ways she maneuvers people."

Shahrazad nodded. "We'd come to a similar conclusion."

We love you, our queen.

The voices whispered in her head, much softer than in her horse form, but she couldn't help but run her fingers to her temples.

"Are they coming for you?" Tahir asked, taking her hand in his.

Shahrazad nodded.

"I hear them, too. They continually invite me to rule them," he said in a tight voice.

"We must tell my father," she said. "Even if he wants to behead me, he must prepare the armies. The *shitani* are more numerous than we ever considered. Even with the Raj's support, we might not defeat them."

"The Warqueen Abbesses could help," Tahir added, looking at his sister.

Kalila thought for a moment. "Princess Shahrazad's palace stands between the *shitani* and the Land of the Sun," she noted. "If we place the Warqueen Abbesses in the Land of the Moon, they'll protect the Land of the Sun."

"We'll all fly to the Land of the Sun," Shahrazad said, deciding.

"But I'm not going home," Queen Kalila said. "I can't."

"But you must." Determination hardened Tahir's jaw. "You can't abandon your home."

"Tahirdro," she said, caressing his face. "I was never going to be a good leader. And if I leave, perhaps Queen Kulwanti will grow a spine and establish you in my place. You are the leader. Just because you have a cock . . ."

"You can't—" Tahir started to say, but Shahrazad interrupted.

"Will you go to the magician then?" she asked Kalila. "She's been pushing your brother and me to her arms. Has she been pushing you?"

"I've been pushing myself," Kalila said, shaking her head so that her dark skin shimmered in the noon light. "I've never wanted to rule the Land of the Sun. Perhaps I could rule the demons."

"But Badra," Shahrazad said. "She's evil."

"She's not as evil as she is tired. If I replace her, perhaps she'll leave the rest of you alone." Kalila gave a weak smile and added, "Although I cannot imagine a future more loathsome."

Tahir looked at her a moment, then struck her. The blow was firm, but not overly hard, and Kalila crumpled to the ground like an empty sack.

Shahrazad gasped in horror, but Tahir shook his head and rubbed his hand. "She really wasn't a good leader," he said.

"But to bring her home and force the issue?" Shahrazad couldn't justify the unfairness of it. "Against her will?"

"I doubt my mother will make her rule," Tahir said. "I'm sure Kalila will slink away at some point."

"But then why?" She gestured at the unconscious woman.

"For my mother. She believes her auguries like you believe the sky is blue. If I didn't return my sister and the *shitani* invaded, she would always believe she'd failed her land, that she didn't do enough to restore Kalila to the throne." He paused and then said, "She'll think I failed the land."

"So now she'll know the truth."

Tahir shook his head. "Who knows what the truth is. I'll still do everything in my power to stop the *shitani* invasion."

"The Warqueen Abbesses?"

"Exactly." He slung his sister over his shoulder. "If you fly us to the Land of the Sun, I will procure us one more army."

Come to us, Tahir heard in his head. *Be our Dark Father. Fuck us. Rule us.*

He shook his head in consternation, pushing their voices from his head. To get to the Land of the Sun from here, they'd fly over the Amr Mountains, a first for him. If they'd been riding or walking, they'd have gone around the jagged monstrosities.

For a heartbeat, a heady thought rolled through his mind as his sister clung unhappily to his waist. Forget lands ruled by men, or lands ruled by women. What if they established a land where men and women ruled together, side by side? Young girls wouldn't need to learn to keep their eyes downcast like Princess Shahrazad did. Young boys wouldn't be castrated like the boys in his land were.

His utopian thoughts were brushed away by the swoop of Shahrazad's wings as she banked steeply.

"What is it?" he asked, looking down. They were over the Amr Mountains now, mountains too rugged for most people to cross on foot or by horse, and a huge flat valley opened in their center.

And then he saw.

"What is that?" Kalila asked from behind him.

An enormous palace existed in the center of the valley and dozens of outlying buildings dotted the perimeter. What looked like horse or camel paddocks decorated an area, and a cool, blue pond filled nearly a third of the valley. Even from this height, he could see white ibis plumes as the birds fished the water. But no human dwelled in this secluded land.

"It's fantastic," he said, and Shahrazad beneath him nickered in agreement.

We love you, our king. Come to us. Come to us!

Tahir looked down, amazed at how loud the voices were. And then he saw the reason why. What looked like every *shitani* ever spawned was scrambling up Amr's first cliff, heading directly toward Shahrazad's land, just as she'd said.

"If it was their land, it isn't any longer. It looks as if they're leaving," he said.

Our king, he heard, *we love you!*

As if she were in pain, Shahrazad shook her head and whinnied.

"What's wrong with her?" Kalila asked.

"She hears the *shitani*. I think the voices hurt her." He leaned forward, urging her to speed. They needed to get away from them now.

Then a thought occurred to him. He'd seen Kalila's face in the spinning orb. "Don't you hear them?" he asked.

"Not very clearly, and they're easy to block out," Kalila said. "Do you?"

"Yes, and the closer they are, the louder they are. I think it's even worse for Shahrazad, especially when she's in horse form."

"That's terrible," Kalila answered. "And here we are flying over a writhing nest of them."

"We're leaving."

"You didn't have to hit me, you know," Kalila said, jabbing his ribs. "I would have come with you."

"I was afraid you'd go to the Cavern of Thieves."

The two demons cackled in his hand despite the fact they should have died long ago given the way he squeezed their wretched necks.

"Would that have been such a bad thing? Perhaps the demons would have left the lands in peace."

"The magician is a liar," Tahir said. "Nothing she says can be believed."

"So what do you suggest?" she asked, archly.

"War. We will kill each and every last one of them. We'll vanquish them, erase even the memory of them."

Kalila said nothing for a moment, then she hugged him tightly. "If anyone can accomplish such a task, brother, you can."

Her confidence in him choked him. He could forgive Shahrazad for believing in him—she didn't know him, not really. She didn't know his home, his mother, his weaknesses and failures. But Kalila did. She'd known him since the day he'd been born.

And she believed in him.

"Look," Tahir called. "Home." Their palace appeared on the horizon, its tall blue minarets welcoming.

"Does it feel like home to you?" Kalila asked. "It doesn't feel that way to me."

"I'm sorry I ran you off. I didn't mean for you to leave. I just thought you could pick your own Impregnator without mother's help."

"Oh, Tahirdro," she said, running her hand over his shoulder. "You didn't make me leave."

"Of course I did. All those queens chasing after you to get Impregnated by their sons. I thought if you put your foot down, they'd give you some room to breathe, live your own life for a few years."

"You gave me the strength to leave," she corrected. "I knew no matter how firmly I resisted, I'd never gain any freedom. And then I heard mother scheming with Queen Casmiri to Impregnate me against my will . . ." Her arms, wrapped around his waist, moved as she shrugged. "I ran. Or rather, the magician took advantage of my discontent."

"I'm sorry still," Tahir said after a moment of silence.

"I'm still running back to the Cavern of the Sixty Thieves the first chance I get."

"That will be mother's problem."

Rule us! he heard again. *We love you. Come to us!*

But he was going home. By the time they reached the center of their land, a gaggle of laughing girls ran beneath them, accompanied by toddling boys. He knew the older boys were inside, many of them working or recovering from their dreaded surgeries.

By the time they approached his palace, the swooshing sound of Shahrazad's wings reverberating in his head, his mother and her entourage waited in the courtyard, her blue robe immaculate in the early afternoon sun.

"I would be pleased if you landed here," he told Shahrazad, and she did, with as much grace as she had the first time in that oasis all those lifetimes ago.

His mother bore herself with such a regal air that Tahir was not at all surprised when Shahrazad oriented toward Queen Kulwanti and stopped just before her.

"Mother," Prince Tahir said in his public voice. "I'm rejoiced to see you again. May God hold you in his eyes." With a grand gesture, he added, "I've brought your beloved daughter, Queen Kalila."

He watched his mother take Kalila in, and her gaze returned to him. He saw . . . surprise at his success. "Son," she said finally, "I too find my heart gladdened at the sight of you. I praise God for holding you as dear in his eyes as I do."

He blinked at her warm greeting, surprised at the public showing of her affection. He slid from Shahrazad's back and then helped his sister dismount.

"And daughter," Queen Kulwanti said, "it is also a delight to see you. I hope your year of meditation brings you home in a peaceful mind."

"It does." Queen Kalila curtsied to her mother. "I'm rejoiced to see you, mother."

An awkward silence held court for a moment, and then Tahir said, "I bring you a gift." He held up his fist of demons. Obligingly, they cackled, although how they did that through his death grip around their necks, he didn't know.

Do not abandon us, our king, he heard as their eyes locked on his. *We love you. We worship you.*

"Thank you," Queen Kulwanti said. "I trust they bring some . . . benefit."

"Besides the beauty of their faces?" he asked. "They do. But perhaps it is a feature best described in private." Especially if she planned to use their invisibility spit to spy on the other houses as he would have.

She nodded and gestured toward Ayoob the eunuch, who stepped forward to retrieve them. "Is the glorious *pegaz* a gift as well?"

"She is not," Tahir said, slipping the bridle from Princess Shahrazad and allowing her to transform for all to see. "This is Princess Shahrazad, daughter of the Sultan of the Land of the Moon." Once her transformation was completed, he added, "Princess Shahrazad, this is my mother, Queen Kulwanti, ruler of House Kulwanti and the Land of the Sun."

"Ah," the old queen said, nodding to the princess. "I've longed to meet a daughter of the moon."

"Greetings, your majesty," Shahrazad said in a clear voice that rang throughout the courtyard. She curtsied with neat grace. "I bring greetings from my land to yours. Your son, Prince Tahir, has made a great impression, and we greatly anticipate working together to rid both our lands of this scourge."

Tahir paused. Shahrazad had made the "we" in her statement sound royal, suggesting that she and her father found Tahir in their favor. It was a good tactic with his mother, and it made Shahrazad seem more powerful than she might actually be.

It made Tahir sound powerful, too.

"By scourge," the queen asked, "I understand you to mean *shitani*. Is that correct?"

"Yes, my lady."

Queen Kulwanti's eyes met his, and he could feel the question she didn't want to ask in public. Was the worry of this scourge warranted?

And his mother, the most powerful ruler in several generations, wasn't asking Queen Kalila.

"Perhaps you would like to refresh yourselves," the queen said, "then join me for an early dinner?"

Tahir approached his mother and kissed her hand formally. "We don't have time, mother, but we need to speak." He said these words for only her to hear.

She nodded briefly, then bade him to stand. She linked her arm in his and began to walk toward the palace. With relief, Tahir saw that Shahrazad seemed perfectly at ease with this arrangement, falling in next to Kalila and Ayoob.

"You have found your sister," the queen asked him, her voice low. Tahir saw the worry in her expression. "No doubt you brought her back expecting a reward—despite your disobedience."

"I brought her back because the augury suggested we'd be overrun by *shitani* if I didn't."

"You brought her back because it was the honorable thing to do." Was she sneering at him?

"Mother," Tahir said, keeping his temper under control. "Have I ever behaved in a manner contrary to that?"

"No." She sighed. "You haven't. Tell me of the *shitani*, then."

"We flew over an abandoned keep in the Amr Mountains."

"I've heard of that place," she said. "But I wasn't certain it actually existed. Did you see *shitani* there?

"Thousands of them, hundreds of thousands. They were leaving the keep, scrambling over the crags toward the Land of the Moon."

"After which they could hook around the pass and invade the Land of the Sun."

"Exactly."

"And what exactly was Kalila doing there?"

Tahir considered the long answer wherein he described the state in which he'd found his sister, and he opted for a different truth altogether. "She was being held prisoner by Badr the Bad."

"The magician. Did you fight and defeat him?"

"No."

"No?"

"The magician lives." He shook his head in frustration. "I believe the magician is manipulating more than we can see. He—or she—gave us Kalila."

"What does Badr want in exchange? Perhaps we should send out Warqueen Abbesses to kill him."

"She wants a replacement, and killing her isn't easy because she seems to vanish at will and take any form. She also controls the *shitani* to some extent." Tahir paused, meeting her gaze so she could see the importance of his request. "Besides that, we have something more important to do with the Warqueen Abbesses."

"And what is that?"

"We need them at the Sultan's palace."

His mother blinked her heavily lidded eyes at him and then said, "Never."

"Never?" He tried—and failed—to curtail his anger.

"I cannot leave our home exposed, not with the demons so close. We need the Warqueens here."

"With the Warqueens at the Sultan's palace, the *shitani* will never arrive here."

"Do not patronize me, son," she said. "I know what you're thinking, but your job isn't to decide, it isn't to rule. Your job is to impregnate the Houses of my choice."

At her words, he expected rage, but that wasn't what washed over him. Instead, cold certainty filled him. He couldn't allow *shitani* to overrun the Land of the Moon.

"I want you to go from here to your quarters. Wash up there, and then go to the Impregnation chambers of House Nouf. You were suggesting that we ally with them, and I believe you're correct."

"If you don't send the Warqueen Abbesses to the Land of the Moon," he said, hearing tightness in his voice but leaving it there for his mother to hear, "your daughter will revolt against you."

"Pah," the queen snorted. "She's more interested in riding and dancing than in fighting. She'll be drinking her way to oblivion before she takes an interest in this problem."

"I don't think you understand the depth of her loathing of the creatures. Kalila might not long to rule, but she longs to fight for this cause. She'll not allow you to leave the Land of the Moon unprotected. She's already agreed it's the best use of our resources."

"Given the insolent way in which you are addressing me, I

should have Ayoob take you to the dungeon. However, I am a loving mother, and I understand that you are hungry and tired. I will excuse you—this once—and I will tell you to wash and go fuck the representative from House Nouf."

Tahir simply looked at his mother. Finally he said, "You're wrong." He extricated his arm from his mother's and turned around, back toward Princess Shahrazad. Her black-as-night hair had never seemed so beautiful to him. He took her arm and led her back toward the courtyard.

"Tahirdro!" Kalila called. "Where are you going?" *Take me with you*, he heard in her tone.

"I'm leaving. Apparently, you are to lead the Warqueen Abbesses to—"

"I'll lead them to the Land of the Moon and nowhere else."

"I suggest you tell that to Queen Kulwanti," he said, marching back to the courtyard.

For a moment, the royal retinue seemed confused. Should they remain with the queen, who appeared dumfounded, or should they follow the prince? Since they'd never in their lives followed a man, Tahir took their hesitation as a good sign, but he didn't gloat. Instead, he walked toward the open area, where Shahrazad could leap into flight without any difficulty.

Suddenly, he realized that the royal party was following him toward the courtyard, and fear lapped bitterly in his blood.

His mother would forsake him now, in his moment of greatest need, simply because he'd finally spoken against her. Would she order him to stop and then fill him with arrows?

He took the emerald-studded bridle and handed it to Shahrazad. "This may turn ugly very quickly."

"Then let's leave." She was already sliding the headstall over her hair and the bit between her teeth.

"Yes."

"Stop!" The queen ordered in her most imperious voice. "Prince Tahir of the House Kulwanti, I command you to stop."

206 / Lucinda Betts

Tahir considered leaping onto Shahrazad's bared back, ignoring his mother and flying away forever. But what good would that do? Instead, he climbed deliberately onto his mount and turned to look back. The time had come for him to make a stand.

"I am going, my queen," he said, looking down at her from astride the *pegaz*. "I'm going to protect the Land of the Moon, the land of my beloved." He felt Shahrazad quiver beneath him but paid her no heed. "In doing so, I'll protect our own land—and I'll do this with or without your blessing."

"Then you will go," the queen said, her voice ringing through the courtyard and beyond, "as General of the Warqueen Abbesses."

She nodded to Ayoob, who approached him, bowed respectfully, and offered him a gift Tahir wouldn't have expected in a hundred lifetimes: the Torc of the Warqueens, which gleamed dully in the noonday sun.

15

She rode a borrowed mare behind Prince Tahir on his stripe-legged stallion. Unlike her mount, his wasn't beautiful, but there was something impudent in his eye, and Shahrazad knew he was wise.

Leading the Warqueen Abbesses around the Amr Mountains to the Land of the Moon, Tahir seemed happier than she'd ever seen him. Or perhaps that was simply the effect of the kiss she'd given him in front of his mother and the entire peerage. Now, his back was straight, and his dark face calm. The torc added to his beauty. The *shitani* should fear his might.

The *shitani* should also fear his army, she thought, casting a glance back at the battalion of Warqueen Abbesses, but God's eyes, what would her father think of an army of women on their identical horses? Bearing their long bows and arrows fletched in the black feathers of the saker falcon, the Warqueen Abbesses looked fierce.

Suddenly his hands went to his head, as if he were in pain.

"Tahir," she said quietly.

"Yes, beloved."

"Is she here? Does the magician approach?" She reined in her mare. "Or is it the demons?"

"The magician." He nodded. "Perhaps this is the time of reckoning."

"Look." She pointed. A figure appeared in the distance, almost too far away to see—but Shahrazad recognized her immediately. It was the magician—Badra—in the form of a woman.

He immediately called the Warqueens to a halt with an efficient hand signal—as though he'd been commanding them his entire life.

"Badra," he said. She watched his thigh muscles tighten around his stallion. "That's her, waiting for us."

And Shahrazad's stomach roiled because she didn't know what to anticipate. She didn't know what to demand. She no longer wanted the curse lifted from her, not now that she could control it. She no longer wanted the tattoo gone from her back. The Raj would ally his army regardless of her suitability. She could no longer demand that the magician call the demons away—because she understood the magician barely controlled them any longer, and Tahir's sister was returned to the throne.

All was set to vanquish the *shitani*.

Tahir turned toward the Warqueen commander, a tall, spare woman with a narrow nose and even narrower eyes. Her hair was pulled tightly against her scalp and tucked into a gray helmet.

"Wait here," he ordered. "If we fail to return before the sun moves one length, continue to the Land of the Moon. You're to report to the Sultan in that case."

"Very well, Prince Tahir," she said.

Tahir reined his horse in next to Shahrazad's, and he held out his hand to her. She took it, and together they galloped toward the magician, spewing thick plumes of desert dust into the air, her horse's hooves pounding in tandem with those of his stallion.

"You," Tahir roared to the magician before his horse fully stopped. "I should kill you on the spot for all the havoc you've caused."

The blond-haired woman merely shrugged at this threat. "You believe it's a weakness, Prince Tahir, but it's actually your strength."

"Don't engage her in conversation, my prince," Shahrazad said. "It only brings tribulation."

"What is?" he asked the magician, perhaps unable to ignore her. Shahrazad wasn't surprised. Neither her father nor the Raj had been able to ignore this magician either. "What's my strength?" he demanded. "Tell me so I may use it against you."

"You're unwillingness to use violence except in the most exceptional circumstances. It is a characteristic you will pass to your children, and they will all become good leaders because of it."

"I have no time for this, Badra," Tahir said.

"Your sister lacks that strength," Badra said, her violet eyes glowing in the afternoon light.

"If you remain in the center of this path," Tahir said, "you'll be trampled beneath the hooves of the Warqueens' mounts."

"I've no fear of the Warqueens, Prince Tahir. It's the *shitani* I dread."

He scoffed. "I'm surprised to hear such drivel from you, given all you've done to make my land and the Land of the Moon vulnerable to their attack."

"Me?" she said, arching an elegant eyebrow and touching her chest with a tapered fingernail.

"Yes, you. Every augury that warned against something, you brought to bear. No man may touch Princess Shahrazad, so a male magician—you—touched her. The Raj may fuck no woman, so he fucked a female magician—you. I needed my sister to prevent the *shitani* invasion, and who kidnapped her? You."

"Save me and I'll save you."

"You'll save nothing," he growled. "We're on our way to re-pulse the demon horde we've seen scrambling toward us. And your actions brought the demons here. We read the books—you woke them."

"The *shitani* would have come anyway. They woke. They'll invade. It's what they do."

"Camelshit. You control them."

"Look at your life before you judge."

"I look at you and judge."

"You think you can control them better than I?"

"Yes!"

"Then do it. Come to me."

"Never," he spat, but the magician wasn't looking at him any longer.

"And you, Princess Shahrazad," Badra added. "You stand there knowing you can fly away at will, to the farthest ends of the earth if you so desire. It is your turn to help me."

"I think not. I'll save my land using more conventional means. You're no model for the kind of person I strive to be."

"Are you certain?"

"Go rule the nine hells, you evil bitch," Tahir interjected.

"But why?" Shahrazad asked the magician. "If you wanted our help, why did you ruin our lives?"

"Your lives were already ruined, tied and bound by the most ridiculous mores." The sun's light changed ever so slightly, and fine lines under the woman's eyes became visible. Shahrazad could see that the magician's forehead wasn't as smooth as she'd believed.

"That is no answer," Tahir snarled, and again he turned away from her.

But Shahrazad paused for a moment. "Oh, Badra," she said, seeing the answer. "Those mores weren't so stupid in the end, were they?" Her voice was just barely louder than the sand blowing over the dunes. "You've had no one for so long—you can't remember the art of giving for others."

"Don't pity me, little princess."

But she did. "You thought we'd flee when our lives became hard—but we didn't."

"You will."

"I don't believe our lives can be more difficult than they are in this moment, Badra," Shahrazad said. "And we're not running."

The magician stepped back, her chin pointed haughtily. "You have no idea. And when you realize you cannot kill every *shitani*, then you will come to me—but it will be too late."

"I'll never replace you," Tahir said.

"Go torment your other candidates," Shahrazad told the magician.

"But Prince Tahir," the magician said. "My demons favor you and you bear no mark." Badra pulled up her billowing ruby skirt to show her beautifully muscled thigh. A snake, much like the one across Shahrazad's back, slithered around and up, disappearing between the magician's thighs.

"I don't want one," Tahir said.

But the magician struck. Badra flew through the air like a dervish. She caught Tahir by the back of his neck and pulled him from his horse. She embraced him then, twining her arms around his neck.

Tahir resisted at first, seemingly oblivious to the long tapered fingernails raking his hair—but then he gave in, melting into her arms, giving himself to the pleasure. His powerful hand wrapped around Badra's neck and pulled her toward him. The kiss wasn't gentle; it was savage.

And Shahrazad hated it.

In that moment, she knew exactly how she felt about the prince. All equivocal feelings were gone, replaced by certainty.

He was hers, and not for one night as the Raj had offered; he was hers first and foremost. He was hers and only hers. Badra's lips did not belong on his.

"Badra," she commanded, kicking her mare so it nearly rammed the couple. "Stop it now." She leaned over and grabbed the magician's shoulder, jerking with all of her strength.

The pair split apart, but it was too late. A snake tattoo wrapped around Tahir's neck, its fanged face posed to strike from his cheek.

"Now," Badra said with a calculated smile. "You're marked like the others."

Tahir wiped his mouth, his expression of disgust unhidden. "I'll never help you, Badra." But his hand ran over the new tattoo like it burned him—as Shahrazad knew it did.

"When you see the *shitani* roiling over your land, you'll change your mind."

"I'll die first—" he started to say. But a dust devil filled the narrow path, and when it cleared, Badra had vanished.

When they galloped into Shahrazad's beloved courtyard, her first thought was panic. They needed soldiers filling the area and spilling into the neighboring desert, but she saw no one. Her ears heard the clanging of no swords, which meant only one thing: the Sultan and the Raj were not prepared for the impending invasion.

As his stallion—Kateb, he'd told her—slowed to a stop, Tahir leaped from his back.

"I need to tell them," she said to him. "I must convince the Sultan, the Raj, and his men to prepare now."

"*Your* men," he corrected.

Her men. She liked the sound of that. "My men, if you insist."

"Wait for me. I'll go with you to your father. He's not to be trusted."

"I can—"

"He wants to behead you, beloved. And the Raj may betray you."

"We don't have time. You must see to your troops. I must see to my father."

"I don't like it."

She shrugged, acknowledging that she didn't like it either but life gave them little choice. "The barracks are on the north side," she told him, adjusting her sandals, which had been tugged loose in the ride. "Your troops will find food and water there. They'll also find soldiers . . . my father's soldiers."

"And no warm welcome."

She shrugged again, knowing it was true. "The Warqueens look capable." Her father's men—her men—would need to bury their arcane opinions of women if they wanted to survive the next two days.

"They can handle it."

"You may meet me in my father's chambers when you're finished here," she said, meeting his gaze directly. The snake tattoo around his neck and across his face made the angular planes of his cheeks even more gorgeous. She paused for a moment and caressed the new scales. "They're very lovely."

"When we were walking back from the oasis and I told you you were smoldering," Tahir said to her, "I had no idea what you were going to change into."

"You knew I was a *pegaz*. What do you mean?" she asked, insecurity stabbing her in her heart. She had crossed the line, been too bossy for his male ego. She should never have looked directly at him.

"I mean this," he said, stepping toward her. He wrapped one powerful palm around the small of her back and the other around the back of her head, and he kissed her right there in her father's courtyard.

She didn't resist. How could she? His kiss tasted like something from a dream—sweet and powerful. She gave her mouth to him, luxuriating in the velvet caress of his lips and tongue.

The glide of his lips over hers made her aware of her breasts, her thighs. Her breasts wanted his touch, his tongue and lips. The molten feeling between her thighs was becoming insistent.

But fear rode in on the waves of surrender. Fear they were running out of time—not fear of discovery. As long as she had her bridle, her head would not end up on a pike, no matter what rules she violated.

"After we vanquish the *shitani*," he said, "will you consent to marry me, Princess Shahrazad?"

"I—"

"No," he said, putting a finger to her lips. "Do not answer me now. You must think on this. Your father may desire your head for this choice. The Raj may desire mine. My mother herself may object."

"I will think on it then," she said. But she knew the answer.

He nodded, a rakish grin on his face. "We'll finish this properly, in a bed of teak and silk."

She nodded, closing her veil over her face in deference to her father. "I'll see you in the Sultan's study."

"Don't let him arrest you or take your head. I have enough demons to kill without him adding to their numbers."

She held up her bridle. "No one will control me again."

He touched her hand and strode toward the commander of the Warqueens as she watched. Tahir, Prince of House Kulwanti, did not appear afraid.

She remembered that bravery as she walked past her father's guards. They didn't try to stop her. They didn't try to question her. In fact, they didn't even acknowledge her.

Which was not right. Shahrazad had never in her life roamed

these halls without an escort, had never walked unchallenged through a guarded entryway. Fear snaked through her stomach.

When she arrived at her father's door, she debated whether she should knock. Duha always had, but she was not her nurse. Marshalling her inner strength, she opened the door and walked through exactly like she was a man.

"Princess Shahrazad," her father said formally, not standing from his cushion. "We've been waiting for you—since you evaded my guards with the help of a strange man, an invisible man."

"Father," she said, rushing toward him. The blue smoke from his *huqqa* coiled around him, obscuring his features. "May God hold you in his eyes, I'm—"

"I'm sorry God has failed to hold you in his eyes," the Sultan said. His own eyes were as sad as she'd ever seen. "Guards!" He clapped twice. "Take her to the prison."

"Father," she said, refusing to acknowledge the fear in her stomach. "You must know that the *shitani* invasion is upon us."

"Take her now."

"But you don't understand," Shahrazad said, stepping away from the guards who eyed her warily. Perhaps the idea that they were to grasp royal flesh—a woman's flesh—unnerved them. "The *shitani*. They're coming. They'll be here tonight or perhaps in the morning—hundreds of them. Thousands! You and the Raj must prepare to fight them."

"How dare you speak to your father in this way," the Raj said. She hadn't seen him clearly in the smoke-filled room, but she saw him now as he leaped from his cushion and approached her.

"Father," she said, falling on her knees before him. "I've always been a dutiful daughter, served you and our land in my thoughts and in my heart and actions—I've seen the demons myself. They're swarming over the Amr Mountains as I speak to you."

"You!" her father roared. "You dare call this land yours when your actions brought these very demons to our doorstep."

Shahrazad shot a glance at the Raj ir Adham, meeting his gaze in bold defiance. If her defiance had brought these demons, his had as well.

"Yes, it was he who told me," the Sultan said, perhaps catching her glance and misinterpreting it. "My spies told me he was to blame for this cursed invasion, but the Raj himself has clarified this point. By your own admission, you've touched a man, succumbed to the temptations of the flesh."

A flash of fear crossed the Raj's broad features. If she mentioned the Raj's penchant for men now—and her father believed her—they'd accompany each other to the Pike Wall. *Rakeb* men were never forgiven.

But Shahrazad understood his choices: it was either her neck or his, and like most people, he'd chosen her neck.

Well, she didn't care. She had her bridle, her freedom.

And if the Sultan beheaded the Raj, they'd have one fewer army at their disposal.

"What you say is true, father," she said, shoulders back and chin high. "I have allowed a man's touch, and I have allowed affection for a man other than you into my heart. Prince Tahir of House Kulwanti is a great ruler, and at great expense to himself, he's brought you an entire regiment of Warqueens to help you battle the encroaching *shitani*."

"I have all the alliance I need with the Raj ir Adham, who's pledged his fidelity to me despite the failure of this marriage."

"No doubt," she said. She looked at the Raj, but he wouldn't meet her eye. "You should both be preparing your armies. Should I inform Prince Tahir that his armies will not be needed?"

"You dare speak to me of matters of which you know nothing." The Sultan had nearly shouted the words, but then his anger fell away. "You'd always been the perfect daughter, Shahrazad. You were always my favorite. What happened?"

"Father." She embraced him, but he remained stony beneath her hands. She took a step back and nodded, knowing there was no way back into his heart. "Did you ask yourself the same question when your tattoo appeared?"

For a moment he stood in silence. She watched the muscles in his forehead freeze, the fine skin around his eyes tighten. Then he broke. "Guards," the Sultan ordered. "Take her away."

The soldiers marched toward her, spears at the ready. This time she didn't resist, not even when they grabbed her arms and touched her flesh.

"Wait," the Sultan said. "Turn her toward me."

For a moment, hope rushed through Shahrazad's blood. Her father had changed his mind!

"I want to be very clear on one thing," he said. "The *klerins* will take your case first thing in the morning, and your head will join Haniyyah's on the Pike Wall."

But Shahrazad refused to be daunted. "As you wish."

True fear still hadn't penetrated her heart, even as the guards marched her through the maze of halls. No doubt, they'd put her in her own bedchamber. Even Haniyyah had been housed in her own bedchamber before her execution.

And once the guards closed her door and locked her inside the safety of her own chambers, she'd slip the bridle over her head and fly away, out the window. She'd find Tahir, and they'd escape. They'd escape the demons and their parents and the wretched magician, and they'd fly over the mountains until her father's treachery was nothing but a memory. She'd done all she could for her father—and her land. She could do no more.

But the soldiers didn't take her to her chambers. Instead, they led her to the bowels of the palace.

"Where are we going?" she asked. "Take me to my chambers!"

But the guards didn't answer, and her mind raced to make sense of this. Then she remembered. Both the Sultan and the Raj knew she'd shift form at sunset—and they were stopping her.

The guards opened a huge gate with a black iron key and locked it behind them. They used a second key to open a smaller door.

"The *shitani* are coming," Shahrazad told them in a desperate attempt to keep her freedom. "They're coming to this palace as we breathe. I myself killed three of them in the desert. Prince Tahir killed one by the library. Who knows how many are already here? If I were you, I'd prepare the men."

But they didn't answer. Instead, they shoved her inside the dark room and slammed the door. She heard the lock click as they turned the key, and then she heard their footsteps clap down the hall toward the larger gate.

She was alone in the smallest, darkest place she'd ever been in her life, and she had no idea how to escape.

As the commander explained in her no-nonsense voice, the Warqueen Abbesses had no interest in sharing quarters with the Sultan's men. Instead, they pitched small tents in the sand outside the palace walls, maximizing the wall's ability to shade them.

"Ah," a man with a fine-boned face said as he approached Tahir. "You've settled your men, then. I'm glad to see it."

The speaker looked so much like Shahrazad that Tahir knew immediately this was the Sultan. "Sire," he said, bowing deeply. "My mother, the Queen Kulwanti, sends her greetings to you. We are glad to assist you in this time of darkness."

"But is it so dark?" a second man asked. Tahir recognized him too, despite his clothing.

"Greetings, Raj ir Adham," Tahir said, bowing almost as deeply to this man, even as he wondered at the game. "You must know it's a dark time. You yourself have seen a *shitani*."

"When did this happen?" the Sultan asked, eyes alert. "When did you see a demon, my friend?"

"I found this rogue skulking through your palace, my lord. And while it's true I saw a demon at this time, who's to say this man didn't bring it himself? He held it in his own hand."

Tahir paused, studied the Raj for a moment. He'd seen the man naked, fucking another man in a land where such things meant death. Was the Raj trying to tell him something, or had he decided Tahir was an enemy to be eradicated by the Sultan? Probably the latter—the magician would do anything to run Tahir and Shahrazad from the comfort of their homes. Why should the magician have treated the Raj any differently.

"Come now, Raj," the Sultan said. "We have a true enemy to fight—the *shitani*. Let's not waste our precious resources battling each other. We need as many allies as we can marshal in these dangerous times."

"Wise words," the Raj said. "My apologies."

"None needed," Tahir said, bowing again. The Sultan's words were wise, but there was something calculated in them. And the magician's warning rang in his head. The magician had said the Raj was not to be trusted—but she'd told so many lies. "May I ask after Princess Shahrazad?" he asked the Sultan. "I believe your devoted daughter sought your counsel. Did she warn you of the demon hordes we saw scrambling this way?"

"She found us," the Sultan said, straightening the sleeve of his embroidered robe. The dark blue of it matched his complexion well, and Tahir assumed that was no accident. "She is dining now, enjoying my finest date-palm wine and goat cheese. She seemed very tired and hungry."

"Yes. Our last hours have been busy," Tahir said, hoping

neither man sensed his fatigue. He hadn't slept since they'd left the oasis, and that seemed like a lifetime ago.

"So we've heard," the Sultan said.

Mentally reviewing the preparations needed to fight this battle in his mind, Tahir said, "This may be our last moment of respite. Shall we use it to make a battle plan?" That he could plan and speak—and think—sent liberating joy to his gut. "Perhaps the commander of the Warqueens has information regarding *shitani* weakness that you lack—or vice versa?"

"A fine idea." The Sultan nodded at this. "Why don't you come to my study?"

"We have little time to spare, my Sultan," Tahir said. "As I'm certain the princess told you, when we flew over the Amr Mountains, we saw thousands of the demons swarming the crags heading this direction. The ground was so thick with *shitani* we couldn't see the earth beneath their claws."

"That does sound dire, but they have some distance to travel, no? And you must be tired and hungry. You cannot command your troops—not even girl troops—without food in your stomach."

Tahir realized he hadn't eaten since the night in the oasis, either. "Very well," he agreed. "Dinner would not go amiss. Please allow me to send for my commander. She should take part in this conversation."

Tahir didn't miss the dyspeptic expression crossing the Raj's face, but the Sultan's expression remained closed. He merely made an accommodating gesture with his hand. "Very well, young prince."

She'd decided to batter the door down with her hooves. She didn't care if the guards heard her. She didn't care if they saw her and came running to stop her. She'd run them down, lash them, pummel them like she had the *shitani* in the desert. Their blood would coat the floor.

Remaining in prison was not a viable option, not while the *shitani* roamed this world unfettered. She would not allow them to swallow the palace children or enthrall the palace men. No woman of the Land of the Moon would tolerate demon tongues lapping their flesh.

She slipped the bridle over her head. The first time she'd done this, she'd felt ridiculous, like a child playing with stable tack. But now, now, the cold metal in her mouth tasted not of iron but of freedom. And her hooves felt like power as they formed. Her tail was a flag, an emblem of her freedom. Her muscles showed her strength; her teeth showed her might.

As her human body gave way to *pegaz* form, the walls crushed in around her. Her *pegaz* form completely filled the small chamber. The dank bricks smashed her wings against her, but she didn't care. She'd changed with her hindquarters facing the door, and that wasn't an accident.

With a powerful kick, she lashed at her prison cell. She wasted no time splintering the heavy old wood, kicking her powerful hind feet into the door like she wanted to kill it.

The voices in her mind began nearly immediately. Even as she pounded away at the door, they chanted at her. *My queen! Come to us! We will love you. We'll adore you, never lock you away. Our queen! Come to us!*

Coming to them was the last thing she wanted to do as she galloped down the narrow hall. She rounded the corner to the large gate where she assumed the guards stood. She'd batter down that gate and anything else that stood in her way.

But the soldiers had a different idea—they waited for her, ropes swirling.

My queen! We love you, my queen.

She reared onto her hind legs with an angry squeal. Her front hooves sought bone and flesh, but it was no use. The ropes lashed out and snared her forelegs. Another rope snaked insidiously around her neck. She leaped back, but the guards pulled the ropes tight, so tight she couldn't breathe. She couldn't run.

Quick as a night jackal pouncing on a hare, they'd tied her legs together and stuffed her head into a grain sack. She couldn't move, couldn't see. She inhaled barley dust and began to cough.

"The Sultan said she'd try this," she heard one guard say.

Leave your vicious land, my queen! Join us. Come to us! We love you.

"Save your words and help me drag her heavy ass into the next cell."

"She doesn't have a heavy ass—she *is* a heavy ass."

Together the two men pulled her over the cold flagstone, carelessly bruising her tender flesh. With much grunting, they slid her into an even smaller chamber, knocking her hip on the iron doorjamb.

They stepped on her withers to get out of the cell. They crushed her tail and her wings. But that didn't cause as much despair as the sounds they made. She heard clanging as they closed the door—it was iron.

Despair washed through her. Even if she could free herself of these cruel ropes, get the sack off her head, what could she do? Not even her powerful hooves could batter this metal door down.

Our queen! the voices said. *We will save you.*

Leave me alone! If she'd used her human voice to say those words, they would have left her mouth as a shriek.

But we'll never leave you, she heard. *We love you too much. Your womb calls to our cocks. Come to us!*

16

"Flight would help," the Warqueen commander told the Sultan as he wiped nonexistent crumbs from his lips with a silk napkin. She herself did not eat, and no one invited her to do so. "Shahrazad can fly. Use her."

The Raj looked at the Sultan at these words, his blond braid coiled around his shoulder. To Tahir, both men looked worried.

"My daughter is too precious to risk in warfare," the Sultan replied after a prolonged pause. "Too precious."

The Warqueen said nothing, and Tahir knew how she felt. The truth of her words was so obvious that no further explanation should be necessary.

And yet it appeared the Sultan needed to hear them.

"My lord," Tahir said, replacing his goblet carefully on the table. "The *shitani* cannot harm her as she soars above them. They have no projectile weapons—their weaponry lies in their ability to enthrall their victims, and I've found that requires both touch and eye contact—books from your own library confirm this."

"He's been in your library," the Raj pointed out.

But the Sultan didn't seem to care. "As both you and your

Warqueen come from a land where women are not loved enough to merit protection, I understand that this is a difficult concept for you to grasp—but I cannot permit my daughter to parade herself as an absurd flying horse for all to see."

"Even if it protects all those who see her? Even if it prepares your men, lets them know the location and timing of the enemy?"

"Even so."

To control his anger, Tahir took a date, let its soft sweetness explode over his tongue. He believed he knew Shahrazad well enough to guess that she'd sacrifice this small portion of her safety and dignity for the safety of her land. "Perhaps this is a decision we should leave to Princess Shahrazad," he suggested.

"Nonsense!" the Raj said. "A woman cannot decide such a thing."

Tahir was pleased again with his Warqueen. Her face remained implacable, and she remained silent. "I know," Tahir said in what he hoped was a calming voice, "that women aren't often consulted in your land. But fate has touched your daughter."

"Someone touched her," the Raj said, almost under his breath as he allowed the servant to put more jasmine rice onto his dish. The words sent alarm racing through Tahir. What had these two done with Shahrazad?

"I would like to see her," Tahir said, standing to make his point. The Warqueen stood as well, her hand on the hilt of her sword. "You might consider me a paranoid man, but I feel a sudden concern for her health."

"Now, Prince Tahir," the Sultan said, his dark eyes peering at him, "there's no need to be hasty. Finish your dinner, and we'll go to the women's quarters if you wish. You'll see her there, dining with her cousins and her beloved nurse."

"There's no time to waste. We need Shahrazad now. If nothing else, she's a resource we can't afford to squander."

The Sultan gave a big sigh. "You may lead your inhuman women against the *shitani*," he said, glancing at the Warqueen.

"But you will never command my daughter—or me." He flicked a hand toward the chamber guards, and they withdrew their swords. "Now, sit and eat."

Tahir looked at his Warqueen and realized she asked a question with her eyes: Should we kill them? Between the two of them, they might be able to do it. Kill the Sultan and the Raj first, and the guards might flee.

But then what? The Land of the Moon would lack a leader, and the Raj's troops would rally to a camel before they'd rally to Tahir and the Warqueens.

No, to defeat the *shitani*, they needed to work together.

He sat.

Come to us, my queen.

She slid her nose toward her knees. She could almost reach. She cocked her head and tried again. If only she could get this bridle off, she could loosen the ropes.

We love you. The voices sounded stronger now, thicker. More demons were chiming in together for their wretched song in her head.

Yes, she answered them, rage roiling through her heart. *I love you, my pets. Come to me, and I will do as you ask. I will bear your king and teach him to rule.*

You will love us! You will spread your legs for us! You will give us your womb!

Come to me, she said in her mind. *Come to me, and I will be yours.*

Be ours!

But send only your best specimens. Send only your lords, and send no more than three.

Only three? But we all adore you. We all want to taste you and raise you to our dais. And we are many more numerous than three!

But you endanger yourselves, she said. *I cannot have your*

*deaths on my conscience. Send no more than three. Then we
shall be free to take over the Land of the Moon.*
    And then the Land of the Sun.
    And perhaps the entire world.

The opulence of the Sultan's study would have impressed his
mother, Tahir thought, although she would not have approved
of the liberal use of the *huqqa* so close to a time of important
decisions. Thick *khansari* perfume filled the chamber.

The Sultan pointed to an elaborate map that filled most of a
spacious wall. "They can come from any of these three mountain passes."

"Which is perfect," the Raj said. "Since we have three armies.
We'll place one army at each pass."

"We could put all our armies in one place if we knew which
direction the *shitani* were going to use," Tahir's Warqueen said
in her dry voice.

"I've said I will not endanger my daughter, and I won't."
The Sultan slammed his fist against his thigh. "I also refuse to
repeat myself yet again—for a woman."

"This is a wasted discussion," Tahir said, rising from the embroidered pillow to stalk around the room. "Not only is the
Warqueen correct, but all those passes lead to one place—here.
If we don't stop the demons at the pass, we'll fight them all in
your courtyard and in your palace. You couldn't possibly believe that a good strategy."

The Raj shook his head in disagreement. "It won't happen
that way."

"Why not?" It took all of his self-control not to yell. "Look
at the layout of those passes and valleys. They will funnel every
single *shitani* into this very basin. That is the only logical prediction."

"Here, young prince," the Sultan said, trying to pass the
huqqa to him. "Smoke. You'll feel better."

"No, thank you. I'd like my wits about me." He looked at the map again. "Do you really mean to endanger your children? The women whom you claim to love above all other things?"

The two rulers looked at him blankly. Finally, the Sultan said, "Our children are not endangered by this."

Tahir shook his head. "And you accuse those of my land of not loving their daughters enough."

"Our outriders assure us we have at least until noon tomorrow."

"And are the *shitani* so predictable?"

"They're not human," the Raj said, as if explaining something to a very simple child.

"That's exactly my point," Tahir shot back. "We don't know what we're fighting. No one has battled *shitani* in eleven generations."

"Our guest seems to feel strongly about this," the Sultan said to the Raj.

"He feels strongly about too many things." The blond man muttered this almost under his breath.

"If his feelings are so strong, perhaps we should respect him. Let us go prepare our armies," the Sultan said, his eyes red from the *khansari*. "Perhaps it is time."

She heard the three demons chuckling in her head as they approached. She tasted their thoughts, their desires. She saw through their eyes.

We love you, our queen! she heard. *We're almost to you.* And they were; they were in the hall now, sneaking past the guards— just as she would in a moment or two, if all went well.

And I love you, my little darlings, she said to them. *Come to me. Free me. Take the key from the guard.* She filled her mind with an image of the key, the heavy weight of it. *I hope you're strong enough, my darlings. I hope you're worthy of your new Dark Queen.*

We can do it, they cried, and they did. She tasted the thought of a demon as it stole a key. She saw the dull gleam of metal, just as the demon saw it. The guard didn't know, hadn't seen the green hand reach up and wrap overlong fingers around his key ring. The guard hadn't felt the weight leave his hip. The guard didn't hear the demonic cheer inside her head as the *shitani* capered down the hall. *We did it*, they cried. *We are worthy of you!*

As she heard their small feet scurry down the hall toward her, she slipped off the bridle. In three heartbeats, she lay huddled in human form on the cold floor, but the bridle was hot in her hands—just where she needed it.

"My darlings," she crooned. They wouldn't be able to speak in her head so easily now that she was no longer in *pegaz* form. Oh, God's eyes, she hoped they wouldn't be speaking in her head at all. "My darlings," she said quietly as she stood. "I'm here. I'm waiting for you, my lovelies."

The key turned in the lock. How they managed to reach it with their short height, she didn't know. She didn't really care. But as the three of them swarmed in to her, she bent down to them, let them scurry up her arms like large kittens. "You're so lovely," she said, kissing each of them on their cold green heads. "So lovely."

And, ignoring the dagger Tahir had given her, she tightened her grip on her bridle.

The creatures on her arms cackled and lay their ears flat against their heads. What might be smiles crossed their thin lips, and they . . . they were almost cute.

Hardening her heart, she stroked a warty back. "I am yours," she said.

The creature on her shoulder caressed her cheek with its lizardlike fingers. Its eyes glowed orange as it met hers, and then it cast its dark spell.

In a heartbeat, her blood turned thick with desire—like it had when Tahir had kissed her in the courtyard, like it had when Tahir's hot tongue lathed her breasts in the Flower Taker's chambers.

Her lips craved Tahir's, as did her breasts and thighs—her core. She imagined his smell so clearly it was like his arms were wrapped around her, her nose buried in his shoulder. She imagined his face so well she could almost trace the curve of his cheekbone, the slight hook of his aquiline nose, the glory of his dangerous new tattoo. She imagined his skin and hair so well she could almost feel the warmth of his skin beneath her palm. She could almost feel the silky weight of his hair as she brushed the dark strands away from his face.

She wanted him to fill her, to complete her.

"I am yours," she said to him, knowing he was nothing more than an illusion brought about by the dark *shitani* magic. "Lick me."

And they did. She knew their overlong fingers were sliding her clothing from her. She knew their alien skin slid over hers. But it didn't feel that way. Instead, she felt Tahir's warm fingers undress her. His warm lips caressed her shoulders. His cock pressed against her thigh, and his hand slid through her hair.

"Oh," she said as his lips traced the curve of her ear. "I love you, Tahir. Where are you?"

Our queen! she heard in her head. *We love you. Let us give you our seed!*

Shahrazad wanted to cry. She'd thought they wouldn't be able to invade her mind when she was in human form, at least not yet, not so easily. But they could.

With dread in her heart, she realized that they'd already scaled the Amr Mountains. The demons were already invading her land.

Lick me, she said, and if she sounded curt, they didn't seem to notice. *My toes crave your tongues.*

Our seed, they countered. *You need our seed. Your toes don't need us.*

But they want you.

And by God's own eyes, she wasn't lying. As their tongues slid erotically over her ankles and wrists she desired their spell. It was like *heit* coursing through her blood. It was like the *khansari* she'd smoked with the Flower Taker.

Except it wasn't. It was more.

As her hand grasped the cold metal of the bit, she craved more. *My toes first*, she managed. *My hands. My neck, my breasts . . .*

Breasts, they agreed. *So delicious. So full. So firm. Think of the milk they'll make for our new king!*

For an instant, she saw Tahir's face, his eyes locked on hers and loaded with intention, with love. He smiled for an instant, and the sides of his eyes crinkled. She melted into the delicious brown of them. She melted into his arms. *And then your seed . . .* she said. *And then I want your seed.*

The Warqueens were impressive, Tahir knew. Even the Sultan would have to agree. As they rode in formation, their horses moved in perfect synchrony, as if they were linked with their minds. One left front foot rose, and all such feet rose. One rear right, all rear rights. Each woman wore an implacable expression and identical uniforms.

Beside them, just outside the palace walls, the Raj ir Adham's army galloped their horses in crazy circles, shouting and yelling and sending the dust swirling. They swung their spears and scimitars above their heads, shaking them as they galloped. Some of the men threw their spears with mighty force into the sand dunes, wasting them.

"Look at them," the Raj said, admiration clear in his voice. He rode an overly muscled dun horse with a beautiful head.

The creature's lines bespoke a noble lineage. "They thirst for battle."

"Prince Tahir," his commanding Warqueen said to him with a bow as she interrupted. "Since the *pegaz* cannot help us, may I have your permission to send out two riders? Perhaps they can determine if the *shitani* have arrived."

He nodded. "If your riders find them," Tahir instructed, "don't look them in the eye. Don't let them touch your riders. That's how they enthrall their victims."

"Very well," she said, and she started to ride back.

"Wait," he said.

She rode back toward him.

"I'm going to insist now that the Sultan release Princess Shahrazad," he said so only she could hear. Over the whooping of the Raj's men, that wasn't difficult. "Please send two warriors—I doubt he'll acquiesce."

"I'll send the two best."

He nodded, and she left.

Within heartbeats, two Warqueens rode toward him through the pack of yelling men. "Have you been apprised?" he asked, and they nodded as one. "Then let's find the Sultan of the Land of the Moon."

"He's on the far side of his courtyard, Prince," the darker skinned Warqueen said.

"Lead the way."

And they did, bringing him through the raucous soldiers to the Sultan.

"My lord," he said, Kateb prancing proudly beneath him.

"Yes, young prince." His own bay horse looked as fast as the wind.

"I must insist that I see your daughter now."

"But . . ." The Sultan held out his elegant hand, indicating the thousands of soldiers. "We're about to ride to war."

"And yet I must be assured of her safety."

"You doubt the safety of my palace?"

"With humble apologies, I've seen what you do to recalcitrant women. I've seen Haniyyah's head—your own niece's head—on your Pike Wall, and although your daughter seeks nothing but the future safety of her land, I fear for her."

"I won't tolerate such impertinence," he said, reining in his horse until it pranced in place. "I won't stand it. I—"

"Sire," one of the Sultan's men shouted. "The demons! They're here!"

"I want Princess Shahrazad released right now."

But the man ignored him. "Attack!" The Sultan shouted with all the strength of a younger man. "Ride on and attack!" He galloped off, leaving Tahir in his cloud of dust.

Tahir turned toward his two soldiers. "Go inside the palace, and find Princess Shahrazad."

"How do we find her?" one asked.

Tahir ran his hand through his hair. "The palace guards will know. Choke one until he tells you."

Their tongues hypnotized her, filled her with a sleepy sexual energy. They wrapped around every part of her body until she was lost to herself. When her half-closed eyes focused enough to see, she saw . . . nothing. No skin. No braids tumbling over her shoulder. No tanzanite in her belly button. They'd lapped her until she was soaked, from both their juices and her own.

Which meant the time was now. Now.

Now! a *shitani* cried. *Now, we fill you with our seed.*

The floor beneath her back and thighs was no longer cold. It burned with her heat. *Yes,* she answered. *Fill me.*

Long fingers grabbed her thighs and tugged. *Finally we can enter! We can enter!*

Yes, she answered. *Enter.*

The weight of Tahir's dagger still rested at her hip, but that wasn't the weight she sought. She sought the bridle, and her fingers brought the bit to her mouth. The coppery taste of the iron filled her mouth, as cleansing as cool, pure water from a well.

But she could see their green cocks. By God's own eyes, all three of them were planning on fucking her at once. *We love you*, they cried. *Our Dark Queen, our Black Mother, we love you!*

Before they could penetrate her, before their long, green cocks could pollute her womb, she changed.

Our queen! one cried as her expanding equine form squashed it flat against the flagstone floor. *Save us! What is happening? Save us!*

But she would not.

Sharp pain attacked her invisible wings. Was it demon teeth or the crushing walls? She didn't care. Instead, she barreled out the door they'd opened, demon spit dripping off the tips of her wings. She squashed a second *shitani* beneath her hooves. The third clung to her back, but only for a moment. She scraped it off on the door frame and then pummeled it with her hooves. Not one of them managed as much as a squeal in their death throes.

"What was that?" she heard a guard ask.

"I don't know. Get the ropes ready in case it's the princess again."

"She can't knock down that iron door."

"Well, I heard something."

Shahrazad stood silent as the soldiers retrieved more ropes. But then they walked around the turn into her hallway. On invisible legs she raced toward them with the speed of the Sultan's fastest courser, wings tensed and outstretched.

Her feathered appendages hit them in the chest like battering rams, knocking them to the ground, gasping. But she wasn't finished.

When she reached the end of the corridor, she spun around, waiting for the men to stand. She'd crush them beneath her hooves if necessary, but if they left on their own accord, so much the better.

"What . . . was that?" one of the soldiers asked the other.

"Can't . . . breathe."

"You think this is what happened to Khufu?" the first soldier asked, slowly climbing to his feet. "Before the *shitani* disemboweled him?"

"You see . . . *shitani*?"

"I don't see anything," the first soldier said. "But something knocked me right on my ass—and you, too. And why does the place suddenly smell like gardenias?"

"My granny used to tell me that *shitani* smelled of gardenias."

"Why would they smell like—"

Shahrazad screamed, using parts of her vocal chords no horse had ever used. The eerie sound pierced the brick walls and echoed down the hall, making bits of adobe fall from the ceiling.

"I'm getting out of here," the first soldier said, his voice clearly shaking.

"I'm going with you."

For good measure, she ran down the hall again, screaming like some supernatural being. She held her wings higher so that when she passed the men, they felt the breeze—but they saw nothing.

And by the time she reached the opposite end of the hallway, they were gone.

Which was a good thing. Because when she inhaled, she smelled *shitani*—thousands of them. And she heard them in her head. Not their voices—no, she heard their feet scrambling over palace walls. She heard teeth gnashing. She heard them pouring through the small, barred windows into this very corridor.

Collecting her hooves beneath her, she ran like lightning through the summer sky, praying to God that he held her dear in his eyes even as her father didn't—because if the soldiers had closed that huge gate locking the prison off from the rest of the castle, she was doomed.

But she needn't have worried. The gate stood wide open, and Shahrazad ran under the arch, the pounding of her hooves echoing the pounding of her heart.

As she galloped through the corridors toward the main gate, her wings brushed against the walls. She ducked her head to get through some of the doorways, but they all stood open. Where were her father's guards?

As she entered the palace's main entryway with its graceful stairs leading high into the minarets, she found two Warqueens, fierce with their swords drawn. One held the soldiers who'd been guarding her.

She needed to warn them, tell them to leave before the *shitani* poured down the hall and swarmed them like evil locusts. What if they flooded the married women's chambers? The children would be slaughtered.

"You'll tell me exactly which cell she was locked in, you puss-ridden camel cunt," one of the Warqueens was saying to the Sultan's soldier.

"Don't make me go in there!" the soldier pleaded. "The *shitani*! The *shitani*!"

"It's by order of Prince Tahir, you blubbering anus." Neither Warqueen Abbess seemed perturbed by the idea of meeting a demon, although the sound of the demons' claws clattering over the flagstone rang in both her head and her equine ears.

Hating the loss of time, she stopped and rubbed off her bridle. "Warqueens, run!" she told the soldiers even before the transformation was complete. "It is I, Princess Shahrazad, and I am safe, but *shitani*—thousands of them—are coming this way."

"If that's true, if you are safe, where are you?" one of the Warqueens asked.

"I'm invisible, as are some of the demons. Their spit smells like gardenias and it renders invisibility. Now run!"

"I'm not running until I see you."

Shahrazad ran toward the tenacious woman and grabbed her shoulders. "I am here. Here! Now go! Lock the married women's gate and protect it. All the children are inside those chambers."

"I think we should listen to her," said the Warqueen in her grasp.

"Good idea," said the Sultan's man. "Let's all flee."

"Not so quickly, vermin," the Warqueen said. "You'll show me the gate for the children's area."

"Where is Prince Tahir?" Shahrazad asked. "Is he safe? Did he rally the troops against the demons?"

"He's working with both the Sultan and the Raj, and each has his army," the second Warqueen said. "He was concerned for your well being, though. The commander wanted you on the battlefield to tell us where the demons were, but the Sultan wouldn't have anything to do with it."

Because he was too interested in chopping off my head, Shahrazad thought. But she only said, "Very well. Leave now. I will find him."

"As an invisible, flying horse, I imagine everyone will want you out there," the first Warqueen said. "May God hold you in his eyes."

Beneath him, Kateb skittered left as a demon leaped toward them, its angry hiss filling the air despite the overwhelming noise, the cries of pain and the clanging of swords. The *shitani* missed Tahir's shoulder, landing on a Warqueen's horse instead.

Her chestnut horse broke formation, and her sisters attacked the creature before it could enthrall the rider.

The fighting techniques of the Sultan's men didn't help them. Three strides in front of him, he watched a demon leap from a rock and land on a soldier's back. His horse bolted and bucked, but no one noticed, not even as the demon sank its brass hooks into a soldier's lip and kick him forward, jabbing vicious spurs into the man's sides. Within heartbeats, the soldier was the demon's creature—the soldier had his sword drawn and was poised to slice a comrade.

Tahir rushed forward, still trying to part the crowd to stop the man. He was too late, but it didn't matter. Black fletching shining in the setting sun, a Warqueen's arrow found the demon first. Blood pumped from the creature's neck to the sand. The *shitani* screamed like a jackal, and the man it'd been riding slid to the ground like someone had pulled out his spine.

Tahir would have gone to retrieve the man if he could have—perhaps save him—but two demons swarmed the soldier next to him. Tahir lashed out, lopping two demon heads off before the man could fend for himself.

"Thank you," the Sultan's man said. "I have your back if you have mine."

"Very well."

Beneath him, Kateb snaked his head out and grabbed a demon from the ground. As Tahir slashed another demon off a foot-soldier's neck, his stallion crushed a *shitani* skull with his massive teeth.

Even as the melee enveloped him, Tahir cursed. If the Sultan and the Raj had listened to him, they could have cut the demons off at the pass, before they swarmed this area surrounding the palace and the palace courtyard itself. So many more men would die this way.

Slash. Another demon head rolled away. Crunch. Kateb killed another. *Pffft.* A Warqueen's arrow penetrated another *shitani's* chest. *Slash.* His sword flew and hot blood splattered him. *Dear God, hold me in your eyes,* he thought. Would this never end? *Crunch.* Kateb smashed something beneath his oversized hooves.

Two demons landed on the man next to Tahir, plucking out the eyes of the man's horse before the man could even raise his weapon. *Slash.* Tahir's sword separated the demon's head from its body. *Slash.* The second demon fell. A third *shitani* landed on Kateb himself, who jumped and twisted until the thing flew through the air. The wise old horse caught the creature and crushed it just as Tahir's sword flew from his sweat-slicked hand.

Tahir drew his second sword, and none too soon. Next to him a demon jerked the brass hooks it had sunk in a soldier's nostrils, and the soldier was drawing his weapon on him. Tahir cut off the *shitani's* head, and the soldier collapsed to the ground.

Was it his imagination, or were the demons getting thicker? No one individual was hard to kill, but the sun was setting and there seemed to be no end in sight. *Slash. Crunch.* And where were the Warqueens? *Slash.* Blood squirted into his face, and when he wiped it away he found a demon sitting on his lap, reaching for his face, its orange eyes locked on his.

Love me, he heard.

Kateb would have none of it. He bucked and twisted like a colt and the creature went flying. This time, Tahir managed to keep hold of his weapon, but Kateb landed on something—a corpse most likely, but perhaps a demon's head. For a heartbeat, the noble horse was on his knees. When he regained his feet, Tahir could tell immediately that something was wrong. The best horse ever born had hurt his foreleg.

For the first time, he wondered if he shouldn't have traded places with the magician.

* * *

Carried on huge invisible wings, Shahrazad flew over the bloody mess that had replaced the dunes around her palace. Everywhere she looked, she saw weapons and bodies and death. The coppery scent of blood filled her nostrils.

You could have stopped this, a voice in her head told her. It didn't belong to the demons; it belonged to her conscience.

The Warqueens were the exception to the decimation; their arrows stopped the demons before the demons touched them. The soldiers near the Warqueens fared well too. Sadly, none of them were positioned near the main palace gate, and demons poured into her courtyard. Toward the children.

She winged over the Warqueens one more time. Where was Tahir? He could stop this.

As she flew around the palace's perimeter looking for him, she saw something that made her heart freeze. *Shitani* were streaming into the back entry. If they made it past the few remaining guards, they'd penetrate the women's quarters.

For a moment an image of women and children filled with brass hooks and ridden by green monsters filled her mind. If she had taken the magician's place . . . No, she told herself. Manipulating people to peace wasn't the answer. She'd stop these demons by honest means. And she'd stop them now.

She swooped down on her invisible wings toward the nearest Warqueen and snatched a rein from the Warqueen's hand. Without remorse she dragged the warrior's reluctant horse away from its herd, toward the breach in their line. If the Warqueens knew about the breach, they'd stop the *shitani*.

But the warrior's horse refused to budge, not for some invisible monster, and the Warqueen agreed with her steed. She slashed blindly at Shahrazad. And with an equine cry of dismay Shahrazad released the horse.

She circled the battle below, looking for anyone to help. And found Tahir! He commanded the Sultan's men in their assault against the *shitani*. As he called to a soldier, she caught a glance of his face and he looked mighty. The striking snake on his face looked like it belonged there, like it'd been there his entire life. His coppery torc gleamed.

She swooped down toward his horse and grabbed the rein. For a moment, Kateb snorted, and Shahrazad could almost hear him thinking. And then he shook his head free and began to follow her, muscling his way through the demon-ridden crowd, snatching *shitani* skulls where he could as Tahir cut them down with his sword.

"Shahrazad!" he called. "Is that you?"

She could only neigh in response.

Within moments, they reached the breach in the wall. Hundreds of *shitani* were trying to funnel through it now, but Tahir and his horse seemed undaunted. Blood splattered his face so that it looked like it dripped from his snake's fangs. "Warqueens!" he shouted, his mightiness making her heart ache in pride. "To me!"

Shahrazad didn't think he could be heard over the death cries, the grunts, and the clanking weapons. She didn't think he could be heard over the gnashing of demon teeth. But the lead Warqueen heard, and she rallied to his side, easily falling in under his command. Others followed.

Soaked in the light of the setting sun, the Warqueens, Tahir, Kateb, and Shahrazad became a *shitani*-killing machine. Shahrazad landed and followed Kateb's example, smashing with hooves and crushing with teeth, dealing death to the forsaken demons in a way not remotely possible in woman form, not even with her wicked dagger.

Demon blood coated her legs and face, her chest and withers. Blood coated her tongue, but she didn't care. She'd killed tens of demons, perhaps even hundreds. She smashed yet another beneath her hooves and pulled one from Tahir's shoulder with her teeth. A Warqueen's arrow pierced it before she could toss it down. When she looked up for the next *shitani*, she saw . . . no more.

She whirled around, seeking the next demon, hungry for its skull. Her hooves longed to smash and pummel. But all she saw was Tahir's blood-splattered face looking at her across the sea of dead demons. Two Warqueens lay in the dust at their feet, and Kateb was holding a demon, its dead corpse dangling from his teeth.

Suddenly a new wave of *shitani* was upon them, pouring in from the dunes toward the passage leading to the women and their children.

Shahrazad didn't stop to think. She pulled demons from the back of Kateb and from the Warqueens' mounts. She crushed them underfoot and crunched them between her teeth. Once she glanced up to see Tahir slicing off three demon heads with one swoop just as another landed on his back. She tried to lurch to his rescue, but a *shitani* landed on her head, right between her ears.

Unnerved, she shook her head. The demon clung tenaciously, wrapping its long fingers around her ears and its long toes around her headstall. She lowered her head and shook again.

My queen! she heard. Her head had been free of their voices for so much of the battle that this call brought her up short. *We will have you, my queen, whether you desire it or not.*

You won't! she cried, tossing her head and bucking like a wild-caught horse.

We will, it said, wrapping its fingers around the headstall next to its toes. *We will, and we'll do it now.*

With those words, it yanked the headstall from her head, and within moments, she'd regained her human form—her helpless, soft human form.

"Help!" she cried as the *shitani* scurried up her leg. She grabbed her dagger and slashed. The demon fell to the sand writhing, but another took its place, scurrying up her leg like a rat. "Tahir, help me!" The sound of war buried her cry.

You need no help, the demon cackled. *You have us!*

She sliced at the *shitani*, but it ducked out of the way and scuttled to her shoulder. "Help me!"

Just look at me, my queen, the thing crooned. It ran a loving tongue over her cheek. *And love me as I love you.*

I won't, she said, but its orange eyes burned into hers, and its long fingers pulled her violet riding pants from her hips. All around her Warqueens fought other demons, and no one noticed her. "Tahir!" she called. "Tahir!"

Lay here, my queen. Forget your Prince Tahir. He is occupied. Let me be your prince. Let me be your Impregnator.

And God help her, she obeyed. Ignoring the thrashing, she lay in the sand. A Warqueen's horse nearly stepped on her head, but a demon appeared just in time. It lost its head to a sword, but the demon wrapped around her neck cackled in deep satisfaction.

No time for niceties now, my queen. Just spread your legs. Let me have you.

And she did. She had no choice.

Just one taste before I plant my seed, it said. It scuttled back down her and extended its vile red tongue. The hot length of it traveled up her thigh, toward that most sacred spot.

And then the demon's head exploded from its body.

"My apologies, Princess," Tahir said with a small bow. At least she assumed it was Tahir from his voice. "I tried to arrive more quickly." His face was so painted with blood that he could have been anybody, but the tenderness in his hand as he reached for hers and pulled her to his feet was uniquely his.

"Thank you," she said, feeling naked and vulnerable in this unclothed female form. Quickly, she retrieved her riding pants, refusing to acknowledge her embarrassment of losing them to the demons. "May I have your dagger? I seem to have lost mine."

He laughed. It was a ragged sound, but it was a laugh. "You've no need," he said. "They're all dead."

"Who's dead?" He couldn't mean the demons.

But he did. With exhaustion etched in his movement, he waved a tired arm around the dunes. Shahrazad looked around the area in amazement. Tahir was right. The only *shitani* she saw were corpses.

The Warqueens and soldiers seemed equally at a loss. "We did it," one of the women said, disbelief in her voice. "I thought—" She took off her gray helmet and ran her hand through her short-cropped hair, which was soaked with sweat and blood. "I mean, I didn't think—"

"I thought you were amazing," one of the Sultan's soldiers said to her, his voice husky with fatigue—or perhaps emotion. "I've never seen such fighting as your regiment showed. Without you, we would have lost the day."

The commander of the Warqueen Abbesses nodded regally, the bone-white moonlight gleaming off her dark features. "Thank you. Your men fought valiantly as well."

"Is it over?" one of the Raj's men asked. "Are they gone forever?"

No one answered, and a strange silence filled the courtyard. "I believe they are gone," Shahrazad finally said. "I hear no more of their voices in my head."

Suddenly, a huge dust devil rode over the dunes, stirring plumes of dust and throwing *shitani* corpses like they were made of parchment.

"God's eyes," a soldier swore. "What is that?"

"Badra," Tahir said, pulling Shahrazad next to him. His arms felt strong, but she knew—they weren't strong enough to protect her from the magician.

She'd thought the magician would vanish as the united armies slaughtered the last demon, but it wasn't so. Badra had come to collect her dark payment.

17

_____

"Who among you bears my tattoo?" the blond woman asked, shaking sand from her luxurious red cape.

Nothing but silence met her, a silence made more eerie by the fact that battle cries still rang through Tahir's head.

"Come now," she chided, striding directly toward him— and Shahrazad. "You cannot hide from me. I know whom I've touched. Speak up, if you please. And even if you don't."

"Badra," he said, "I know what you want, but you won't find it here. No one will help you."

She shook her head so that the full moon rising behind her cast strange shadows on the dunes before her. "Prince Tahir, in due time you will thank me for all I've done for you. But mankind requires a magician, and I am finished with the task."

"I don't trust you, Lady Casmiri, Badra, Badr—whatever you're calling yourself in this moment."

"I don't ask for trust. I ask for help. I've managed the _shitani_ for twenty generations, and I want to stop. This duty belongs to someone else. I can no longer control these demons."

"Your control of them is no longer needed," Tahir said, his

words filling the night. "We've killed them. Together, we've slaughtered every last one."

"And perhaps we have enough resources to slaughter one more," the Sultan added, walking toward her as he pulled his sword from its bloodied sheath. "You."

Silence filled the dunes as the exhausted fighters waited for a reaction.

And then the magician laughed. She laughed like she'd lost her mind, like no shred of humanity remained in her heart. "Oh, my naïve innocents," she said, "the *shitani* are not dead. They're not vanquished."

"Then what lies before you?" Tahir demanded. "Figments of our collective minds?"

"Oh, no," Badra said, her blond hair gleaming in the moonlight. "These corpses are as real as you are, my handsome prince. But they are but the merest fraction of the number rushing toward you."

"I do not believe your lies," the Sultan said. "You weave them like a spider weaves it webs."

"Then listen, dearest Sultan," the magician demanded. "All of you who bear evidence of my touch, listen. Not with your ears but with your minds. Do you hear them calling? Do the voices of the *shitani* not grow louder in your thick skulls even as we stand here?"

"I hear them," Shahrazad said quietly to him. And a lance of fear stabbed his gut. The princess always showed the most sensitivity to their calls, and these human warriors were nearly spent. They couldn't battle the demons again, not without rest and food.

"I do not believe you," the Sultan said again, but his words quavered this time, and Tahir knew he'd heard the demons.

"You," the magician said, pointing at the Raj ir Adham.

"Me?" To Tahir, the man looked terrified by her attention.

Badra swung the tip of her cape, and the Raj ir Adham flew

through the air, landing on the sand between Shahrazad and Tahir. "It's your turn to manipulate," the magician said. "You wear my tattoo, and you've proven yourself capable."

"Capable?"

"Yes, capable. What does the Sultan believe about his daughter, thanks to your rotten tongue? What do you know to be the truth?" The magician morphed into her male form. Her small breasts gave way to a wiry chest, and her face lost that soft look. Her long gold hair didn't fall out, but it changed to short, dark stubble. And he smiled, something lascivious and threatening. "I granted your heart's desire," Badr said to the Raj. "Now you must grant mine."

"Yours?"

"Yes," Badr said, walking toward the Raj with all the coiled power of a tiger. Badr grabbed the Raj's cock over his loose clothing. "You liked our trysts. You loved them."

"That's not—" Tahir saw the abashed expression on the man's face, and he realized this supposed ruler had sacrificed Shahrazad's reputation to save his own. He would have seen Shahrazad's head on the Pike Wall for his selfishness—just as Badra had predicted. "You'll get me beheaded, you perverted creature. You were never my heart's desire."

The magician looked down at the hardened cock. "And the people of your land name me the queen of lies." She pushed him away. "You're too weak to take my place." Badr morphed back into feminine form. Tahir realized that this woman's form must be the magician's true form—if such a thing existed.

Come to me, he heard in his mind. The voice was faint—but clear. And it sent that fear through him. What would happen if he killed the magician? Would the demons vanish with her? He didn't think so.

In fact, he was beginning to believe the words he'd read in the ancient tomes.

"And you?" the magician demanded, pointing her finger at

the Sultan. Like the Raj, invisible hands seemed to lift him, speed him toward his daughter, and dump him in the sand.

"What rule did you break to get your tattoo, father?" Shahrazad asked. "I've been wondering since I learned of it. Have you done something that would land your head on the Pike Wall as I have? Did you seek forgiveness and understanding, or did you try to hide it? Did you earn that tattoo in a rush of selfishness, or did your heart long for—"

"Silence, daughter!" The Sultan might have seemed more intimidating if fine grains of pale sand weren't plastered to his forehead and his white turban wasn't stained and askew. "You've no right to question your father!"

"But she's earned the privilege," the magician said. "Every sacrifice she's made, she's made for you, for the Land of the Moon."

But the princess just shook her head. "I don't want to know. It's enough to know he has the tattoo. Not even he lives up to the perfection he expects in others."

"Sultan!" Badra demanded of the man. "Will you save this land you claim to love? Will you give your life for it?"

The Sultan spat in the sand at the magician's feet.

"You reject me although you've been exposed to all your soldiers, to your daughter, to the rulers of the Land of the Sun, as a fraud, as a hypocrite?" The Sultan spat again.

"How could either of you be worthy?" Badra said. "Neither of you volunteered for this; neither of you came willingly. Which brings me to Queen Kalila," the magician said. "She has a snake on her skin, and she came to me willingly." The magician nodded, the rising moon casting odd shadows across the planes of her cheeks. With a flip of her cape, Kalila flew through the air.

She landed in the sand at her feet with a thump. At first Tahir thought his sister was dead, and his thoughts flew to his mother. Her heart would be broken.

"Kalila," he said, squatting to touch her shoulders. "Kalila!" But she lived. "Where am I?" she asked.

"At the magician's reckoning," Shahrazad said.

"Will you replace me?" the magician demanded of her, her voice ringing over the sand. "Among those here, you're the one who knows my work the best. And you are a queen among manipulators—we can ask your mother about that."

"I—" Kalila started to say. Tahir knew she couldn't agree to any leadership role, especially one that would last hundreds of years. Well, she might agree to it, but the world might live to regret her largess.

"Stop." Shahrazad spoke the word so softly that Tahir was surprised the magician heard. But she did.

"Do you have something to say, Princess?"

"Stop. You're destroying these people, making them face the things they hate the most about themselves." Her honeyed skin glowed in the moonbeams, and her expression was bleak. "I will do it. I will take your place. I will guard the land against the *shitani* when they next invade. I know them and loathe them. I will accept this task—if God will hold me in his eyes."

"You cannot do this, Princess Shahrazad," the Sultan said in the most commanding voice Tahir had ever heard. "I forbid it absolutely."

But she just shook her head, pulling out the gold tips binding her braids. "I renounce you, father."

Never had a woman seemed more beautiful to him. And it wasn't her hair or her skin or her breasts and thighs—although all those things delighted him. It was her courage that caught his heart and refused to let go. She shied away from no hard choice, even when it cost her.

"Is it that easy for you, Princess Shahrazad of the Land of the Moon? To give up your life and walk away?" the Sultan asked, his voice gentler now. Tahir had never seen him appear more fatherly than he did now, but it was too little. And it was too late. The princess had needed a dependable father yesterday, and instead the Sultan had locked her away.

Shahrazad looked at her father. "Yes." Her voice was as bleak as her expression. "It is that easy."

"Daughter," he said, his tone pleading. "Don't do this."

"Shall I stay, then? Let my head join those of the other disobedient women on the Pike Wall?"

"Perhaps I was too hasty. I love you. I've always loved you."

Shahrazad walked toward him, took his hands in hers. "That may be, but there is no place for me in your life any longer. You've forsaken me."

"I forsake you no longer." He turned toward the crowd. "I love my daughter."

"And I love you, but I must go." She turned toward the magician without looking back. "Will you accept me?" she asked. "I'll bring honor and truth to this role. No more tricks. No more manipulations to meet dark needs." She looked at the magician, her face calm. "Will you accept me?"

In that moment, Tahir realized that Shahrazad—his princess—was leaving. He'd thought . . . Well, he thought the Sultan would forbid her. But instead she'd followed her heart.

Could he do less?

"Princess Shahrazad," he called to her back. "Princess!"

She paused and turned toward him. A slight night breeze caught her purple silk and rippled it over her lush curves.

"I'd accompany you, if you'd have me."

She looked at him like she'd never seen him before.

"Let me share this burden," he told her. "We'll rule side by side, man and woman equally."

Queen Kalila stood, perhaps finally understanding the situation. "Mother and I will send you unwanted boy children." She looked at the princess's father and said, "And perhaps you could send your unwanted women to your daughter rather than decorating your Pike Wall with their heads."

Shahrazad looked to the magician. "Shall we go?"

But the magician just threw back her head and laughed, the white moon gleaming off her long neck. "As if it is in my hands."

A dust devil blew into the corpse-ridden area. Inexorably it swirled toward the princess, who stood expressionless, accepting her fate.

As the dust devil approached her, he heard his sister cry, "My snake!" In the pale light, Tahir didn't quite trust his vision. A snake slithered over his sister's forearm and tumbled into the sand. It squirmed away into the darkness. Next to him, the Raj and the Sultan were shouting and writhing as their tattoos came to life and deserted them.

Suddenly the tattoo on his face started to burn. Tahir realized the snake was coming to life. He looked toward his princess and realized she wasn't struggling. Her snake, like the magician's, remained in place. She was stepping calmly toward the dust devil.

"No!" he cried, knowing the woman who completed his heart was leaving him behind. "No!"

He vaulted toward the dust devil, damning the consequences. He would not remain behind, not without Shahrazad.

But he was too late! Swirling sand coated his teeth as his arms reached for the maelstrom. He reached for her but felt nothing, nothing but sand.

"No!" he called. "Shahrazad, no!"

But the concentrated sandstorm sucked him into it—and thrashed him to oblivion.

18

He woke without moving; his eyes barely opened. But when they focused, they focused on her. She was sitting in a chair next to him, reading a book.

Golden sunlight poured through an unfamiliar window and bathed her in its light. Her skin reminded him of the richest honey, and a nimbus of black hair billowed past her shoulders. When had she taken out her braids? Was it an act of defiance against her father?

But it wasn't defiance he saw on her expression now. Now he saw peace. Now he saw just how kissable her lips were, and how serious her rested expression was.

This woman was not someone to take lightly.

But he'd already known that.

"You're awake," she said, turning those amber eyes toward him. Her thick dark lashes made him long to kiss her, feel their feathery texture under his lips.

"I'm awake." He looked around the bed in which he found himself. It was decadent and comfortable. Suddenly he realized he felt fantastic. His wounds were gone, his bruises vanished. He felt like he'd been fed a sumptuous feast, bathed, then curled up in the presence of the most outstanding beauty. "Where are we?" he asked. "Why do I feel so damned good?"

She held up her book. "I'm just reading about that. It seems we're in the abandoned palace that we flew over."

"That's the—" He sat up. "Is that the book we sought in the library?"

"It's the missing spellbook. Badra gave it to me before she left."

She left? He wanted to know more about that, but a more urgent question presented itself. "And the *shitani*?"

"Badra and I pushed them back into their caves."

"Without me?"

"I needed to convince her that two would be more suitable to replace her than one."

He swallowed, understanding her implication. He'd won her heart. "Will . . . your spell hold them?" All he wanted to tell her, and that was the best he could come up with?

"For a short period," she said. Then she flashed him a grin. "We'll have a chance to see how well we work together."

"Shahrazad," he said, searching for the words to seduce her. Not her body, but her mind. "Shahrazad, I—"

Suddenly the room hummed, and she smiled at him.

His cock throbbed. "Do you feel that?" he asked. "What is that strange vitality?"

"I feel it." She nodded. "That is immortality—our immortality."

"It's just us here, then?" he said with a roguish grin. "No husbands-to-be? No fathers?"

"No queens to tell you whom to impregnate? No sisters who vanish when you need them most?" She looked at him, her amber eyes burning into his. "It's just us."

He smiled then. "Are you ready to start this new world? One of justice and equality?"

The tension she'd been holding in her shoulders vanished. A

small smile curled her lips, and he realized her smile transformed her into the most beautiful woman he'd ever seen. "I am."

"Then might I suggest a place to start?" He reached for her and pulled her into the bed with him.

"Are you going to order me to obey if I object?" she asked.

Tahir leaned so close she could see the fall of his lashes against his cheek. The scales on his snake tattoo glittered in the sunlight, making him look dangerous . . . and delicious. The length of his dark hair threw his face into shadows. "I'd rather seduce you," he said. And his husky voice made his intent all the more clear. "I'd rather seduce you, but I won't."

Her heart paused for a minute. "What do you mean?"

Tahir took her hand in his and stepped from the bed. "Princess Shahrazad," he said, falling to one knee. "For your entire life, you've been forbidden to make important decisions, but I'm laying one at your feet."

"And what is that?" she asked, fear making her heart pound crazily.

"Do you choose me? We have tens of lifetimes to spend together, but if you wish I will leave. If you crave freedom and independence, I will leave. Should you change your mind, find me, and I'm yours to command, but I refuse to be foisted upon you by the magician—or my own stubbornness. You are capable of living here without a male ruler."

"I've fought to bring you here," she said. "Are you asking me if I want you?"

He looked up at her, his dark eyes shining. "Yes, my princess, that is exactly what I'm asking you."

As his words heated her core, she looked up at the golden light pouring in the window. Now she understood something—she'd been made to yield to the Flower Taker; she was sent to her bed without being asked for an opinion. The Raj ir

Adham had been foisted upon her, too. Even having Tahir here with her now had been foisted on her. When he'd flung himself into the dust devil, he would have died—if she hadn't convinced the magician to use the last of her *prana* to bring him here.

But now, she had a choice. And she knew what she wanted.

"I want you," she said. And she did. Her lips remembered the taste of his. Her tongue remembered the velvet of his, and she craved another lick, another nibble. "And if I want to seduce you?" she asked.

"You already have. My heart and soul have been yours since before we met. In your hands I'm helpless. In the moonlight and in the sunlight, I am your slave."

She wanted him to touch her, to show her. She knew it was right. "You want me," she said to Tahir. It wasn't a question.

"Your heart has captured me. Your loyalty to your family, your willingness to sacrifice."

Shahrazad realized that this man, this prince, saw her for who she truly was—and liked her. No, he loved her. He melted her very soul. She leaned toward his face, letting a wicked grin dance over her lips. "Then kiss me."

Tahir stood and gently pulled her body to his. Her arms met his, embraced him in return, pulling him toward her, feeling him along the length of her body.

Where the Flower Taker's body had been soft and giving, his was hard muscled and unyielding. His was strength itself.

His eyes locked on hers, asking permission. *Can I kiss you? Oh yes.*

He lightly touched his lips to hers, almost as softly as the Flower Taker had done. With a brush of tongue, he took her mouth with his. He tasted real—like strength and like truth. He paused his tongue on her lips.

Tentatively, she touched him.

Then, he sucked her in, sliding his tongue over hers. His kiss was truly as good, as enveloping, as she remembered. Her lips sought his, wanting to drink his strength. She gave her mouth to him. She caressed him with her tongue. She gave him her breasts, her nipples. Use me as you will, her body said to his, and his agreed.

With deliberate hands, he unbuttoned her bodice, letting the backs of his fingers caress her midriff. Slipping his hand inside the silk, he brushed an erect nipple. With the side of his hand, he tantalized her areola. Then, sliding the bodice off her shoulders, he nuzzled his head between her breasts before grabbing a nipple between his teeth.

She lost her ability to breathe. Who was this woman she'd become? Who had she been when she sought Tahir's heat in the Flower Taker's chamber? Shahrazad arched her back, offering him her breasts. Her heart.

He traced her erect nipple, nibbling, and she moaned in pleasure. A direct connection existed between his tongue and her core. They pulsed in the same rhythm to the tempo of his tongue.

Under his hands, the remainder of her clothing melted away, leaving her naked in the golden sunlight washing through the oversized window.

For a moment, he looked at her, admiration clear in his expression. "You're breathtaking."

"Come to me, then."

And he did, quick as lightning in the summer sky and just as hot. Their bodies pressed up hard against each other, their hips moving in tandem. Shahrazad sighed to feel his thickness through his clothes. His hardness and her wetness reflected the power of their desire for each other.

Her night with the Flower Taker had given her confidence in her beauty, in her desirability. But she hadn't been able to see his expression, covered as he'd been in demon spit. Now, when she saw the heat in his eyes, his consuming desire to have her, her confidence became unshakable.

"Remove your clothes, Tahir."

"Already you order me around." He laughed, but he unbuttoned his loose white shirt. "Are you secretly from the Land of the Sun?"

"Perhaps." She laughed. "But you can tell me to stop. You commanded the Warqueens and my father's soldiers like you were born to it."

He stood and removed his trousers. Shahrazad sat back down on the bed, savoring the sight of his naked body gleaming in the sunbeams.

He walked toward her and wrapped her in his arms. "I'll never hurt you."

Shahrazad looked up at him, her prince, and drank in his features. The snake tattoo that marked him as the one of the two magicians suited him, warned that he was dangerous. His hawk eyes were kind now, not fierce, and the dark planes of his face begged to be traced by her lips.

But it was the depth of his eyes that called to her—that won her heart.

He brought his head down and kissed her. Not hungrily like his previous kisses. This kiss was loving, filled with promise.

Against her stomach Shahrazad became aware of his throbbing erection. The tip of his cock glistened.

"Every part of me wants you," he said, following her gaze.

Bold now, she began to kiss him, taking his lower lip between hers and sucking, running her tongue over it, moving until his tongue met hers.

She moved to lie atop him. Their bodies touched only pubic mound to erection. He thrust his hips up, pushing his hardness against her belly. She leaned into him, savoring the pressure.

Tahir moved his hand over her body, slowly, like he was memorizing the texture of her skin, the curve of her ribs and hips and belly. Then he cupped her vulva, rocking her.

Two skilled fingers parted her, and he slid a finger over her sensitive nub. "Tahir," she gasped. He slid a finger inside of her. With one finger inside, he ran a gentle fingertip over her nub, electrifying her. With his other hand, he slid inside of her, faster and faster.

As his finger danced over her nub, he arranged himself atop of her. Her body trembled, anticipating the burst. His cock nestled between her thighs, and she felt it throb against his fingers.

She opened to him, pushing hard against him, raising her hips to meet his cock, welcoming him. Inviting him despite her fear. She burned with such exquisite feeling. "God's eyes," she gasped. "That feels so good."

She squirmed and bucked underneath him, urging him to go deeper, to slake the passionate sensation with his pounding cock. Hot flames of desire scorched her, licked at her like a bonfire.

He stopped, tearing a small mewling sound from her lips. Tahir buried his face between her thighs. His tongue slid over her nub. She couldn't help herself. She opened her thighs wider for him, bucked her hips toward him.

But he stopped. When he looked up at her, his eyes were black with desire. "We could start populating our new land, if you wish. Our first new citizen might arrive in nine months." He licked her again. "If you wish."

"Yes," she answered. "Oh yes." With a sigh, Shahrazad closed her eyes as Tahir stroked her nub. His fingers languidly dipped inside.

She started to quiver, nearing that point, and he sensed it. He straddled her and slid his cock as far as it would go, filling her, filling her completely.

When she met his gaze, she saw love, pure and simple. And she melted into him, pressing her hips toward his. He began to move faster, and she wanted, needed, more of him. Tilting her hips, she urged him for more. She wanted him buried in her.

Again and again he thrust into her, and with each motion she moved to meet his tongue and lips, breathing herself into his mouth, making her part of him. She lost the ability to know where her skin ended and his began.

Under him she could feel his sweat mix with hers, and she wrapped her mouth around the side of his neck. He cried out and shuttered, and the force of his desire together with his pounding thrusts made her come with him.

Huge waves of ecstasy surged through her veins. Every muscle in her body quivered with delight, starting deep inside her belly and reaching her fingertips, her toes, her eyebrows. A heartbeat later, Tahir joined her in the orgasm. He emptied himself inside her.

Twined around Tahir, Shahrazad savored his scent, the weight of his body draping hers. The scent of him, the scent of sex, filled the room. A series of tiny ripples reverberated through her vagina. His shaft throbbed in response.

The quiet moment filled her with inner peace. In this moment, she knew she'd chosen correctly.

Turn the page for a preview of
CARNAL DESIRES,
by Crystal Jordan!

On sale now!

1

The snow tigress was in heat.

His nostrils flared. He could smell her desire from across the ballroom. Her scent called to him, tempting him to cast off the veneer of civility and take her in any way he could.

Mahlia Najla Mohan.

His mate.

Longing warred with sadness at the thought of her. Of their lost child. Pain exploded in his chest, choking him. *No.* He would not think of that. He could not. The agony would drive him to his knees.

"Amir Varad." His manservant's voice pulled him back to the present. Varad pasted a charming smile on his face, appearing the besotted male who would soon have his mate begging him for the surcease only he could grant her. And possibly conceiving an heir to the Vesperi throne. A new heir.

"Welcome back, brother." Taymullah's hand clapped on his shoulder.

Varad quirked a brow at the shorter man. And he was a man; the boy he'd left behind six months ago had grown into someone Varad hardly recognized. The last half turn had been a difficult time for all of his family.

Taymullah's face settled into serious lines as he turned to look over at his brother's mate, Mahlia. "You have a great deal of work before you, Varad."

"I know."

Varad swallowed, his gaze tracking her movement. Mating on Vesperi was a complicated affair, only lasting from a woman's heat cycle to the next. Because Varad was here, no one would touch his woman. Had he not returned in time, it would have been a different tale. However, she could always choose to mate away from him. His gut clenched. *No.* Mahlia was *his.* Had been his since the moment he'd looked into her ice-blue eyes, so rare among his people. His treasure. She would have no other for as long as they both lived. Whatever tragedy they shared could not destroy the depth of emotion that had always pulled them together.

Gods, he was tired. Six months on a spacecraft for the trade run was more than he cared for, but he doubted the werebears on the planet Alysius would trade with anyone except him personally. Lord Kesuk was not a man to trust.

A genuine smile tugged at Varad's lips as he thought of the Arctic Bear clan leader. He wondered how the enormous man had fared after Varad had encouraged the tiny human woman to return to the werebear's caves. The man hadn't stood a chance. Lady Jain would have seen to it. Varad's grin widened. Mahlia would like Jain immensely.

And Kesuk would try to kill him when Varad returned next turn, no matter how happy the werebear lord was with his lady. It would be an interesting fight. Varad flicked a barely visible piece of lint from his sleeve as he wondered who might be the winner. A tiger versus a bear. Yes, interesting.

He shook his head, marveling again that a spaceship could have drifted among the stars since before the Earthan sun had died. Two unaltered humans, Lady Jain and a young scientist, Sera, had survived a crash landing on the werebear planet. Humans were extinct now, having had no way to survive the harsh environments of the four colonized planets. Only gene-splicing with different animal species had made it possible for humans to survive at all.

He wondered how the two women would fare. Lady Jain had her new Bear clan to contend with, but Sera had insisted on journeying to Aquatilis, the planet that maintained the greatest level of technology from old Earth. He suspected her choice had more to do with her fascination for a certain merman ambassador than her need for machines.

"Amir, your guests await you." Varad's valet bared his teeth a bit at the word *guests*. Varad chuckled as he descended the curving staircase from the wide balcony. Unlike Taymullah, one of the few who had supported Varad's expeditions, his manservant disapproved of the trade relations with Alysius.

"Well, we shouldn't disappoint our *valued* visitors." A warning was in Varad's tone. He was the king here, the Amir, and his wishes would be obeyed by all. If he bore the responsibility of leadership, he demanded the respect that came with the position.

"Yes, my Amir." His servant bowed and backed away.

Trade had always been maintained between Vesperi and the Harenan weredragons, but many had thought Varad mad when he set out to find the other two planets. It had been a risk, he admitted. But what was life without risk? None could deny that the new flood of goods from the werebears and merpeople were good for all four planets. No matter how much his doubters might like to protest. He tried to cover his laugh in a discreet cough.

He sobered abruptly, the grin falling away from his face. Many of his people agreed that trading with the seemingly barbaric werebears was a mistake. They were a rough people, but he'd grown to respect them, especially Lord Kesuk. He sighed, the weight of his responsibilities riding heavily on his shoulders. He shrugged as if to shift the burden, but nothing could ease his troubles.

A sweet laugh rippled across the ballroom, and he wasn't the only one who turned to smile at the source. Mahlia. Another challenge to face. Whether it pleased either of them or not, he would soon have her.

The room gleamed with white marble and wildly colored swaths of fabric—all the ostentation a feline could need. He worked his way across the vast ballroom to her side, nodding to his guests, noting the flashing scales of the Harenan weredragons, the imposing bulk of the first Alysian werebear ambassador, the violently colored hair of the Aquatilian merpeople. An interplanetary gathering, just as he had hoped. Excellent. When he reached Mahlia, she was entertaining a merman and the werebear ambassador with a story about her inability to master the waltz as a child.

"Amira Mahlia." Varad's hand stroked down the length of her bare arm, tracing the tan stripes on her creamy skin with a fingertip. He savored the feel of her, enjoying the way her servant had gathered her long cream-and-bronze-striped hair on her head, leaving her shoulders bared in a laced black corset. One of her legs was exposed by the filmy deep-blue skirt slit to her waist. His cock hardened, the need to have her fisting his gut. A deep breath dragged her scent to him yet again. Only because he was so focused on her did he hear the soft catch in her breath before she turned icy blue eyes on him. The natural black lining that surrounded all weretiger eyes made hers stunning.

"Amir Varad." She attempted to curtsy before him, but he quickly squeezed her elbow to keep her upright. Even after a Turn, she was not accustomed to her role in society. Or perhaps she was still uncomfortable with him. It mattered not. His mate would not bow to him. She was his equal—the only true partner he had in his world. He inclined his head to her, and after the briefest of pauses, she followed suit.

"Your Amira was just telling us an amusing story, Amir." The sub-bass rumble of the werebear split the silence; a white smile flashed in his dark face. The hammered metal circlet welded around his massive bicep, a mark of his standing among the Bear clans, glinted in the light from the glowlight chandeliers.

"Yes, the Aquatilians wish you all felicity in your return." The merman's nasal tone and sophisticated speech demonstrated the difference between the merman's culture and that of the werebear. Only Mahlia could have charmed the two into maintaining a peaceful conversation for more than a few minutes.

"Welcome home, Amir." He turned to see Katryn, his mate's closest friend, approaching their group. Her dark hair rippled to her hips, and her golden skin was set off in a stunning white gown reminiscent of an ancient Grecian toga. The weredragon was beautiful, but the first thing one noticed about her was the purple scaling that crept from her wrists to her biceps.

Still, no other woman had ever called to him as Mahlia had. Anticipation tensed his muscles. Soon. Soon he would have her. Would have her legs about him as they rode each other, her slick heat tight on his thrusting cock. He bit back a groan and then traced a finger down the lacings of her corset. Her breath panted as her scent increased, surrounding him, commanding him.

The hunt would begin soon.